WOLF'S BANE
MONSTERS OF THE NEXUS 1

NANCEY CUMMINGS

Wolf's Bane

Monsters of the Nexus
Book One

Nancey Cummings

Copyright © 2020 by Nancey Cummings

Cover art by Phantom Dame (2023)

All rights reserved.

No part of this book may be reproduced in any form or by any electronic or mechanical means, including information storage and retrieval systems, without written permission from the author, except for the use of brief quotations in a book review.

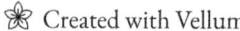 Created with Vellum

About Wolf's Bane

A human colony lost in space.

A century ago, colonists crashed on a distant planet. Technology failed and strange energies caused catastrophic mutations. Now every generation slips away from science, into superstition and darkness.

Solenne survives among the broken relics of the past, trying to protect her family from the mutated beasts that wax and wane with the moon. When her father is injured, she turns to the one man she swore never to speak to again. The man who kissed her vowed he'd return and broke her heart.

Can this be their second chance?

A man lost to the beast.

Since being bitten and cursed to shift into a werewolf every full moon, Aleksandar has lived in exile.

Until he receives a letter from Solenne, the woman he promised his heart to years ago. She's the only thread that keeps him anchored in the chaos, the only memory that keeps him sane.

He must protect her from creatures that stalk her family, but how can he protect her from himself?

The monster within him won't be denied.

The beast will have his bride.

An Introduction to the Nexus

Centuries ago, humans looking to make a new life left Earth on colony ships. Most ships safely arrived at their target destinations, and humanity spread across the stars.

One ship, however, became lost. Very lost.

The crew woke to find themselves on a planet that occupied a spot in the universe with unique properties. Technology failed. Power surges fried computers, and the ship that sailed the stars was grounded. The worst was yet to come, they discovered.

The wall separating parallel universes fluctuated with the moon. What came through were creatures spawned from nightmares.

Surrounded by the worthless technology of their colonial ancestors, each generation of humanity slides into darkness and superstitions.

How long can humanity keep the darkness at bay? Can the hunters save them?

Chapter One

Solenne

Boxon Hill

Marechal House - The Kitchen

"Grab your kit!"

An icy wind swept through the house as Luis carried in the bleeding form of their father, Godwin Marechal. Servants hurriedly opened doors, clearing the way into the warmth of the kitchen. Hastily, the worktable had been cleared just as Luis laid down his burden.

Under the dim overhead lights, Solenne examined her father. Flickering light from the fireplace cast an orange hue over his skin. A gash sliced across his face and left eye. Blood matted in his hair and soaked through the layers of his coat and tunic.

"Was he wearing any armor at all?" Solenne hissed. Godwin's abdomen had been viciously slashed in an unmistakable pattern. Claws.

"The material failed," Luis said.

Solenne bit her tongue to hold her snarky comeback. *Obviously, the armor failed. Useless old relic.*

"Hold him down," she ordered. Her brother placed his hands on Godwin's shoulders. The elder hissed as silver shears cut through cloth.

"Are they deep?" Luis stood near, barely breathing.

"I need hot water and a paste of honey and onion," Solenne said. She wouldn't know the severity of the wounds until she cleaned away the blood. At least the bleeding had slowed. The eye injury concerned her the most. They needed to call the doctor, but none would venture out during the night of the solstice.

"Don't worry about me," Godwin hissed. "The beast is out there with my blood on his muzzle, and we've hours left before dawn."

Solenne shared a look with Luis. Their father needed immediate attention, but if the estate was under attack, she could deal with her father while Luis hunted the monster.

"I hit it with my pistol. It'd be mad to come back," her brother said.

"I loathe that old pistol," she grumbled. The pistol took forever to pack and only held one shot. *Useless*.

"Well, that old pistol drove off the beast tonight." Luis looked exhausted, covered in dirt, blood, and gunpowder. The sleeve of his jacket had been slashed, exposing the matte black material of his armor suit underneath.

"Did it get you too? Did your armor hold?"

"No, and yes. This time." Luis ran a filthy hand through his hair. "Father shoved me out of the way. He saved me. I shouldn't have—"

"None of that," Godwin moaned. Solenne wished she had a sleeping draught on hand to put him to sleep.

"Wash your hands and bring me the bottle of wolfsbane," Solenne said, pointing to the scullery. "Might as well get the whiskey too."

The kitchen maid brought a bowl and a pitcher of hot water. Carefully, she removed debris and washed the wounds clean. The cook supplied freshly diced onions and ground them into a mixture with honey under Solenne's instruction. Luis poured Godwin a generous measure of whiskey and encouraged his father to drink.

Solenne indicated that he should drink half a glass of the wolfsbane tonic. No one in their family had ever suffered the curse of the beast's bite, but there was no sense in testing fate.

"Hold him down. This will hurt." Solenne held up a bottle, and Luis nodded, leaning forward to use all his weight to keep Godwin pinned in place.

"I'm sorry, Papa," she whispered as she uncorked the bottle of eyewash and poured it carefully over her father's injured eye.

The older man thrashed and cursed enough to turn the air blue. The lights flickered briefly before fading. Godwin, thankfully, had passed out from the pain.

Small favors, perhaps. That seemed to be all the universe doled out to the Marechal family.

"Fucking batteries," Luis complained. "They won't hold a charge in the cold."

"They don't power properly on cloudy days. We can use a lantern," Solenne said. At least the lanterns held a charge decently.

By the soft light of the ancient lanterns, Solenne tended to her father. Luis ran down the events of the evening. He and Godwin hadn't even needed to track the bestial wolf. It waited for them beyond the estate's gates, which showed a disturbing intelligence, in Solenne's opinion.

She dreaded the turning of the solstice and equinox, when the nexus energies surged and monsters prowled the night. Everyone knew that. The Marechal family had hunted those monsters for generations, since humans first arrived on the planet. Their ancestors had been granted land near a nexus point, marked by strange stone circles crafted by an unknown intelligence, and a charter to protect the neighboring settlements.

Monster hunting, however, wasn't lucrative, and equipment—all silver-tipped and plated—had to be replaced frequently. Their estate was marginal land and last year's drought had been hard on the sheep herd. Thankfully, being close to the nexus point meant their land held unique plants and herbs. The tonics and remedies she made supplemented their income, and she feared that it would be the entirety of their income if lambing season or the wool harvest disappointed.

Whenever Godwin brought up their finances to the village council, they made noises about taking the charter away. Modest compensation came with the charter, yes, but it had not been adjusted in decades. The council made it very clear that the Marechals were expected to sustain themselves with their land.

The situation was endlessly frustrating. Sometimes Solenne wished the council would take the charter and let someone else worry about keeping the village safe from the nightmares that prowled the night.

The Marechal name still commanded respect, for what that was worth.

Solenne applied the last of the bandages. She sagged into a chair with exhaustion and gratefully accepted a mug of hot tea. Six years ago, she had been at the university in Founding, determined to pursue botany. She never imagined that'd still be in her father's house, worrying about sheep shearing.

"We must clean it again in the morning and apply more paste," she said.

"He will survive," Luis said.

"If we avoid infection, yes. I won't be happy if he spends less than a week in bed."

"Which he won't allow."

"Probably not, but his two children will nag him until he relents," she said. "It's his eye that's the problem."

Luis nodded. The siblings did not need to say that a monster hunter with one eye was as good as dead. No depth perception meant he couldn't fight, or at least win a fight.

"We'll send for Dr. Webb in the morning." She'd worry about how to pay for the doctor tomorrow. In the past, he accepted a trade of a tonic of poultice. If not, the house was large and full of useless decorations. She'd rather have her father alive and possibly blinded than silver-plated candelabras.

Colonel Chambers had attempted to add one of the Marechal's many defunct weapons to his personal collection, but Godwin had always refused. Perhaps he could be pursued to part with a piece. Various plasma pulse rifles and pistols, even something called an EMP cannon, gathered dust. None were operational. Godwin probably wouldn't even notice if one went missing and the ready money would fix a good number of problems, like the broken glass panes in the greenhouse.

Solenne pushed the thought away. Selling a weapon—even a broken, inoperable weapon—behind her father's back would be wrong. Godwin noticed little, but she knew that if she suddenly had money to spend, he'd notice.

"Scarring is in a bad place. He'll be stiff," Luis observed. They both knew what that meant.

Godwin could not be injured. Farmer by day and monster hunter by night, no one else could pick up the mantle. Luis, while large for his age, had only graduated from boarding school months ago. He was too young and under trained. Tonight's mishaps proved that.

In her youth, Solenne had trained in the family's profession, but so much changed when Mama died. Her training ended with a fractured wrist and arm. Then Godwin packed her and Luis off to school.

Unconsciously, Solenne rubbed her left wrist.

She wondered if Godwin regretted, as the wolf nearly gutted him, sending his children away, ending her training and delaying Luis'. Another set of eyes, another blade or bow, could have prevented this.

A howl sounded in the distance. A dish shattered on the floor.

"Oh, my nerves," Cook said, bending to retrieve the fragment.

"It's my fault," Luis said.

"No, it's that beast's fault." She looked down at her father's bandaged face. Unless the beast was exceptionally old, therefore strong, it would be inactive until the summer solstice. "We have some time to prepare. We need help."

She had letters to write.

THE DOCTOR ARRIVED SHORTLY after dawn. The news wasn't good, but not as bad as Solenne and Luis feared.

Godwin would live, but he would lose the use of his eye. They had to wait until the summer solstice to determine if he suffered the effects of the wolf's bite. Until then, Solenne would keep the wound clean and pour wolfsbane tonic down her father's throat. He'd drown in the stuff.

Heartened by the doctor's prognosis, she pressed two silver coins into the man's hands.

He pushed them back. "I will not accept your coin. Godwin Marechal has given more to this village than we can ever hope to repay."

It remained unspoken that her father gave his sight. So many Marechal ancestors gave their blood to protect others, and Godwin could add his name to their ranks.

She lifted her chin, stubborn to her very core. "You deserve compensation. Goodwill and smiles do not put food on the table."

"Indeed. I will gladly accept a tin of your rosehip tea."

Solenne nodded, her pride assuaged.

"Another reply." Luis broke the wax seal and unfolded the letter. "Miss Marechal, we are saddened to learn of your father's injury. As you know, ours is a dangerous profession…this goes on for a bit," Luis said, skipping ahead. "Regretfully, we cannot spare—" He balled up the letter and tossed it in the fireplace. The paper crackled as it burned. "That was Bornau."

"We'll write to others," Solenne said, though honestly she did not know to whom. In the last week, she had written to the closest towns with hunters. All sent their regrets. They, too, were strapped for time, money and manpower. Fallkirk's letter came back unopened with a note that the town had been without a hunter for nearly a year.

A year.

"There are no others." Luis sank into the chair by the worktable.

The familiar scent of dry herbs and lemon filled the room. The stone floor was still cool, but the fire would warm the room soon enough. Part of the original house, the room had once been the kitchen but now served as her workshop.

"Get to grinding if you're going to sulk," she said, waving a hand to the mortar and pestle on the table next to her brother. She turned her attention back to her own mortar and pestle.

There was one other person she could write.

Her pride demanded the idea be rejected. Aleksandar—

She sighed, setting for the pestle and rubbing the ache in her wrist. The old injury always twinged and complained in the damp weather.

Her pride didn't matter, nor did the lingering heartache of a sixteen-year-old girl. She barely even remembered being the girl who had fallen for her best friend, the boy her father took as an apprentice, and they swore to a secret engagement as they knew Godwin would forbid it.

How her father discovered them, she did not know. What she did know was that Godwin turned Alek out from their home when she broke her wrist turning a training mishap. He held Alek responsible, despite it being an accident. Alek swore he would return for her when she was old enough to do as she pleased. She believed him.

More fool her.

Years had passed since she received even a letter from him.

Hurt had faded with time. Even her anger eventually left. All that remained was a sense of loss over her oldest friend. She didn't care about anything else, the pity over being a spinster or the gossip about dabbling with plants and herbs. None of it mattered.

She knew what she had to do.

"I could send a letter to Snowmelt," she said, breaking the silence.

"Snowmelt?" Luis scrunched up his nose. "Does the post even go that far north?"

"I daresay we'll find out." If Aleksandar was even still alive.

ALEKSANDAR

Snowmelt

Hardwick House - The Beast's Den

EMBERS GREW cold in the grate, and the lights dimmed. Rain pounded against the window. The room, once elegant, lay in tatters. Great gashes tore into the wallpaper and plaster. Furniture lay smashed on the floor. Iron chains and a collar sat in the corner, waiting.

This room had been his jail for some years. The housekeeper left food outside his door and, more importantly, ignored the snarls and howls that came from his den.

The rest of Hardwick House was not in such shambles, though it was far from a fashionable or even a comfortable house. Closed for several years, a small team of staff kept the house repaired and free of vermin. The estate manager handled the business with tenants. The housekeeper did as she pleased. Alek cared not. If anyone had concerns over the landlord's reclusive behavior, no one dared mention it to him.

They left him alone, especially during the solstice and equinox events, which was all that mattered.

Sitting on the bare floor, Alek reread the letter. Again. The name signed at the bottom claimed to be his old mentor, Godwin Marechal, but he knew who truly authored the letter.

Solenne.

Each time, he swore he could smell perfume, a clean mix of fresh-picked herbs and ink. Years had passed, but he could still hear her laughter, bright and clear as a bell. He held the letter up and breathed deeply.

She had been his friend then, but it's easy to have friends when you have a handsome face. If she could see him now, scarred and disfigured, she'd recoil in horror.

Growling in frustration, he crumpled the paper and tossed it into the dying fire.

Godwin and his family needed him.

Alek did not like to dwell on his past. His family had been slaughtered in the night. Godwin Marechal arrived like a savior to rid the small village of its monster infection. It seemed the fucking sunlight even gleamed on his golden hair when Godwin pulled Alek from the steamer trunk he had been hiding in for days.

Alek had been entranced. Godwin appeared so noble, so admirable, that the new orphan followed the hunter in a desperate case of hero worship.

Fortunately, Godwin Marechal was as good of a man as he appeared to a starry-eyed child. He took in the scared child, gave him a home, taught him a profession, and treated him like family. Until—

Alek could not say no; he owed too much to the Marechal family.

Unfortunately, much had transpired in the decade since he left the Marechal home. He hunted monsters, like the one that slaughtered his family, but paid a price. At the time, he had been happy to pay.

Now? He could not find it within himself to regret his choices. A cursed half-life for the lives of innocent people? A bargain.

If the Marechals knew of his curse, he doubted they would welcome his help. He could barely keep himself contained. Leaving would endanger the very family that sought his help.

And yet he yearned to see the only family he had, the people who needed him. Wind rattled the windowpanes and the house groaned.

Aleksandar retrieved the letter from the fire, batting at the charred edges and blowing away soot. There had to be a way to help. He would find it.

Chapter Two

Solenne

Boxon Hill

Marechal House - The Undercroft

The iron key rattled as Solenne shimmied it into place. The locking mechanism groaned in protest as she turned the old key and pushed the door open. At one time, the Marechal family had many functioning treasures of the old world. Now they had a room full of broken junk. Some still considered the useless machines to be treasures, which was why Solenne picked through the shelves.

The armor Godwin and Luis wore was a genuine treasure. Made of a lightweight and super-strong carbon, the ability to fabricate the material had been lost to time. The pieces were battered and failing. Fortunately, the blacksmith in the village had developed a technique to repair the carbon material. The mended fabric was not as strong, but still better than anything else. Leather was not durable enough, and metal, even chainmail, was too loud and too bulky for the family's work. By this point, the Marechal armor was mostly composed of repairs. Solenne would eat her hat if more than 50% of the original material remained.

She moved aside defunct slabs made of a material as clear as glass but stronger and shatterproof. Sometimes, if she left them in the sun long enough, they glowed with an internal light.

Godwin would never part with a weapon, inoperable or not, but a long-range communication device that had not worked in decades? That could be bargained away.

Solenne found it difficult to believe that the machines of the ancestors ever worked, that technology could be reliable and dependent. It seemed like a fairy story.

The artifacts disturbed her. She knew it was not magic, but a lost technology. Electricity and circuits. It worked on a principle of gears and levers, heat and steam, or pressure and valves: the same as any machine. Still, images and symbols that she couldn't decipher ghosted across the surface. She would rather leave well enough alone.

However, Miles, the blacksmith, couldn't get enough.

She passed over non-functional pistols—or that's what they looked like to her—and mysterious black boxes. At the back of a dusty shelf, she found a spheroid object, flat on the bottom with a handle. Once white, the casing had yellowed with age. The material was plastic, which, while no longer produced, was common enough. The oldest houses had entire dinner services made of the stuff. The ancestors had used it for practically everything, even trivial, single-use products. Discarded plastics were shredded into chips and melted to be reused. The end product was a crude but durable material, perfect for roof shingles and the like.

Carefully, she wrapped the item in cloth like a sacred relic and added it to a basket along with the damaged armor. She did not need to convince Miles to accept the item as payment for repairing the armor, but she could prevent it from being damaged during the journey.

A week had passed since the events of the full moon. Godwin refused to stay in bed and rest. Luis pored over old texts and fiddled with broken weaponry. The household was almost normal, if one could ignore the underlying current of worry. Every night brought them closer to the summer solstice when creatures prowled the night.

Alek had not replied to her letter, but it had not been returned as a person unknown, either. It had been delivered, presumably read. She had to be patient.

Time was not on their side.

Luis perched on a stool in the library, holding a small crystal to the window. Solenne knocked on the open door's frame.

"A new gun will not help you," she said. The ancestor's weapons discharged searing bolts of energy. The weapons had little effect on the monsters and more often than not exploded in the operator's hand. They were too dangerous to use. "You'd be better off practicing with the crossbow."

"I did. I have the callus to prove it." Luis held up his other hand, the palm red. The family had a crossbow made of a flexible carbon material similar to the armor, but they also had an armory full of models made from humbler material.

The weapon did not matter so much as the silver-tipped arrows did. Silver injured the beasts better than anything.

"I'm going into the village to see Miles," Solenne said.

"I'll walk with you."

She thought he might.

Luis sprang from his seat. Tall and athletic, the morning sun picked out golden highlights in his dark hair. Solenne knew her brother much preferred history to fighting, but they were not given a preference for their lot in life. Solenne had once wanted to learn archery and become a swordfighter. Godwin forbade his daughter from such pursuits—bet he regretted that now as Luis was unequipped to handle such responsibility on his own—so she learned the uses of the plants of the forest.

"No worries. I just wanted you to know to expect me back in the afternoon. I'm calling on Charlotte for lunch," she said.

"Let me."

"Luis—"

"Solenne, please. I know nothing will happen during the day, but I need to know you're safe," he said. "Please."

Her brother stood a few inches taller than her. Somehow, in the last winter, he shot up and filled out. At the end of every term when he returned home from boarding school, he was taller, broader. In the months since graduating, he shot up. The scrawny beanpole she remembered now rivaled their father in stature. He was eight years younger than her, but somehow Luis had grown into an adult without her noticing.

"If you must," she said.

"I enjoy the way you make it sound like a hardship for yourself." He grabbed an overcoat from the rack in the hall, and they made their way into the village.

The sun had finally pierced through a rainy spring, although a damp chill hung in the air. Rain was a constant for the season. Soon enough, the afternoons would grow warm and the greenery would explode in the valley. At the moment, mud colored everything.

The Marechal estate sat midway on Boxon Hill. A standing stone circle loomed above, at the very top of the hill. The top of the hill offered panoramic views, if a person could tolerate the humming from the stones.

A ring of old-growth trees surrounded the bottom half of the hill, and denser forest growth lay to the south. To the east, the village was a brisk walk away. Pastures suitable for grazing were to the north and to the west. Beyond the pastures were the plains, the West Lands, where the terraforming of the original settlers ended and the wild, indigenous planet began.

As removed as she felt from the defunct technology the original settlers brought from the old world, it defied comprehension to think the flora and fauna were also from another world. Another planet. Various histories all agreed that a portion of the world had been *terraformed*, whatever that meant. Livestock was revived from frozen cells. Seeds planted in newly transformed ground. All that humans farmed and harvested came from the old world. Even the forest and the wild plants were planted by the settlers.

Humans were aliens here.

It seemed impossible that humans had so much technology, so much power to change the face of an inhospitable planet, and it slipped away. Nexus energies caused havoc on machines and humans alike.

The settlers had changed the planet, but the planet had changed them as well.

In the sunshine, a sparkle at Luis' throat caught her attention. Now interested, she studied his wardrobe. Luis wore his typical tan trousers and white shirt with a plain white waistcoat. The greatcoat was made of heavy wool and dyed a deep navy that hid many stains. His dark hair had been pulled back and tied with a red ribbon, but wisps had escaped. He very much had the air of a gentleman farmer.

That cravat though...

"Are you expecting to be attacked by a blood drinker in broad daylight?" she asked, keeping her tone light and jovial.

Luis touched the silver-infused cloth and blushed. "I thought it looked nice."

She hummed and straightened the fabric. Pressing her lips to hide her grin, she looked away and said nothing.

She counted Miles as a friend and he would make a suitable match.

Sneaking a glance at Luis, she approved of the excited gleam in his eye.

Just not for her. Luis' crush on the blacksmith had been obvious for years, at least to her.

"Miles is awfully clever," she said. Luis nodded. "Awfully handsome too."

A furious red blush took over his face. "It's not like that, Solenne. He thinks I'm a child," he sputtered.

Luis had grown a lot over the winter and filled out his frame. Solenne suspected that Miles might reevaluate his opinion of Luis when they met.

"Have you spoken to him since you returned from school?"

"Once or twice."

"Well, sometimes it's easy to think of people as they had been, instead of noticing how they are," she said.

"Trying to make him notice anything that's not broken tech is impossible." The sulk in his tone spoke to his youth.

Solenne turned her attention to the undergrowth near the edge of the trees, hiding her amusement. Her baby brother had it bad.

A purple blossom caught her attention. "Hold a minute." She pushed the basket into his hands and drew out a small silver blade. The slight curve made it ideal for collecting plants.

"Lungwort," she said, folding her collection carefully into a handkerchief. Luis rolled his eyes. "You'll be thankful when you have a cough."

The path emerged from the trees, and the air felt lighter. Luis tugged at his ear, like he had water stuck inside.

"Is it bad?" she asked.

"It's background noise mostly, except during events."

The family was, to varying degrees, sensitive to nexus energies. It was, according to family lore, why the family had been given Boxon Hill and the surrounding land. They instinctively sensed any fluctuations in the nexus energy and could track its movements.

Well, Solenne could not. Luis described it as chasing fish in a river, which did not clarify things at all.

The strength of the gift varied from person to person. Solenne sensed nothing unless she stood directly on top of the nexus point at the stone circle. Even then, it was faint; a tingly, zipping sensation that grew into sparks, like static electricity discharging when she shuffled her stocking feet across a carpet. Leaving the immediate vicinity of a nexus point, however, always felt like a relief, like silence replacing a constant buzzing noise.

Open pasture stretched from the foot of Boxon Hill to the outskirts of Boxon village. Other than a small herd of sheep, livestock didn't thrive on the hill—too skittish. The animals that lived on the hill were wilder and, sometimes, otherworldly. Solenne would be skittish too.

"You should practice archery with me," Luis announced.

"What?"

"You used to be good with a bow and arrow, right? Back when Mama—"

Silence fell between the siblings. Injured while conducting one of her experiments, Amalie Marechal succumbed to her injuries. Solenne had been fifteen, Luis just seven.

Godwin immediately forbade Solenne from continuing her training. He lost his wife to an accident, and he would be damned before he lost his daughter to monsters.

Solenne pressed her lips together. Godwin's actions, spurred on by love and fear, condemned them. Godwin would never regain his vision. Luis could not protect the entire valley on his own. If her father hadn't been so stubborn—

"Father will be upset," she said.

"What he doesn't know won't hurt him. Practicing with a long-range weapon is smarter than giving you a little dagger and hoping you never have to use it." Luis frowned at the blade in the basket.

For months after their mother's death, Godwin reluctantly allowed Solenne to continue her training. The day she broke her wrist, however, ended his tolerance.

Solenne rubbed her wrist. She shifted the basket to cover the motion. It had been an accident. Alek hadn't known his full strength, but Godwin wouldn't tolerate it. He sent Alek away.

She lost several things that day. The full use of her arm was only one.

Luis noticed. He noticed everything. "You were hurt, but he was wrong to stop your training." His voice took on a deep firmness that Solenne had never heard before. For a moment, she got a glimpse of the man her little brother would grow into.

"He was scared and angry," she said. A badly placed hit fractured her left arm and her wrist. Godwin's reaction, though.

Godwin had not been himself, lost to grief and alcohol. That was the first and last day he ever raised a hand in anger to his apprentice, Alek. He never touched a drop of alcohol again, but the damage had been done.

Alek was beaten and sent away, despite Solenne's pleading. Alek was her oldest friend and the man she loved, and it had been an accident.

While her arm healed well enough, she lacked the strength to hold a sword. The only thing that hurt was the sense of incompleteness from her absent friend, and she learned to ignore that. After a decade of living with the loss, her resentment had mellowed.

"He's a stubborn asshole," Luis said. "He was wrong to send Aleksandar away and wrong to send us off to that boarding school." Youthful anger and certitude colored his voice.

"Papa's not a saint. We all make mistakes," she said, thinking of how her time at university had been cut short because the funds ran out. When she returned home, she found the estate badly managed and the accounts in shambles. "A lot of mistakes."

Luis huffed.

She leaned in until they bumped shoulders. "Hey," she said.

He grumbled a reply.

"I think it's a good idea, but I don't know if I have the strength in my hand for a bow. Maybe a crossbow. Or I can practice with my left." Training to use her non-dominant hand would be difficult, but his idea was sound.

Luis nodded. "There's the blacksmith."

On the edge of the village, the forge billowed out steam in the cool morning air. Luis fidgeted with the lapels on his greatcoat.

So cute.

"Come on. Let's ply Miles with our treasures so he can work a miracle for us today," she said.

Aleksandar

Snowmelt

Hardwick House - The Study

Words failed Alek; he tossed his original reply to Godwin Marechal, curt and quite rudely so, into the fire. He scratched out another response, filled with vitriol and a touch of gloating. That also joined its brethren in the fire.

He then wrote to Solenne, as he often did, because she was never far from his thoughts or his heart, and that went into fire. He had hoped that time would lessen the pull, but a thread connected them, always had, and it hooked directly into his heart. They were tied together. Sometimes he could go days without thinking of her, then some sound or a flash of color would spark a memory and the pull intensified.

Foolishly, he'd pen another letter, which ended up in the fire like all the letters he had written to Solenne over the years.

The beast inside him howled with hunger, impatience, and wanting. Always wanting.

Staying in exile as he had done for years was the best way to protect her from himself. Yet she needed his protection from others.

Either he left Solenne defenseless against the beast that attacked her father, or he endangered her with his own hungry beast.

There was no good choice.

Alek snarled with frustration and flung the pen and ink pot across the room. It splashed against the door and rolled onto the rug. Dark ink soaked into the sage-and-cream-colored rug.

He felt a moment's worth of shame at his behavior. His tantrum punished no one but Mrs. Suchet, his patient and aging housekeeper, with her creaking knees. This room—a gentleman's study, though he never used it and certainly never considered himself a gentleman—was not his den. He could not do as he pleased and ruin the furnishings.

Alek flung open the door. "Suchet!"

"Yes, Master Alek?" The aging housekeeper made slow progress down the hall. She called him by his childhood name, but he did not complain. Mrs. Suchet was one of the few people who remembered his parents and how alive the house had been before a monster invaded.

"How do I—" He waved a hand to the rug and the spreading ink stain.

"Oh, dear," she said. "I'll fetch the vinegar and a cloth."

"Tell me its location and I'll fetch it," he said, not out of kindness but necessity. If he waited for her, he'd be there all night. "And don't you dare get on your knees to scrub. This was my handiwork and I'll clean it."

In short order, Alek was on his hands and knees, scrubbing at the stain but only making it worse.

"Blot," Mrs. Suchet said.

"I am," he snapped. His teeth felt sharp. If the housekeeper noticed, she said nothing. She had seen worse behavior from him, no doubt. Since his return to Hardwick House, they carefully avoided the subject of his curse. She didn't ask about the room with the chains or why he locked himself in there. He had no inclination to explain.

"It's that letter. You've not been yourself."

Alek laughed bitterly. "I haven't been myself in years."

"You've got more than a little of your grandfather Maksim in you," she said in a knowing tone. "Keep blotting, not scrubbing, and I'll bring in your dinner."

He continued his ministrations until he was certain the rug could not be saved. What did he care about a rug, anyway? It kept the chill from the floor and would continue to do so admirably with a great gray stain. And why did he need to send a letter? That spring had been rainy and travel would be slow. If he took a coach as far as he could and then hired a horse, he'd arrive at Boxon as quickly as a letter.

Yes. He'd do that.

After his meal—long cold—he informed Mrs. Suchet of his travel plans and left instructions for the estate manager. The two had handled his affairs well enough without his input and would continue to do so.

He packed a trunk, taking care to don leather gloves before stowing his weapons away carefully, and tossed in whatever garments seemed decent enough for society. He'd leave in the morning, so there was no time to worry about wardrobes. If Godwin Marechal took offense, then he could fight off the beast on his own with his one working eye.

The beast inside him took notice, hungry and wanting.

Solenne

Boxon Village

The Blacksmith

They found Miles by the forge, with the collar opened on his shirt and his sleeves rolled up. Damp blonde hair stuck to his brow. The furnace was cold, but a stove in the corner heated the workshop to a balmy temperature.

Miles smiled when he spotted them, and Luis gulped audibly. He inspected the damaged armor, accepted the item for trade, and Solenne helpfully suggested that Luis would be interested in observing the repair process.

"Really?" Miles blinked, as if surprised, but then gave Luis an assessing gaze. "An extra pair of hands is always helpful, but you'll ruin your coat."

Solenne leaned in, whispering, "He's interested in your hands."

"I don't mind," Luis said in a hurry, blushing and stumbling over his words. "About the coat."

Miles took Luis' coat and hung it from a peg on the wall.

Solenne enjoyed watching her brother, the monster hunter, stumble awkwardly around his crush. It was too precious for words, yet she dug deep down and found a cheery, "I'll stop by after my visit with Charlotte."

She didn't wait for Luis to answer. Miles had turned his attention to the damaged armor, and Luis watched the blacksmith work.

The mill dominated Boxon. The nearest river lay several hours' journey to the west, which meant the village relied on overland transport for the delivery of raw wool and linen and the shipping of finished goods downriver to the capital. Overland travel left a lot to be desired. Pavement wasn't always a guarantee, and the further away from Founding a person traveled, the more likely the road would be mud. Still, while industry didn't thrive in Boxon, it brought in steady income and a steady supply of fresh goods.

Solenne ambled through the open-air market, enjoying the crowd and the noise. She took a fair amount of pride in knowing that Boxon's stability was thanks to her family. Other settlements as close to a nexus point rarely fared as well. Such proximity created uncertainty. Farmers lost livestock and crops. People feared going out after dark. Industry shuttered at sunset.

An uncontrolled nexus point was a death sentence to a settlement. It was more than a passing curiosity that most abandoned settlements were always found near a nexus point. They were abandoned for a reason.

Boxon had a modest industry, and its citizens felt safe.

Sometimes the provincial government would send in forces to secure the area. Sometimes they considered the settlement a strategic loss. With no easy access to transportation or valuable resources, she had doubted the province would be motivated to send aid to Boxon if her family failed.

The threats came from all sides. If they could just make it through the next full moon, if Luis could defeat the wolf and not get himself killed in the process...

She needed a lifeline.

"Miss Marechal."

Chapter Three

Solenne

Boxon Village

A Street

Solenne turned at the deep voice, familiar with its owner. "Good morning, Colonel Chambers."

"Always a delight." Colonel Chambers stood with a younger man with a thin, pinched face. The young man gave her a bored once-over. "Permit me to present my nephew, Mr. Parkell. How is your father?"

Chambers leaned on his cane, and a gloved hand touched the tip of his hat. A leg injury forced him out of the military and into the occupation of the gentleman farmer. He was pleasant enough, Solenne thought, if a bit pompous. He had renamed his house Vervain, after all. Vervain, as in the legendary sword, said to slay werewolf and vampires in a single blow.

Honestly.

Chambers seemed to hold her in high regard, though Solenne could not imagine why. She had only ever been civil to the man and made pains to avoid him.

Godwin, however, placed several not-so-subtle remarks that Colonel Chambers was not so much older than her—only fifteen years!—and she could do far worse for a match. He had enough money to revitalize the Marechal's fortunes and understood their responsibility, even supported their mission.

The family needed a lifeline. She wasn't sure if this was the correct one.

"Healing slower than he would like," she said. Over the last few weeks, it became apparent that Godwin would lose sight in his eye. He could be handling it better, but Solenne thought her father was allowed to be a grumpy bastard, considering the circumstances.

"Any news of the creature that attacked him?" His gloved hand gripped the silver handle of his cane, the leather creaking.

"Luis tracked the creature, but the rain has slowed down the search," she said. Rain obscured any trail the creature made with freshly churned mud. Thus far,

Luis had not discovered the creature's den, if it had a den. If not, the creature transformed into its human form and now hid among the crowd. It could be anyone.

"It was injured," she added.

"With silver?" He grimaced as he said the word.

"Yes, so that should slow down its regeneration." The silver shot from Luis' pistol, to be precise. If the wolf hid among the flock, so to speak, they would be wounded. She had no one way of knowing how an injury in wolf form translated into a human form, but new and unexplained injuries were something to consider.

The clock tower struck noon.

"I'm afraid I have an appointment to keep," Colonel Chambers said.

"Miss Wodehouse is expecting me." She gave a quick dip of her head and turned away to make her escape.

"How delightful. That is our destination as well."

Disappointed at her failure to escape Chambers' attention, Solenne kept a pleasant smile on her face. "Oh, splendid of Miss Wodehouse to plan a little soirée."

There. She was positively rude to imply that Chambers was imposing himself on a private affair.

His grin did not waver. "Just so. Shall we?" He held out an arm, and she found herself unable to refuse.

The Wodehouse home was a tall stone house off the main street. A footman led them to the back garden, where Charlotte sat reading. A halo of sunshine and vivid spring greenery surrounded her, complementing her pink dress and bronze complexion. Her curling hair had been pulled back into a loose bun. Sunlight picked out warm russet highlights in her brown hair. She made an extraordinarily pretty picture, Solenne thought, even if fashion said that her plump frame and spectacles were unbecoming.

"Interesting book?" Solenne asked.

"Oh, it's horribly dry. A ship's manifest, believe it or not, for Papa's research. Hello." Charlotte closed the book and smiled at her visitors. Mr. Wodehouse once taught at the university in Founding, but his health made it necessary to leave the city for the country. He had an impressive library, but half the volumes were histories and terribly dull, in Solenne's opinion.

Charlotte disagreed, being an avid historian herself. She always had her nose in a book, researching some obscure fact. Solenne's taste in literature veered more toward popular fiction or books on botany. Reading histories reminded her too much of the school reading assignments: something to be endured and then promptly forgotten.

Colonel Chambers made the introductions while the table was prepared on the veranda. "I was hoping to speak to Mr. Wodehouse today. There's a book I'd like him to track down."

"Papa is in Founding on business. He'll be home tomorrow," Charlotte answered. Her eyes sparkled behind the spectacles, because there was nothing she enjoyed better than books, or perhaps it was the sunshine.

Honestly, it surprised Solenne that they were such fast friends. As children, Solenne had Alek as a companion, and every moment spent in the village school was a trial to be endured. Charlotte had been the model student, always with her nose in a book and never interested in exploring anything exciting.

That changed at university, when two young women who were barely acquaintances were thrown into the same dormitory and several of the same classes. Late nights and early morning classes forged their friendship.

Charlotte turned her attention to Mr. Parkell. "Are you in Boxon long?"

Mr. Parkell watched as Charlotte carefully poured out the tea and served up tiny sandwiches cut into triangles. "My physician prescribed fresh country air. Uncle obliged." He picked up a silver spoon, then removed a cloth from his coat's breast pocket to polish it. "Everything is delightfully rustic."

His snobbish tone belied his words.

Colonel Chambers ignored his nephew's rudeness. "I'm glad to have the company. I'm tired of rambling about that big house all on my own." He tossed a look her way.

Solenne focused on her tiny sandwich. The bread was thin and the filling nothing but cucumbers and butter. They were a rather unsatisfactory experience, and she wondered how many she could politely eat before raising eyebrows. Probably not enough to sate her stomach.

"Life in the country must be so dull after the military. I can't imagine it compares," Charlotte said.

"Things were exciting enough on the equinox." Chambers glanced to Solenne.

Rather than exchange the polite sympathies about her father, Solenne said, "Tell me all about the West Lands. Is it true that there are plants that will swallow a person whole?"

"Oh, yes! The land there is the planet's natural habit. Is it wholly unsuitable for humans?" Charlotte leaned forward with rapt attention.

Chambers told them about flowers that changed colors based on the temperature, and the person-swallowing plant actually swallowed insects, not people.

The West Lands was native habitat, free from human alteration. Every child learned the story in school. After the ship landed, computers deployed terraforming equipment, but the energy fluctuations from the nexus broke the machines. By the time the crew and the settlers woke—again, the stories never really explained what this sleep was but implied it was something other than the regular eight hours a night sleep—they discovered they were on the wrong planet and only a small portion of the continent had been made suitable for human habitation.

Surprise.

The knowledge to reform a planet in your image. To move between the stars…it all seemed like a fairy story.

"Did you see the city in the mountains? Is it true a second ship landed there, but none of the crew or settlers survived? Machines built a city for the dead?" Charlotte shivered at the grotesque image.

"My company never made it that far west."

"And you found the sword Vervain?"

Solenne's interest perked. The sword, one of several empowered weapons created by early settlers, were common bedtime stories. She did not have the enthusiasm for history like her friend, but she relished stories.

"Is that true? It was lost," Solenne said.

"I have an old sword, ancient, in my collection, but not that sword," Chambers said.

"Collection." Mr. Parkell made a derisive noise. "It's like living in an armory."

"I thought we might have a dance," Chambers said, once again ignoring his nephew's rudeness. "A summer solstice dance, before the event, of course."

"How exciting! I do so love a dance." Charlotte clapped her hands, legendary swords forgotten. Which was a shame, because Vervain was one of the few interesting points of their conversation.

Colonel Chambers nudged his nephew with his foot, who sputtered out, "Oh, yes. I'm intrigued by what passes as entertainment among the rustics."

Not even Charlotte could ignore the disdain in his voice. She looked rather awkwardly at the floral centerpiece on the table. "I am rather pleased with the tulips this year. Such color."

Solenne would have none of the pompous twit sitting, a guest in Charlotte's home, and looking down his nose at them. "I'm sure life on the fringes out here must be a change for you, Mr. Parkell. I rather enjoyed the noise and bustle of Founding, when Miss Wodehouse and I attended university."

"Academics. I should have known," he scoffed. "I much prefer ladies with other accomplishments."

"Jase, that's enough," Colonel Chambers warned, nearly growling.

"Accomplishments?" Charlotte asked, her voice sweet. Solenne recognized the trap as Mr. Parkell blundered in. Even Colonel Chambers sensed the danger, and leaned back in his chair, content to watch the scene play out.

"Amiable, amenable and charming, for starters. Singing, playing an instrument, painting or sketching, and needlework. Those sorts of accomplishments." He examined a butter knife and must have decided it clean enough to spread cream on a scone.

"Oh, I daresay that between us we can do a passable sketch," Charlotte said, sharing a glance with Solenne.

"My needlework is decently good," Solenne added. "I always thought sewing and embroidery was rather like stabbing the cloth with a tiny little dagger."

"You're skilled with a dagger in any setting," Charlotte said in a conversation tone.

"Any sharp object, really. You've any impressive recall on what you've read," Solenne replied.

"That's the trouble with you academic types," Jase said with a sigh, explaining nothing about the trouble with academic types. "You ruined your eyes reading. Still, you'd be pretty if you put some effort in."

"Such flattery. I hardly know what to think," Solenne said dryly.

"Jase, enough. Apologize," Chambers said.

"What are your accomplishments, Mr. Parkell?" He might be more amiable than a boil on a bottom if he put some effort in. She felt rather proud of herself that she held her tongue.

"I am a gentleman." He sat straighter. The leaf green silk coat and darker green trousers might have done for Founding but they made him look ridiculously fussy sitting next to his uncle in a sensible brown coat and tan buckskins.

"And your occupation?"

"I am Uncle's heir," Mr. Parkell announced, as if that were a real accomplishment.

"Your only accomplishment is breathing, then." A gasp went around the table, followed by a chuckle from Chambers. Solenne continued, "But I'm a simple rustic, so I'm not sure what the people of quality do in Founding."

"And I've ruined my eyes. Ruined," Charlotte repeated for dramatic effect. "How will we get on, Solenne? Why did no one *tell* me of the dangers?"

"I'm sure you think you're very amusing—" Mr. Parkell started, but was interrupted by Chambers laying his hand on the young man's shoulder.

"I think you've delighted us enough with your opinion. It's time for us to take our leave. Wait for me outside," Chambers said.

"But, Uncle—"

"Now, Jase."

The man snapped to attention, made a hasty bow and left.

Charlotte huffed, tossing her napkin to the table. "I'm sorry, Colonel Chambers, but your nephew is awful."

"It's his mother's influence. She spoils him." Chambers leisurely finished his cup of tea. "I must say, I did enjoy watching you ladies eviscerate him."

"Eviscerate? We were positively polite," Solenne replied.

Charlotte nodded in agreement. "We went easy on him, as it was an unfair fight. Imagine, picking a battle of the wits when all he brought was his..." She waved a hand, as if searching for the correct word.

"Arrogance? Snobbery?" Solenne supplied.

"His fashionable coat." A grin spread across Charlotte's face, then she sobered. "Don't tell Papa. He'll be horrified."

"You ladies have my word," Chambers said. "Miss Marechal, may I have a word before I leave?"

Solenne froze. "Yes?"

"I'll just clear these things," Charlotte said, loading up a tray and returning it to the kitchen.

Chambers cleared his throat. His cheeks were ruddy, from the sun or the embarrassment of his nephew's behavior, she could not tell. "Please do not let Jase's conduct keep you from attending my dance. His lungs are only one of things I mean to improve about him while he stays with me."

"You've got your work cut out for you." Solenne was not the most polished of young ladies. Her clothes for going out in society were several years out of fashion and her clothes for working about the house were homespun. Her hair forever refused to stay in a neat plait or in a bun. Regardless, she did her best to be amiable. Manners cost nothing, as her mother always said.

"Just so. I'd like it very much if you would attend," Chambers said. "Very much." The light gleamed unnaturally on his eyes.

The summer solstice seemed impossibly distant. "I had planned to attend, but with my father's condition..." She let her voice trail off, unwilling to let Colonel Chambers trap her into a promised dance or three. Last autumn, at the last dance she attended, he hovered near and scowled at any man who approached her.

"Understandable. Let us hope for a speedy recovery." He smiled; Solenne felt an icy chill that had nothing to do with the spring weather. Perhaps it was the sunlight or the shadows, but his normally affable face transformed into a leer.

He gave an elegant bow and left.

She breathed a sigh of relief. She knew that people called her a spinster behind her back. Twenty-six was not so very old, but the expectation was to marry young. Her mother had been twenty when she married Godwin, who had been thirty. The double standard of men not *spoiling* with age rankled her.

If she were to believe the gossip, she needed to pick someone, anyone, while she still had options. Colonel Chambers might not inspire warm feelings in her, but he wasn't a bad choice.

Just a bit dull. And tedious. And the last person she'd ever want to marry.

"It seems the long winter has not determined Colonel Chambers' regard for you," Charlotte said, returning to the veranda. She had a small platter of fresh cookies, steam still rising.

"Lemon cookies?"

"Cook made your favorite. Too bad our guests left so soon." Charlotte set two down on the plate next to her teacup, then grabbed one for herself directly from the platter.

"I see. Two for Solenne, and the rest for Charlotte," Solenne joked.

Charlotte ignored her attempt to lighten the mood. "He'd be a fine match. Retired but not too old, settled but lively, and wealthy enough for a wife and family."

"The gentleman farmer." Solenne grimaced, nibbling on her cookie.

She refused to be pressured. Any match she made would be purely practical and loveless. Her troublesome heart had belonged to the same man since she could remember: Aleksandar. Two years older than her, he seemed so mature and handsome and clever and a dozen other favorable attributes. But more than that, Aleksandar had been her friend. They trained side by side. He listened to her. He never pressured her into going against her nature. Instead, he made the worst ideas seem like the best. He led, and she very much wanted to jump in after him.

At some point, her willingness to take foolhardy risks to make him laugh turned into a desire to have his approval. She wanted his attention, and she wanted his kisses.

Not that much ever came of it.

Was a secret engagement still valid if your fiancé vanished for ten years?

Solenne gave up hope of Alek returning after her first year at university. He knew her plans. He knew where to find her. He just...didn't.

Yes, she knew it was pitiable to carry a flame for a man she hadn't seen in ten years, but her feelings remained. Her regard for Aleksandar, or her memory of him, prevented her from forming a strong attachment to another. She had simply never met another man she admired half as much.

And he still hasn't replied to my letter.

She was not worried. He would answer the call for help. Aleksandar was a good man. Godwin, unjustly, made him leave, but he would return. She knew it, felt it in her bones the same way she felt the nexus surge with the seasons.

A wind stirred, carrying the bright floral scents of the garden.

She hated this; longing for a man who walked away. She had tried and tried to harden her heart to him, to move on, but it stubbornly refused. She was no longer that sixteen-year-old girl infatuated with her friend, but it seemed her heart very much was.

Ridiculous things, hearts.

She didn't have the time or the luxury for sentimentality. Marechal House desperately needed money for repairs, and Colonel Chambers had money. A husband who could aid Luis would be ideal, but money bought new equipment. Wouldn't it be lovely to have Luis in new armor and not fret about it failing when he needed it most?

Love and adoration would be nice, but those were luxuries for an aging woman in her position.

Colonel Chambers was a good match. The girl she had once been no longer held dominion over her heart. She had to make adult choices now. She had to think of the future.

Chapter Four

Aleksandar

Fallkirk

A desolate road

The horses gave a startled cry, and the carriage lurched precariously to one side. Wood groaned, and Alek shifted to the far side to act as a counterweight, as if that would help. The horses reared back, hooves thrashing as the driver snapped his whip. The wheels on one side left the earth and crashed back down. Alek tumbled against the carriage door. Glass shattered.

Dazed, he pulled himself upright. Broken glass dug into the calfskin leather of his gloves but did not pierce. Wetness trickled down the side of his head.

Using a handkerchief that had once been grand but now was in tatters, he pressed the cloth to the head wound. Feeling the chill of the cold spring air, he pushed open the door and stumbled out of the carriage.

The driver limped badly but stood on his own two feet. The horses reared and flailed their hooves, panic in their eyes. The carriage was in worse condition with a snapped axle.

"The horses were startled, sir," the driver said, his voice panicked.

By the time he grabbed the horses' reins, he had himself under enough control to coo soft words. Gently, he stroked their necks, and his calm demeanor eventually soothed the animals.

"What startled them?" Alek asked.

"A great furry beast. It darted out of the forest, bold as brass."

Alek rolled his shoulders. He had a week until the next event, but he could already feel the pull of the nexus point the closer he got to Boxon. The area had always made his skin sing with awareness. Now it felt amplified. Undeniable.

A growl came from the tree line. The horses whinnied and stamped, nervous.

Yes, that pull again. A creature of the nexus was near.

"Do beasts often attack this road?" he asked.

"Sir?" The driver blinked. "No, sir. It's never happened before. Only when the moon is full."

And the barrier holding back the nexus energies was thin.

Alek retrieved his box from the back of the carriage. The contents were a jumbled mess. His fingers brushed over a wooden box but did not open it to check on the contents. Perhaps the bottles of wolfsbane tonic survived. If not, he had enough time to make more. At the moment, there was a beast stalking them in broad daylight.

Time was of the essence.

Strapped to the inside lid, the war hammer waited. Dedicated use had rounded the silver head of the hammer. The claw end curved wickedly backward, gleaming in the early afternoon light. Inlaid silver decorated the handle. It was a bit extravagant, but Alek had never regretted the purchase. The hammer had a comfortable weight and felt as familiar in his hands as an old friend. This was his preferred weapon, and nothing outperformed it for close combat.

The coachman's eyes went wide at the sight of the hammer. "What do you have that for?"

Alek spun the hammer, tossed it in the air, and caught it with ease. The weight felt good, like it belonged in his hand. He barely felt the sting of silver through the calfskin gloves.

"Four or two?" he demanded.

"S-Sir?"

"Was the beast on four legs or two?"

"I cannot recall. It was a blur," the coachman said, stumbling over his words.

"Stay here," Alek said.

"We're not going anywhere until the horses calm down."

They weren't going anywhere until he dealt with the rogue wolf.

Alek moved away from the mud of the road to the marginally less trampled grass alongside the road. Once the roads had been paved with a black substance that poured out like liquid and cooled to a rock-hard consistency. Concrete was used in the larger towns and cities, but the constant expanding and contracting with the weather made it degrade too quickly for the more rural routes.

He could have taken a boat down the river. Many people preferred to travel via canal and rivers than deal with a bumpy, dusty coach trip. Wanting to keep himself away from crowds as much as possible, he chose the less desirable coach on an infrequently used road.

More fool him.

He should have found a horse and rode the entire way. Alone. No nosy coachmen looking through his trunks or making eyes at his weaponry.

Carefully, he picked his way across the forest floor, tracking the wolf's clumsy trail. Tracks in the mud and disturbed undergrowth gave no doubt which direction the wolf fled. But did it leave? Or was it stalking?

Creatures prowled the nights of solstice and equinox. A cursed wolf, however, could lose control in the days leading to the event. With just weeks to summer solstice, the cursed monstrosity had no control. The Marechals were right to beg for his help.

Solenne, he reminded himself. Solenne wrote to him. No one else. That knowledge pleased the bestial part of his nature. It wanted her to claim him, to mark him as hers, if only as her pet creature.

A twig snapped under his foot. He paused, listening.

This could be an ordinary wolf. Boxon was still two days' journey away. For this to be the same creature that injured Godwin required it to have considerable territory. Alek disliked that prospect. However, the alternative of it being a different cursed wolf was worse. That meant there was a master wolf creating a pack.

A growl sounded, shifting through the dense foliage.

Alek answered with his own rumbling, "Beast, come out now." Cursed creatures, especially ones who could not hold their true form, had no patience to stalk their prey.

He did not have to wait long. A heavy weight landed on his back. He rolled and lay prone, one arm holding back the wolf and the other gripping the hammer.

The wolf snapped, teeth yellow and diseased. Hot, fetid breath wafted over him. To call the monstrous creature a wolf was a kindness. It was a half-finished thing, stuck between a transition from wolf and man. Not half of either and not wholly itself. A snarling muzzle distorted a human face, holding far too many teeth.

The body walked on two legs, despite a wolf's haunches and paws, and defying every law known to nature. Violet-tinged fur coated the body, taller and more massive than a man's. The hands were distorted into grasping talons. The eyes were the worst, still retaining their human shape but glowing violet. What stared out of those eyes was a brutal beast, inhuman and unfeeling.

Alek recognized his own kind.

This thing had been a person, once.

A second snarl, coming from the left, distracted him. He turned to glimpse a second wolf, large and so pale a lavender it nearly glowed in the dim of the forest.

Pack.

Claws slashed across his stomach. The fire of pain flared and burned. Teeth sank into his arm, piercing the coat. Rich and metallic, the scent of blood, even his own, set Alek craving to bite.

His mouth watered as his teeth descended. He forgot about the second wolf. All he could hear was the wolf's heart thudding and pounding. It would be nothing to bite just under the jaw and sink his teeth into the beast's throat. He had not had a hunt in so long, locking himself away during the full moon.

His blood sang. Inside him, an insidious voice whispered that it was not such a huge step to partially shift, to let his claws extend. His strength kept the wolf from seriously injuring him, but he'd be stronger if he was in his other form.

His true form.

The hammer crashed into the wolf's skull. It squealed and lurched away.

Alek rolled to his knees, ignoring the pain in his gut, and grabbed the wolf's back leg. It turned, snapping at his hand, but he refused to let go. Clutching tighter, tight enough that his claws extended and dug through the beast's fur, he brought the hammer down again.

It was not an elegant, efficient maneuver, like the ones he had been taught. The fight was vicious, beast against beast. He shouldn't have enjoyed it as much as he did—as his corrupted, cursed nature rose to the surface—but he did.

The leg cracked with a wet squelch and a whine.

Alek shuffled forward on his knees, one hand holding his stomach, until he loomed over the beast's head.

Another blow ended the beast. The ethereal glow diminished until it ceased to be altogether.

The wolf's body seemed to shrink, to dwindle as it lost whatever power it leached from its connection to the nexus, but Alek knew that was an illusion. The wolf would be the same size and weight as it was in life. It would not shift to its human form, as many believed. Whatever strange power that allowed the creature to shift between forms had left and its final form was just that. Final.

He listened for the second wolf. Now would be the ideal opportunity to attack. He was weak with blood loss. The curse that caused a man to change into a beast affected the mind, but a wolf's instincts would be to attack vulnerable prey.

He waited, aware of his heart pounding in his chest. Every thud affirmed his unnatural existence.

Alive. Alive. Alive.

He did not know for how much longer. Adrenaline coursed through his veins, but he knew he lacked the strength for a second fight.

Birdsong returned. The wolf had left.

He relaxed, even though the wolf's ability to resist the temptation of wounded prey worried him. The wolf was clever and potentially rational. Was it older? How long had the person been cursed that they had so much control over their beast? He disliked any possible answer. He had lived with his curse for years, and control remained a flimsy thing for him.

Alek attempted to clean the hammer with an unsullied corner of his shirt and did a piss-poor job of it. Soaked through, the violet-hued blood was indistinguishable from his own on the shirt and smeared with the matted bit of fur and brain.

The wounds weren't deep, but he had lost a considerable amount of blood. Honestly, his hand hurt worse than his stomach. It stung with every motion, not to mention the beast ruined a pair of expensive gloves that Alek could not easily replace.

Hissing with pain, he lifted the wolf to carry across his shoulders and rose to his feet. He wobbled for a long minute. A good meal and a solid night's sleep, and his wounds would heal overnight. It was the only benefit of his curse.

He followed the sound of the coachman and the horses until he broke through the trees.

The coachman shouted in surprise, causing the horses to stamp their feet nervously. "Sir—"

Torn, the front of his shirt gaped open, exposing the fresh slashes.

Bother.

"Do not be concerned. They are not deep. What is the nearest town?" he asked.

"Fallkirk."

"And does Fallkirk pay a bounty?" He did not wait for an answer, instead lashing the wolf to the top of the coach. The spilled luggage had been secured back in place.

Alek considered retrieving a shirt from his trunk, but his wounds still bled. He could not afford to ruin another shirt. Instead, he stripped down and wrapped the old shirt against his abdomen. The bleeding would cease soon enough. He felt the coachman's eyes on him, watching him with alarm.

"Are you—"

"I am tired and want a hot meal and a bath," he said in a crisp tone that did not invite further questions.

Food. Sleep. Those were his priorities. Tomorrow, he'd collect the bounty on the wolf and find a horse to finish the journey on his own.

Solenne

Boxon Hill

The North Pasture

Her aim left a considerable amount to be desired.

Solenne frowned at the target, then at the arrow planted into the hay bale behind the target. She knew that learning to shoot with her non-dominant arm would be work, but she didn't expect to be so embarrassingly *bad* at it.

"I don't understand," she muttered, retrieving the arrows from the bale. "I used to be decent with a bow and arrow."

"You also used to shoot with your other hand. Your body is relearning a skill," Luis said. To demonstrate, he switched his stance and his bow to his right hand. He notched an arrow and drew back his left hand. After taking a moment to correct his stance and line up to the target, he released the arrow.

It sailed through the air and hit the target slightly off center.

Luis gave a whoop. "Can you believe that? First try. I'm sorry, Solenne, but I am ah-maze-ing."

"Cheater," Solenne said.

"Yes, cheating with my superior skills and techniques." He nodded and gave her a sympathetic, if exaggerated, frown. "Poor Solenne. It must be hard to be so old and incapable of learning new skills."

"Oh, hush." She switched back to her dominant hand. The muscles in her arm ached as she drew the string back, but every part of her ached at the moment from exercise. Repetition would build her strength and relearn the skills she once had.

The arrow flew straight, hit the target, and bounced harmlessly off.

"That's not possible," she said, frustration growing. Desire to toss the bow to the ground and stomp on it until the frame snapped surged through her, but equipment cost coin. She could only trade so many tonics and liniments.

Speaking of, she rolled her shoulder and flexed her hand.

"Did you hurt yourself?" Luis asked. He took her hand, removed the glove, and gently rubbed her wrist.

"It's nothing."

"Lies," he tutted, but released her hand. "You are using the muscles in your hand for all your strength, instead of your arm muscles. Do not do this."

"Don't stand this way. Don't shoot the ground," she said, voice teasing.

"You are very good at hitting the ground."

They retrieved the spent arrows and cleared the evidence of their practice. The upper fields were host to the flock of sheep, leaving the lower field empty and far enough away from the house that no one, namely Godwin, could spot them. Of course, that would require Godwin leaving his bedchamber, a feat he had not done since his injury.

Solenne didn't like the way her father sulked. A fever had kept him in bed, but the illness had passed. It had been weeks since the accident. He should be up and about, especially with the next full moon only days away.

"It will grow easier," Luis said, interrupting her thoughts.

"Will it?"

"Repetition. Build your strength. Get calluses on those soft, ladylike hands."

She huffed with amusement and held up her hands. The pads were red, and she knew she needed to ice her wrist. While her hands weren't as rough as they had been before Godwin ended her training, they were far from soft and ladylike. She worked. It showed.

Luis set the equipment in a disused cottage near the edge of the forest. Once, the estate manager had lived there, back when the house had a larger staff and people were not too frightened of living near the forest. Empty except for dusty furniture, it provided a dry spot to wait out a rainstorm or hide away from her responsibilities for an afternoon. Solenne had not enjoyed that luxury in some time, but she remembered sneaking books away from the library and reading in the old chair by the window.

As they approached the house, she carried her basket as if she had been gathering herbs in the forest. No one questioned her.

Travers cornered her as she left her workroom, a jar of liniment in her pocket. "The master asks to speak with you, Miss Solenne," he said.

The scent of sickness hung in the room. Godwin sat in a chair by the bedside, brooding in the dark. A quarterstaff rested against his legs, as if he had used the weapon as a walking stick. He probably did, rather than ask for help.

Solenne set down a pitcher of fresh water on the bureau. She then drew back the curtains and opened the window to air out the room.

"Can't you let a dying man sleep?" Godwin grumbled.

"You're not dying, and you stink."

He gave a tired chuckle. "Ah, the sweetness of your gentle ministrations."

She regarded the pale figure of her father. He seemed thin, swallowed up by days spent in bed. A brief fever had burned through him. The doctor confirmed that infection had not set in, but Godwin would never regain his sight.

"You're hiding," she said.

Godwin made disgruntled noises, none of which expressed denial.

"But it is good to see you out of bed. I can send up hot water." The house had a heated bathing chamber on the ground level. However, traversing the several stairs that lay between Godwin and a hot bath would be difficult.

"I'll go downstairs. I know you're itching to clean in here," he said.

"True." The bed desperately needed fresh sheets after fever sweats and fitful sleeping.

"I received a letter," he said.

"Oh." Anticipation zipped through her. Solenne focused on keeping her voice light and unworried as she poured water into a clean glass. Her smile was pure artifice as she handed it to her father, along with a pill left by the doctor.

"It seems Aleksandar will return to us in our hour of need."

Solenne turned her head to hide her genuine smile. Aleksandar's return meant nothing. She meant nothing to him. He had said as much. It was unwarranted, unreasonable, and unforgivable how excited she felt thinking about his return.

Ten years had passed. She was not that girl. He was not that man.

She knew that.

She *knew*, yet her heart clung onto the delusion to the point of pain. Aleksandar would be married by now, possibly with a child—children—and she was practically an old maid with few prospects. Well, Colonel Chambers seemed interested, but the notion of an alliance with the retired military man left her cold, like a staring down a plate of sprouts that had to be eaten. Ultimately good for her, but dreaded.

Godwin thumped the quarterstaff against the floor, snagging her attention. "It seems I wrote to him," he grumbled.

"Drink," Solenne prompted, pushing the glass into his hands.

He held her gaze for a long moment, the glare louder than any accusation. Finally, he took a mouthful and swallowed the pill.

"Funny how I don't remember writing."

"You had a fever. I'm sure there's plenty you don't recall," she said, voice placid. She stripped the bed, tossing the soiled linens to the floor.

"I would never ask that coward for help."

"We don't have a choice, do we? Sending Luis to hunt alone would be suicidal," she retorted, heat seeping into her voice. She refused to let anything of the sort happen to her brother because of Godwin's pride.

Silence stretched between them as she remade the bed. Finally, with fresh sheets and a well-worn but clean quilt in place, she turned her attention to Godwin's clothes. He had worn the same sweat-stained shirt for days, and it stank. She tossed a clean set of clothes onto the bed.

"You must think me worthless to ask him to come here, after what he did," Godwin said, breaking the silence.

Solenne had heard this tirade before. Godwin blamed Aleksandar for the death of their mother was the long and the short of it, despite knowing that Amalie took unnecessary risks. Amalie always had. Alek had been in Amalie's workshop the day of the explosion, but he had not been responsible. Anyone could see that.

Well, anyone sensible.

Frankly, Solenne was sick of Godwin's self-indulgent pity, his anger at losing Amalie, and his suffocating need to control his children.

"Marechals hunt monsters. We all know that," she said.

"And now I can't. You're replacing me."

"For the love of—" She rubbed the back of her neck, aware that most of her hair had escaped from her bun. "I don't think you're useless, Papa."

"I am blind."

"In one eye. One!" She grabbed the quarterstaff from him and swung with no real force. He blocked the staff easily, then wrenched it away. It smacked into furniture. "Not so blind after all."

"Do not taunt me, girl. I am useless out there." He waved a hand toward the window.

"Oh, I'm sorry. I didn't realize that your decades of experience and knowledge were contained in that eye. I'm so sorry for your loss, but how extraordinary! We should write to the academy in Founding. Top minds will want to examine you—"

"Enough of your sarcasm, girl," he snapped. With a weary sigh, he rubbed the mostly white stubble on his chin. When had his iron gray turned white?

"There is a wolf out there with the taste for blood," she said. Hopefully, her words would remind him that the situation was bigger than his pride and his injured eye.

"Am I such a failure?" he asked.

"No, Papa." She abandoned her tidying and knelt at his feet, her hands on his knees. "You want to keep us safe, to keep everyone safe."

"It is our duty to guard the nexus point," he intoned, practically chanting the often-repeated phrase.

"Luis cannot do this on his own."

"He's not much of a fighter," Godwin said.

Solenne fought back the urge to argue. Luis was an excellent fighter, but there was more to him than the love of the hunt.

He patted her head, just as he did when she was a child. His rough hands knocked free the last of her hair from the bun, but her appearance was the farthest thing from her mind. In the silence, he was just a man, worried about his family and his declining health. She recalled all the wonderful memories, the laughter and joy that sparked in Godwin with ease before sorrow and grief took that away.

"Do not think I haven't seen you practicing archery," he said, breaking the silence.

He had seen that? They had chosen a field so far away and been so careful. A servant must have reported their activity, probably Travers. He had an uncanny ability for knowing when she was up to mischief. Or Godwin had spied Luis carrying the equipment.

No, she decided. Her father didn't know, not for certain, and waited for Solenne to deny it.

As angry and frustrated as her father made her, Solenne couldn't bring herself to lie to him. "You'll have to leave this room if you plan to make me stop," she said. Not that she would.

"No. Practice in the courtyard. I want to see," he said hurriedly, almost as if he were ashamed. Then, he added, "I was wrong to end your training. But your arm—"

"Is fine, and the other is perfectly functional. I'm not swinging a broadsword, but I don't think I'd be able to do that anyway."

Another pat, then he motioned for her to back away. Leaning heavily on the quarterstaff, he heaved himself to his feet.

"There's no shame in seeking help. We're strong together. Don't you always tell us that? Strength in numbers," she said, gentleness returning to her voice.

Six days until the full moon. She hoped Aleksandar arrived in time.

Chapter Five

Solenne

Boxon Hill

The Woods

Repetition. Repetition. Repetition.

Four days until the full moon.

Solenne drew the bow and waited. A twig cracked. She spun and released. The arrow planted itself into the tree, and the rabbit hopped away.

She had not made superhuman strides in the last few days, but forcing her body to remember what it once knew through stubborn determination helped. Muscle memory unlocked. Skulking through the forest, forced to act fast, also helped. If she thought too much, she favored her wrist and her stance went wrong and she used the wrong set of muscles entirely. Hunting rabbits forced her to move on instinct before she got too in her head. Her aim had improved, even if she still hadn't hit a rabbit.

Sunlight filtered through the forest's canopy, creating pools of shadows. She waited. Listened to the sound of birdsong. The wind made a lovely spring melody with insects buzzing.

This was a waste of time. She could not hunt alongside Luis in four days, and she'd never hit the cursed wolf unless she walked up to it and stabbed it with a silver-tipped arrow. As it stood, she was a liability. Her time would have been better spent preparing tonics and salves, boiling bandages so they were fresh and sterile. How much string did she have for stitching? She loathed dragging needle and thread through flesh, but if Luis needed it, she'd do it. Willow bark for pain and to reduce a fever? She could always use more.

If Luis failed to trap the wolf, if he suffered a severe injury, Godwin would have no choice but to contact the provincial government for support. Familial pride would smart. They would lose the contract to protect the village and they might even lose their home, but too many lives were in danger. The people of Boxon and the valley deserved to live without fear of the monsters that prowled the dark.

Alek said he would come.

Four days until the full moon.

A twig snapped. Solenne finally noticed the stillness in the air. Birdsong had vanished. Even the insects retreated.

Solenne notched an arrow and held the bow at ready. It was not uncommon for a cursed creature to feel the pull of the nexus as the moon approached its zenith. They were known to give in early to the shift and prowl the territory outside their den, which is why she was by herself and not with her brother. Luis searched for signs of the wolf and its den.

The back of her neck crawled with the sensation of being watched. She shouldn't have gone into the forest alone. She should have stuck with hay bales for target practice.

Carefully, she picked her way through the undergrowth, back to a deer trail, and toward the old cottage. She'd run for the safety of the building if need be. The door should hold. Either the wolf would grow bored when it realized she was locked up tight and leave, or someone in the house would realize she was missing. Travers, most likely. He always seemed to know where she was, especially when she was somewhere she wasn't meant to be.

Reach the cottage. She'd be safe in the cottage.

The undergrowth thinned. Sunlight broke through the canopy of leaves. The cottage sat half in shadow, half in the sun. The light made the golden stones glow against the darkness of the surrounding forest.

She had never seen anything so inviting.

A growl came to her ears. Solenne spun, the bow drawn and ready to fire.

A man held up his hands in surrender. He stepped back, holding his hands up. "I did not intend to startle you," he said.

"Who are you?" She kept the arrow trained on the man. Only a few feet separated them, and she felt confident that even she could hit him at this range.

Several days' beard growth covered his face. Dust and dirt covered him too, like he had rolled in the mud. Dark circles hung under his eyes. Hair had been pulled back to keep it tidy, but it escaped in a tangled mess. He appeared thin, in need of a hearty meal and a good night's rest. Those things were hard to get on the road, Solenne understood, especially as far out on the edge of civilization as they were.

More than the man's desperate need for a thorough scrubbing and a haircut, menace dripped off him. He stood with a predator's stance, despite his submissive gestures, watching his prey.

Watching her.

"A traveler," he said. The horse munching on leaves behind him supported that. "I stopped at the well for water."

"We're nowhere near the main road, and no one knows about the cottage and the well." Practically no one, and if they did, no one with sense would use it. That was why the cottage remained empty. "Try again," she ordered.

A look of amusement flashed across his face. An unsettling grin of sharp white teeth spread across his tan, weathered skin. "Well, to be perfectly honest, I thought I might wash up. I am a slave to vanity."

"Water your horse and fill your canteen, then be on your way." She waved the bow toward the well but did not lower it.

"I heard the Marechals welcomed travelers at their hearth. Does that kindness not extend to the water of your wells, Miss Marechal?" His words had the ring of familiarity, yet she did not know this man.

Solenne lowered the bow. "The roads here are difficult to travel. You are welcome to stay the night in the cottage."

"Easy? No. I can't claim it's been an easy journey."

Nor an easy few years, judging by the state of him. Everything about his travel-worn appearance still held, but she noticed the lines on his brows and the exhaustion in his face. He seemed thinner, and in a way that was more than lean and suggested illness.

"You can wash up if you don't mind cold water," she said and headed for the cottage. Inside, she pointed to the tub and soap.

"Using this for storage? Seems a waste," the man said. He stood uncomfortably close as he looked about the one room, making no motion to retrieve the tub.

She shivered and moved a hand to her silver blade. Menace rolled off the man. "It's built to last, but no one is brave enough to live out here on their own."

"I understand this region has a wolf problem." He grinned, somehow baring more teeth than should be possible.

She tapped the flat of her blade against the cake of soap. His eyes followed the movement. "Just a small suggestion. You smell."

"So do you, Solenne." That grin reappeared, sharp and unsettling.

He knew her name.

Something inside her, a thread or a faint warning bell, reverberated in her chest. She needed to leave. Not flee, because running made predators chase, but leave.

Minding to walk at a casual gait, the tension in her chest eased once she reached the cottage's gate. She felt foolish at her skittishness. The man was a traveler, drifting between the settlements on the fringe of habitable land. It was a hard sort of life and he deserved kindness, not apprehension.

"Come to the kitchen in the back of the main house if you want a meal," she shouted.

The man had already pumped water from the well into the tub. First, he allowed his horse to drink its fill. Sunlight picked out the golden highlights in his brown hair.

Then he removed his shirt.

Lean muscles flexed in the sun. The man had a large frame, but hardship made him lean enough to count his ribs. On his chest, over his heart, was a simple tattoo in gray ink, a circle surrounded by a burst of rays.

Sunlight, her namesake. She didn't know why her breath caught in her chest because the man was a stranger and the tattoo held no significance.

Pale scars stood out against his flesh, crisscrossing his belly and back. They whispered of a life of pain and danger. A fierce bite stood out on his shoulder, looking almost fresh and unhealed. What monsters did that to him? Despite the scars, despite the ribs standing out, he had strength yet in his body.

She pressed a hand to her chest and swore that he smirked.

He dunked his head in the tub. Head wet, water rolled down his chest, rinsing away dust and grime.

Solenne slammed the gate closed, her cheeks burning. "I trust you can find the big house," she said, barely pausing for him to answer.

This was dangerous. She invited a dangerous stranger into her home.

Aleksandar

He watched Solenne scurry away, delighted at the obvious discomfort in her tone, and even more delighted in how her trousers clung to the curves of her ass.

He remained enough of a gentleman that he did not express his appreciation. Unfortunately, he was not enough of a gentleman to avert his eyes. He had a wicked beast inside him.

Wash complete, he returned the tub to its peg on the wall of the cottage. Other than the air of neglect, the building had not changed in the last decade. The roof was sound, and the walls were sturdy enough to keep out monsters. Or keep one contained.

Being so close to Solenne, catching her delicious scent, riled his beast. He heard her heart, steady and true.

Thump. Thump. Thump.

She had not recognized him, which stung, but that wonderful smell helped to ease the hurt. He had purposefully removed his shirt, knowing she watched. She had no comment on the bite. This close to the summer solstice moon and the nexus, the bite was red and raw. He suspected that she only failed to recognize the bite for what it was because she felt the same disorienting attraction as he.

Godwin would recognize the bite at once.

Very well. He'd try his best to remain clothed in the presence of his old mentor. In a few days, as the moon waned, the bite would look as unremarkable as of the other scars on his person.

In a wooden chest, he found a medical kit stocked with wolfsbane. He took the bottle and a few more useful-looking tonics. The wolfsbane would be enough to keep him under control for this cycle.

He had such a clever mate.

Chapter Six

Aleksandar

Boxon Hill

Marechal House

The house remained unchanged in that timeless quality he always associated with the Marechal family. They were a fixed point in his life, staying as they had been a decade ago.

It perched near the midway up Boxon Hill, a squat building with honey-colored stone walls and faded green shutters, surveying the lord's domain. The stone glowed in the late afternoon sunlight. He knew from experience that the house was frightfully cold in the winter, but remained pleasant throughout the summer. The scent of a wood smoke drifted from the chimney.

He could not shake his surprise when Godwin limped down the front steps, leaning heavily on a short staff.

"Aleksandar. Solenne said a disheveled traveler surprised her at the old cottage, and she nearly shot him full of arrows," his old mentor said, obvious pride in his voice. He wore an eye patch. The flesh surrounding it appeared red and swollen.

"How bad is—" Alek stopped himself from finishing the question. He knew how detrimental it could be when a hunter lost their vision. Even partially. Skills honed over a lifetime would have to be relearned. Fighting stances and preferred weapons adapted. It was bad, bad enough for the proud Godwin Marechal to ask for help.

Or at least for Solenne to ask for help.

The man aged poorly in the last ten years, and not just from the recent injuries that put the shuffle of pain in his walk. Alek suspected the tragic death of his wife aged Godwin faster than any beast. His hair was more iron gray than dark. Wrinkles and worry set heavy on his face. Godwin Marechal had been fierce and proud, indomitable in spirit and unbeatable in a fight. This man? This man was frail.

Godwin's good eye glared at Alek. For a moment, he thought Godwin would tear away the patch and demand Alek to gaze on his ruin. No such dramatics occurred.

"The last I heard, you went to the West Lands," Godwin said.

"For a time."

"They have not done you any good."

"I disagree," Alek replied. The West Lands were unsettled and wild. Not wilderness, exactly, but lands lost to uncontrolled nexus points. Some smaller farmsteads and villages scraped out a living there, and Alek scraped out his own meager existence, turning in bounties for whatever slipped through the nexus. It hadn't been profitable, but the hard work forged him into a stronger person. He could not have survived as long as he had with the curse if not for the experiences of the West Lands.

"I'm back to my family's land now," he said.

Godwin nodded. That said enough about Alek's fortunes, meaning he had none. "Nothing has changed," Godwin said.

Alek drew his shoulders back to stand at his full height, angry that Godwin had to be blunt. Of course nothing had changed. Alek was still the same penniless hunter he had been ten years ago, when he asked Godwin's permission to court Solenne.

And Godwin was still the proud fucker.

The wound on his shoulder thrummed, and the silver ink embedded in his skin burned. He would never contain his beast during the full moon if he let his anger take control.

He knew Solenne or Luis needed to marry well, to bring an infusion of coin into the family's coffers. The Marechal children would have to be practical. Marriage to another hunter, while common for the previous generations, would not give them the help they needed now. The once proud family could not afford love.

"It seems your circumstances have changed," Alek said, his voice cold. The beast inside him clawed and snarled, wanting out to finish the job at which the other beast failed. Who was this man to tell him no? To decide he was not good enough for Solenne?

To deny him his mate?

The beast would take what he wanted and answered to no frail man.

Alek snarled. His teeth felt sharper, like they crowded his mouth and needed to bite, bite, bite.

"You'll stay away from Solenne," Godwin said. "She has an understanding with a very good match. You'll not confuse the issue or turn her head."

"You sorely misjudge your daughter if you think she can be confused," Alek said, working the words around a mouthful of teeth.

He struggled to contain the beast, to remember that Godwin had saved Alek and took him into his home, mentored him, and gave him a profession. That man, the man Godwin had once been, deserved Alek's respect.

Deferring to an obviously weaker man felt wrong to the beast, whose thoughts were no more complex than the gratification of seizing and dominance. The beast respected only raw strength. Godwin could not defend himself, not half-blind and limping. He should kneel before Alek, thankful that the strength of the wolf wanted to protect his home and family, not claim those for itself.

Civility, tattered and frayed, held Alek in check. This *was* the man who saved him. This was the man who took him into his own home, when Alek's own family had been slaughtered by a monster.

Silver burned, containing the beast. Alek might be more monster than man now, but his rational mind was still in command. The beast might hold dominion over his body, but his mind controlled his actions.

For the moment.

"You will not enter my home until I have your word," Godwin said, either unaware of his peril or uncaring.

"Very well. You have my word." Alek held out his hand to shake as a peace offering.

Having reached accord, they shook.

The beast howled in frustration. Alek knew all the sound reasons a union with Solenne was foolish and doomed to unhappiness. He could not give her what she needed. He could not be the partner she deserved.

"Come inside. You've had a long journey if you came from the West Lands," Godwin said. "You must want nothing more than a hot bath and a good meal."

Alek wanted several things, but he would settle for a good meal and a comfortable bed. "I washed the worst away at the cottage," he said.

"Then a soak, but I suppose you're young enough that you don't feel the miles in the saddle," Godwin said, even as the groomsman led Alek's horse to the stable.

Inside the front entrance, the house remained the same, as if frozen in a memory. The wooden floor had been axed and polished to a deep, reddish hue. Grand doors lined the foyer to the left and right. From memory, Alek knew the drawing room and the other tidy little rooms of social convention to be to the left and the dining room to the right. A staircase curved up and around to the second floor. A corridor tucked neatly to the right side led to the downstairs kitchen and baths. Beyond that, around a corner or two, was the oldest part of the structure.

The fading sunlight filtered in through tall windows that could use a good washing. The draperies appeared a little more worn and faded. A console table sat between two closed doors, a bowl of fresh flowers perfuming the air. Alek bet if he checked, he'd still find his and Solenne's initials carved into the back of the table when he had been eleven and she nine.

"Solenne said you were injured," Godwin said, pausing at the foot of the stairs.

"A beast attacked our coach. I handled it," Alek replied.

"I am sure. I'll send her up with her kit to patch you up."

"Perhaps not, all things considered." The beast inside him howled with displeasure.

Godwin gave him a withering look. "I need you in fighting shape."

"A good night's rest is all I need." Lies. So many lies.

Solenne

Godwin announced that Alek had arrived but would not be joining them for dinner. Instead, he sent up water for bathing, a meal on a tray, and eventually Solenne with her kit. She schooled her expression to remain neutral. Too eager and Godwin would lock her away in her room. Too insolent and Godwin would rage at her rudeness. She struggled not to rush through her meal in her eagerness.

"What is Hardwick like? I barely remember him." Luis followed her, arms laden with every item their guest could require. Solenne herself carried a pitcher of hot water.

The bedroom door burst open, and a large figure of a man filled the frame. He was cleaner now and dressed casually in a clean white shirt and trousers. His hair had been combed, but his beard was as wild as ever.

The traveler at the cottage.

"Alek," she whispered. This was it, the moment she'd been anticipating for years and the moment she dreaded. She felt like the same over eager girl in the throes of her first love, living for brief touches and stolen moments alone. Nothing had changed. It was as if she had been frozen in amber, and she struggled against the binds in frustration, because she had changed and so had Alek. She hadn't even recognized him. "You look—"

"Tired," Alek said. He eyed Luis. "You've grown since I saw you last."

"Puberty does that. Can you even eat with that thing on your face?" Luis responded.

Alek's face remained blank for three heartbeats. Solenne scrambled to apologize because they needed Alek's help—she had begged for it—and they could not afford to offend him. Even if he was smelly and sported a wild beard that made him look more beast than man.

Alek threw his head back and laughed, loud and booming. He stroked the chin of his bushy beard. "Meals are tricky. Sometimes I like to tuck bits away for later." He mimed picked out crumbs and popped the imaginary morsels in his mouth.

"Set that down on the bureau, please," Solenne said, nudging Luis.

Travers put Alek in the same third floor room, tucked under the eaves of the attic as when he apprenticed with Godwin. Narrow and small for an adolescent, the room was too cramped for three adults. The ceiling slanted dramatically, requiring Alek to duck his head. A cool breeze flowed in through the open casement windows.

The furnishings were simple: a bed too narrow for the grown man to sleep comfortably, a desk and chair, and bureau. A battered trunk took up much of the floor space.

"I'll have Travers ready a more appropriate room. This is too small," she said as she pulled out the chair. "Sit. Shirt off."

"Do not bother. The room is adequate." He sat but did not remove his shirt.

"It is a child's room with a child's bed. I need you fresh and limber, Hardwick, not twisted and stiff."

The muscles in his jaw twitched. She raised an eyebrow. He cleared his throat and looked away before saying, "I don't want to be a bother. Perhaps the cottage?"

Luis perched on the edge of the bed, his knees bumping into Solenne. She tripped over his feet as she moved to the bureau.

"If you wished to be exiled," she said, shooting Luis an irritated glare. He shrugged and tucked his feet carefully under the bed.

"I'm used to my privacy," Alek said.

"The answer is no. I'm afraid I won't put the extra work on Miriam and Travers. I'll find you an adult-sized room, but you'll be in the house. Now, shirt. Off." She snapped her fingers. Alek rolled his eyes but complied.

The wounds weren't as bad as she remembered. They appeared less angry but still red and swollen. The scars on his stomach were faded, almost as if they had been there for ages, but she remembered they were red.

She kneeled before him. His knees parted, allowing her space. Up close, the smell of the caustic soap drowned out anything unpleasant. His scent was sweat, green grass, and cool water.

Her fingers brushed the sun tattoo, then drifted down to the tight lines that crossed his stomach, his abdomen muscles jumping. A wolf once tried its damnedest to shred Alek to pieces. But they had been red. Perhaps that had been a trick of the light.

The bite, though, her memory did not fail her. As red and angry as ever, it needed attention before infection set in.

Solenne was aware of Luis watching her as she inspected Alek's injuries. She refused to blush. She refused to let her heart flutter or her breath quicken. This was another injury, just body parts not so different from any of the other bodies she tended.

"You know what? I don't need to be here," Luis said. As he exited, he managed to kick her calf, trip over her foot, put a hand on her shoulder, and nearly shove her head into Alek's lap. To be so clumsy required an amazing execution of grace.

Alek's eyes followed Luis, narrow and calculating. When they were alone, he said, "Is he that clumsy?"

"I think he thinks he's funny." Solenne rose to her feet, resisting the urge to smooth her hair or fuss with the folds on her dress.

"You changed," he said.

"I was covered in mud, same as you."

"I was not referring to your garments." His tone felt mocking, like he expected her to be preserved in amber while he transformed into an almost unrecognizable man.

Anger, bright and furious, anger she normally kept bottled up flared in her. So much about her had grown and matured, but she felt emotionally stuck at sixteen, and it was horrid.

Solenne looked away, needing a moment to collect herself. She breathed in and out. Sweat and green grass and cool water. The scents were warm, like the promise of summer.

Once under control, she approached with a rag soaked in the hot water. Just a shoulder. Never mind the moonlight highlighted the musculature of his upper arms or the cords in his neck. Just another shoulder.

When she dabbed the cloth to the bite, his body tensed, but he remained stoically silent.

"Is this recent?" The bite appeared recent.

"It must be, to look like that," he eventually said.

The teeth had pierced deep. "Any difficulty moving your shoulder?"

"No."

"Show me."

With a put-upon sigh, he raised an arm, then dropped it quickly back to his side.

"Touch your ear," she said. He touched the ear on the same side. "No, the other one."

Moving stiffly, he reached around and tapped his other ear. Then, to be clever, he patted his head and moved his arms in a circle.

Solenne cleaned the bite and slathered on a generous layer of a cream made with wolfsbane. The red rash under his silver necklace and wristband received the same attention.

As she held his wrist, she felt his pulse flutter. He watched her work, eyes sharp and following every movement like a guard dog. There was so much she wanted to say but didn't know how to start. She wasn't the same sixteen-year-old girl, deep in the clutches of infatuation, but in that moment, close enough to smell his soap, she was.

His wounds cleaned and covered, she brought the pitcher and bowl and hot water over and placed them nearby on the trunk. Luis had helpfully laid out a pair of scissors, a razor, a small mirror, lather brush, and a cake of shaving soap. Using a mirror, Alek hacked away at the beard while she worked the soap into a lather with the brush. Just as she raised the brush to Alek's face, he caught her wrist.

"You do not need to do this," he said, his voice thick and betraying the first sign of emotion.

She dabbed on the soap as a means of answering. Slowly, the beard vanished under a layer of white foam. Carefully she dragged the razor across his skin, each stroke revealing a civilized man.

"The house is quiet," he said.

"Indeed."

"It used to be filled with..."

The voices of people not afraid to laugh or otherwise be heard. The house used to be filled with life. She wanted to say nothing, focused on the razor scraping along his cheek. Let him think what he wanted.

Instead, she said, "I guess something has changed after all."

He did not waste a beat, pouncing on the crack in her defense. "Afraid of upsetting your father?"

Her hand jolted with surprise. Alek hissed as the blade nicked him. Quickly, she dabbed the injury with a clean corner of the wet cloth until the bleeding stopped.

"Initially, perhaps, but no. Father gets a piece of my mind when he deserves it."

"Afraid of upsetting your fiancé?"

Fiancé? Hardly. Her nose scrunched at the thought.

"No promises have been made." Unlike the kiss and promise Alek made to her.

She knew her father regarded an alliance with Colonel Chambers as inevitable, and Chambers himself was a pleasant enough man, but she held nothing more for him than friendly regard. If Chambers was of a mind to marry, he never made his intentions clear.

"Not according to your father."

Solenne dropped the cloth and sat back on her heels. "What is happening?"

"You're carving me up like a roast is what's happening," he grumbled.

"You're upset with me."

"I'm more than capable of shaving myself. Leave." He grabbed the razor from the trunk.

"You're upset that I am not the same sixteen-year-old girl besotted with you."

"You promised to wait for me."

"And you promised you'd return, not wait ten years for me to beg you. No letters. Not a single one. I knew writing to you was a mistake."

They stared at each other, as if no longer seeing the shadow of their past selves but each other as they were now for the first time. Alek was not the boy with easy smiles and a warm laugh that she remembered. He was harder now, scarred and burdened by the world. She was no longer a carefree young woman with a world of options open to her.

The razor's edge glinted in the moonlight.

"Who is he?" Alek asked, breaking the silence.

"You do not know him."

"Who. Is. He?"

Solenne lifted her chin, refusing to be cowed. "A gentleman farmer. Military. Retired."

"Old and rich," he said, a sneer in his voice.

"Not so old, and wealthy enough." Solenne pushed, wanting a reaction out of Alek. When they met earlier at the cottage, he acted cool and indifferent, as if he didn't know her at all.

"You must be pleased with such a catch. A spoiled thing like you always gets what she wants. Soon you'll be knee deep in babies and diapers."

Spoiled? What about the tumbledown house and her family's desperate situation implied she was spoiled? Alek sought to wound her. If he wanted a fight, she'd give him one.

"They could be yours," she said.

"No."

"But you left."

"I had to leave," he snapped. She knew that was true, but still she pushed.

"You did not write. Not once."

He surged to his feet, knocking the chair back. "And say what? Dear Solenne, today I cleared a pack of wolves, but the village could not pay the bounty they offered. Instead, they gave me a pair of chickens. I slept in a barn with my chickens." His tone was cruel and mocking.

He continued, "Dear Solenne, I returned to the ruined husk of my family's home. The roof is badly damaged, but the four walls remain upright for the time being. I cannot wait to make you mistress of this hovel. I had nothing to offer you then, and I have even less to offer you now."

"I would have known you were alive."

He held out his arms and turned slowly. Moonlight picked out the pale scars that crossed his abdomen and his back. It seemed as if every part of him had suffered from injury or wound. From the appearance of the situation, he worked very hard to remedy his affliction of being alive.

"Such as it is," he said.

She shoved her supplies into her kit. So this was it. He was upset that her life had moved on and then wanted to make a grotesque exhibit of why she should have never wanted him in the first place.

She took out a jar of wolfsbane powder and slammed it down on the bureau. Bottles rattled. "One spoonful twice a day in tea or water. It's bitter. I'd suggest honey, but I suspect you like to torture yourself so I won't bother."

"Solenne—" His voice almost sounded remorseful.

"No. No," she said, snapping her bag shut and holding it protectively in front of her. "You do not get to have it both ways. Yes, we were children when we made promises to…" She swallowed, unable to say the word love. "*Care* for each other. I won't hold you to that and don't expect you to do the same."

He opened his mouth as if to speak.

She continued on, "What I expect you to do is behave like a gentleman in this house and not insult me or make…aspersions on my character because I have to put my family first." She lifted her chin. "If I must wed a not-so-old and wealthy-enough man for the good of my family, I will do so, and I will not suffer your crass comments or jealousy."

"Jealousy." He growled out the word.

"What else could it be? Are you willing to offer me a better prospect? I'm twenty-six, Aleksandar. My options are limited." And growing more so every day.

"No. I cannot. *That* has not changed."

"Then goodnight. I will see you at breakfast." She paused at the door, unwilling to leave with such unhappiness between them. However far apart they had grown over the years, however much they both had changed, Alek had once been her friend. She believed he could be again.

"I did not know you were such a mercenary," he said.

"Then you truly do not know me at all."

Chapter Seven

Solenne

Boxon Hill

The pond

The day broke with bright sunshine and warmth. Her list of tasks for the day kept growing, but wasting such a lovely day felt wrong. She wanted only to sit in the sunshine.

Gathering a basket of sewing, she stashed a well-worn book in the bottom. "All work and no play," she muttered, then headed to the pond.

She situated herself on a small blanket under a tree, one of her favorite reading spots. Near the water's edge, she got a lovely view, shade, and was hidden from the main path. It was the perfect locale to steal away a few undisturbed hours.

The book opened flat, the spine broken ages ago. Working her way through a basket of items to be mended, she kept one eye on her needle and the other on the book. Her hands worked on muscle memory, pulling the needle through the garments and tying off the thread. Buttons were replaced. Torn seams repaired. Socks darned. The work was tedious but mindless. She soon found herself pulled into the book, the story familiar and welcomed.

Shadows shifted, growing smaller under the tree, and the day's heat increased. It'd be noon soon and someone would be sent to find her.

Someone rustled through the grass, and Alek plopped down on the ground next to her. He placed the basket in his lap. "Apple?"

"No, thank you. I need my fingers clean," she said, eyes fixed on the pages of her book. She refused to pay attention to the heat rolling off his body, how their shoulders brushed, or the noise he made crunching into the apple.

Her stomach rumbled.

"I have cheese," he said in a teasing tone.

Solenne frowned. This situation felt familiar, like how they used to be and how they could be now if they could willfully forget the last ten years. "What is this?"

"Lunch. And I brought enough to share." He waved a second apple at her, red and ripe.

He waved temptation at her, but she remembered the harsh words they exchanged the night before. She'd be damned before she took his apple.

"No, thank you. I am working," she said.

"Suit yourself," he said, around a mouthful of apple. "What's that?"

"It's a book." Solenne pulled needle and thread through the sock, her motion automatic, and barely lifted her eyes from the page. She needn't have bothered, having read the book often enough to have it memorized.

"What is the book called?"

With an exasperated sigh, she lowered her sewing and closed book. "*The Confinement of Twilight*. Are you here for a particular reason or just general mischief?"

He grinned, a bit too broad and toothsome for his face. "I thought lunch and a refreshing dip in the pond seemed just the thing on a day like today."

"Shouldn't you be beating my brother?"

"We're done for the day. We broke for lunch and will reconvene to inspect the weapon stores."

"Well, as you can see, I am working. Please go elsewhere."

"As you wish." In a fluid movement, he rose to his feet and moved to the pond's short wooden dock. Not that she could remark on it, because she was not staring at his position or any other part of his person. She simply made sure he complied with her wishes.

In the sun, he stretched and removed his shirt. The wounds she tended to last night looked mostly healed, and a network of scars crisscrossed his back. Again, she studied him to note his progress and look for signs of infection. It most certainly was not in admiration, and she failed to note or appreciate the way his muscles flexed in the sunshine.

He looked over his shoulder and winked, taking another bite of the apple.

"For goodness' sake, Alek! Put on your shirt," she snapped.

"I do not recall you being the boss of me, sweetpea."

How dare he? The pet name stoked her anger like nothing else. No one had called her that since Mama passed.

"You do not have permission to be so familiar with me, Mr. Hardwick."

He raised a brow and took another mouthful of the apple. "I think you're spoiled and too used to getting what you want," he eventually said.

Spoiled?

Spoiled!

Solenne jumped to her feet. As she stomped toward him, she gestured broadly to the basket of sewing, the ruinous house, Boxon Hill in general. "What gave you the idea that any part of this is what I want? My glamorous life of darning socks? Selling salves and poultices so I have a little coin?" She jabbed a finger at his chest.

Alek growled. Actually growled.

Surprised, she jabbed him again.

He grabbed her finger, hand sticky from the apple. "Do not."

"Unhand me."

"Not if you're going to poke with your boney finger."

"I'll poke you with whatever I damn well please," she said, which was such a ridiculous statement that it did not even register.

He smirked. "See, spoiled."

"You're impossible." She shook her hand, but his grip held tight.

Fine. If he wanted to play that game, she would play.

Solenne planted her free hand on his chest and shoved with all her might.

His eyes went wide as he fell backward. Still holding her pointer hand, his grip tightened and the weight of him pulled her forward.

Into the pond.

Cold water shocked her. They were a tangle of limbs. She thrashed until she freed herself from Alek, kicking and flailing until she broke the surface of the water. She gasped, cold to the bone and furious like she had never been before.

"Stop! Stop fighting me!"

"Unhand me!"

"I'm trying to keep you from drowning," Alek rumbled.

"I can swim. You know I can swim." She splashed water at him and continued until he drifted away.

They stared at each other, wet hair plastered to their heads and both fully clothed.

"You pushed me!" Alek scraped away water from his face and shook his head like a dog, water and hair flying.

Solenne brushed back her own sodden hair, pond water in her mouth and up her nose. "You pushed me first!"

"You were...eleven?"

"Well, it was very memorable." Lifting her chin, she paddled her way to the dock with as much dignity as possible. The weight of her skirts made motion difficult, no matter how hard her legs kicked.

Finally, she reached the dock. Grabbing the wooden plank, she struggled to pull herself out of the water. She could perform the maneuver in a swimming costume, but apparently her garments had absorbed the entire contents of the pond.

"You are a proud creature. Let me help."

"I don't need your he—" Her words were swallowed into a yelp as Alek planted two hands on her bottom and lifted her out of the water.

She flopped onto the dock like a fish and rolled to make room as Alek joined her. Sun warm, the boards leached away the worst of the water's chill.

She turned her head to the side, meeting Alek's gaze.

That was...

He was...

They burst into laughter.

"You're a monster," she said through gasping laughs. "What were you thinking?"

"Lunch and a swim. We used to do it all the time."

"When we were children."

"Yes. I see that." He reached over, brushing back her wet lock. His fingers ghosted over her brow, her cheek and the seam of her lips.

Her mouth opened slightly, she couldn't help it.

He licked his lips.

A strange awareness washed over her, knowing this was the moment he would kiss her and nothing would be the same.

Only he had been so cruel the previous night.

He had abandoned her for ten years and now expected kisses?

Self-conscious, she sat up, hunching her shoulders. The wet dress clung to her and left nothing to the imagination. Not that any amount of fabric layers would protect her from Alek's grin—stop staring at him!—but it did not help to feel so exposed.

"I'll fetch your blanket," he said, rolling to his feet.

She did not twist to watch his confident amble, and she certainly did not admire the way the wet trousers stretched as he bent to retrieve the blanket. Don't be absurd. She was a gentleman's daughter.

And she absolutely did not feel his eyes watching her figure as she retreated to the house.

Aleksandar

What was he doing?

He was a monster. She said the words in jest, but they drove home the point that he had to keep his distance from Solenne.

Last night he had been purposefully cruel. He wanted to drive a wedge between them, to make it clear that whatever they had been, they no longer could be. Clear to her. Clear to him.

And today, when he saw her reading under the tree by the pond, he remembered all the summer days they swam in that pond. He recalled every story Solenne read aloud as he lounged in the grass. They climbed trees and scraped knees and laughed, and it was as if no time at all had passed. He wanted that back with a fierce hunger.

He wanted *her* back.

It was foolish, but just for a moment when they laughed at the absurdity of them falling into the pond, he felt the spark. This was his friend. Whatever time and distance stretched between them, she would always be his friend.

Then the beast had to ruin it.

He had nearly kissed her and would have if she had not jumped away like a skittish colt.

Alek dried his face with his shirt, dressed, and returned to the house. The entire journey, he thought of ways to apologize. Solenne had pushed him, but he had deserved worse. Travers was none too thrilled about the puddles he left on the floor. Once he changed into dry clothes, he snuck into the kitchen and begged Cook for a favor. With promises made to clean and organize the scullery, he took his basket and found paper and ink in a desk drawer in the library.

He scratched out a note.

"Please accept these lemon cookies as an apology for my atrocious behavior last night and this afternoon. Cook says these are your second favorite and that more groveling is required for your favorite. So I apologize for that, as well.

"I understand that we are no longer the people we once were, but I had hoped that our friendship had not changed. Again, my apologies."

He blew over the ink to dry and reread. The apology fell short of his intentions, but anything other than laying on the ground and bearing his throat to Solenne felt inadequate.

Alek delivered the basket to her workshop door and knocked. He hurried around the corner, in case she did not wish to speak to him.

The door opened. Her hair hung down to air dry, and she had changed into a shapeless tunic and trousers.

Shame. He rather liked the breezy yellow dress she had worn. The fabric went nearly translucent when wet. The beast especially liked that fact.

She read the note and folded it carefully. "You do realize you wouldn't have to sneak cookies away from Cook if you behaved," she said.

No doubt, but she had pushed him, and he did not regret the moments he held her in the water.

He scrubbed a hand over his brow. This was dangerous. He gave his word not to interfere with Solenne, and here he was flirting over baskets of cookies. Still, he could not resist the pull of her. He needed to stay away.

Alek retreated down the corridor.

Chapter Eight

Solenne

Boxon Hill

Marechal House - The Library

"I say!" Colonel Chambers shouted, rearing back as he spotted the creature lurking in the shadowy recess of the library. His cane thumped against the floor as he took a defensive stance. "Miss Marechal, are you well?"

"Oh, that's just Tristan. He's quite harmless as he is stuffed." Solenne turned her attention from the window and faced her visitor.

Chambers approached the stuffed monster, radiating curiosity. "Stuffed. Godwin mentioned this curiosity once, but I did not believe him. Fascinating."

"Grandfather hunted him and had him stuffed." Gutted and stuffed with a concoction of chemicals and sawdust, the transformed wolf stood on his hind legs. Tucked into a corner to prevent further degradation from sunlight, he lurked, mostly ignored. Tristan needed a good dusting, but Solenne hated the thing.

The creature had a remarkably human face. Perhaps it was familiarity on Solenne's part that saw the human still trapped inside the beast, because so many natural features had been twisted by the curse.

Tristan's nose and mouth pulled forward into a short snout. Deformed lips had been curled back into a snarl. Age yellowed the teeth, but Solenne knew they were still razor sharp. Faded violet-tinged fur covered his face in a shaggy beard, but the rest of his body was covered in a short pelt.

The eyes, though, remained fully human. Painted glass, they sparkled in the light when cleaned, watching. Sometimes it felt as if he understood his fate, hunted, stuffed, and kept as a curiosity. Dusty as those eyes were now, they stared out blindly from under a gray film. It seemed kinder, somehow.

The fierceness of Tristan's visage was ruined by a silk coat, cut in the fashion of fifty years prior, complete with trousers and a rather limp gray cravat around his throat.

"The taxidermist was remarkably skilled. Was he called Tristan in life?" Chambers rubbed the snout, fingers coming away with a layer of dust.

"He was Grandfather's dearest friend, Tristan Wodehouse." Saying the words made her feel ill. The curse forced her grandfather to end the life of his friend. It was the hard truth of their lives, but he chose to humiliate the corpse of his friend, stuffed and put on display in a costume and a cravat.

"Wodehouse? I say." He peered closer, as if searching for a familial resemblance. "Wodehouse always hinted that something hinky happened with the line of succession." He stood abruptly. "Shame."

"He should have been buried in his family plot," she said, surprised by the vehemence in her voice. Luis knew her feelings regarding Tristan, but few others did.

"I suppose it is educational."

She huffed, not bothering to hide her feelings behind a mask of politeness. "It is a farce. Tristan was a person, once. Whatever misfortune happened to him, he was meant to be a friend, and he deserves respect, even in death. Especially in death."

She couldn't express how much it disturbed her. Slaying cursed beasts was a responsibility, a duty not done lightly. This was cruel.

Godwin had stories that his father used to haul Tristan down to the dining room for meals. He was used as a prop for japes and tricks. It was tasteless behavior, but what should she expect from the same man who squandered away most of the family's dwindling fortune?

"You feel strongly, Miss Marechal. Is it compassion for the beast you feel?" Chambers watched her with interest, the light through the windows giving his eyes a hard sheen.

"I loathe it, Colonel Chambers. It is a cruelty made for the amusement of a selfish man." She took a breath to calm herself. "Father refuses to have it destroyed. He claims it is of historical note." Her eyes drifted to a gap on a bookshelf, evidence of what her father did not have qualms about burning.

Chambers approached the stuffed beast again, as if to examine it once more with this new information. From the coat's breast pocket, he removed a pair of spectacles and slipped them on. "I agree. Whatever the intentions behind its creation, the average man seldom has a chance to meet such a creature face to face. It is unnerving, like one of those carnival mirrors."

About to ask him what he saw when he looked at the beast's face, a loud shout from the window snagged her attention. It was a most intriguing sight in the courtyard.

"Hmm, they are rather loud," Colonel Chambers commented as he joined Solenne at the window. He stood close, the sleeve of his coat brushing against her. "No wonder I cannot hold your attention, Miss Marechal."

She blushed, caught observing Luis spar with Alek. It was rather vulgar to be staring at their sweaty forms, but it was equally rude of Chambers to call out her behavior.

"The solstice is in two days. They must be ready." She turned her back to the view in the courtyard below.

"Yes." A strange look crossed his face. He removed his spectacles, gently folded them, and slipped them into his coat pocket.

"My apologies. Would you care for tea?" Solenne reached for the bell, but Chambers cut her off.

"Thank you, but no. I understand you enjoy a good book, so I came to deliver a novel that recently arrived. Before the rush of the dance this evening, you understand." Chambers pulled a blue cloth-bound volume from his pocket. "I thought you might enjoy it."

"Is that the *Seventh Evil*?" she asked, interest piqued. "They say the mystery is quite riveting, and it is impossible to solve until the end."

"Indeed. It is rather scandalous. Do not inform your father that I am in the habit of supplying respectable young women with less than edifying reading material." His smile was sharp, too angular, as if he had too many teeth for his face. In the distance, Tristan lurked just over his shoulder.

Solenne gladly accepted the book, cracking the spine and running an appreciative hand down the creamy, smooth pages. "This is a true delight, Colonel Chambers." She had read every book in the family's library two or three times, more if the book was a favorite. She had read *Confinement of Twilight* to tatters. Fortunately, when the book would finally disintegrate, she had the contents memorized.

"Your library is most impressive, however. I fear my humble contribution rather brings down the tone," he said, scanning the walls of books next to her.

A genuine smile tugged at the corner of her mouth. The Marechal library had older books, including several diaries from early colonists. Not original. Goodness, no. Books that precious belonged in the national library in Founding, not gathering dust in a country house on the edges of civilization. They had diaries dating back that far written by long-ago ancestors, and a rather unique volume on herbs and flowers that the colonists must have brought from the old world because Solenne had never seen such a thing as a *daffodil*. The illustration made it seem like a wondrous thing, like a little drop of sunshine. Those priceless books were kept on a shelf well away from sunlight.

Selling the library or even part of the collection could fix the family's finances, and she knew that Godwin had sold a volume or two of historical note to Mr. Wodehouse. Emptying their wonderful library filled her with dread, but soon, they might not have a choice.

"Fresh stories are a challenge to find," she said, turning her attention back to Chambers.

"Then I am delighted to be of service." He smiled again. Perhaps it was the morning light or her happy glow at the unexpected gift, but the smile transformed his rather dull face into something pleasant. The light picked out the silver at his temples, giving him a distinguished air.

She...she could do this. Chambers was not unappealing. She could be amiable and amenable and all those other bland qualities men looked for in wives. He brought her books, so he couldn't be all bad. She could...flirt.

She forced a smile and batted her lashes.

"Is there something in your eye?" he asked.

Not the reaction she expected.

A shout from the courtyard snagged her attention and Solenne dropped her flirtation.

Luis rubbed a shoulder but appeared unharmed. Alek lowered his weapon. Somehow, he lost his linen shirt but wore an undershirt. Sodden with sweat, it clung to him.

Solenne gasped.

Old scars ran up and down his bare arms. He wore a silver necklace around his neck. The ornamentation was barely noticeable except for the irritated red skin, almost like an allergic reaction.

Chambers cleared his throat.

With a reluctant sigh, she closed the window, shutting out the sounds of Luis and Alek's sparring.

Solenne knew it was unfair to compare Colonel Chambers to Alek, as the man was a good ten years older and injured. He might not be a prized specimen of athletic prowess, but he was considerate, and he brought her books; that counted for a great deal in her estimation of him.

In the days since her conversation with Alek in her workshop, he avoided her, going so far as to leave a room when she entered. If he wished to avoid her, she did not wish to cause him undue stress. Alek was there for Luis, really, not for her. No matter what her traitorous heart wanted to believe. She could continue to stare out the window and sigh or pay attention to a respectable man who, for reasons she hardly understood, seemed to hold her in some regard.

She turned her back to the window and smiled. "This is a very generous gift."

"I shan't take up any more of your morning. Please, enjoy the book. Tell me what you think," Chambers said with a brief nod.

"Thank you. I shall. Colonel?"

He paused. "Yes?"

"Forgive me for being bold, but can I count on a dance with you at the ball tonight?"

There. Flirtation. Mission accomplished.

That smile again, sharp and with too many teeth. "I anticipate the event with great relish."

Aleksandar

He could feel Solenne's eyes on him. She was as subtle now as she had been when they were clumsy adolescents. Physically, she had changed dramatically from the gangly girl he remembered. She finally grew into her feet and stood nearly as tall as him. She had strength in her, and not just in her body. Her eyes shone with an inner light as transfixing as the moon's cold glow. She had always been pretty with dark hair and velvety gray eyes, but necessity had refined her down to her truest self.

She was a jewel under pressure, and she shone.

Luis' blade smacked him on his shoulder. He hissed in pain, dodging a second blow. The bite, the one that cursed him, fluctuated as the full moon approached. The flesh grew tender and red. Add the constant ting from the silver chain around his neck, and Alek was in a brittle mood.

"Pay attention," Godwin barked from the side.

Right. Focus.

The window above closed. He relaxed. Days from the full moon, his beast wanted nothing more than to rub itself against Solenne. Well, the beast wanted more, but he tried his best to remain a gentleman.

Solenne was from a noble family. She was much too good for a cursed man such as himself. As much as Godwin embraced Alek and welcomed him back into his home, calling him old friend and son, he knew that to be a flimsy thing. If he approached Godwin about his intentions toward Solenne, he'd be tossed out on his ear.

Again.

Time had not lessened the sting.

Blades clashed. Alek pressed Luis, driving him back. The younger man had superior skills, and what training he lacked could only be gained from experience. Alek knew that was his responsibility, to hunt the beast and give Luis enough time to learn how to defend his territory on his own.

Luis fought brashly, rushing and using all his energy. He'd never last in a fight, and hunting under a full moon often took all night. All Alek had to do to win the bout was endure, and he had years of practice. He endured burning pain every month. He endured the call of the beast, craving the hunt that ended in sweet, fresh blood.

He endured the way the beast whined for its mate.

Anger fueled his movements, growing erratic. Luis stumbled but quickly recovered. Alek did not allow the younger man to regain his footing because there were no niceties on the hunt. There was only opportunity and prey.

Alek knocked the blade from Luis' sloppy grip. He looked stunned, glancing at the blade far behind and back at Alek.

He rushed, and the youth raised his arms to defend himself. The flat of the blade landed in harsh blows along Luis' side and back. Every blow amplified his frustration. The Marechals needed him—begged for his assistance—yet Godwin warned him off his daughter.

Solenne needed to make a good match. She could not marry a penniless hunter. More than that, he knew he shouldn't want her. He was cursed. If any of them learned his secret, they would slit his throat, probably with an ornate silver blade passed down through the generations.

"Enough," Godwin shouted.

Alek did not stop, instead tossing the sword. The man's voice infuriated him. The silver chain around his neck stung. His bite burned. Who was Godwin to tell him to stop? Only a partly blinded old man. He would not stop.

He slipped behind Luis, wrapping an arm around his neck and dropping the youth to the ground. A silver blade pressed against the tanned skin of his throat. Up close, Alek saw the faint stubble of several day's growth.

A faint line of red appeared where the edge sank into skin. His very being trembled with the desire to lick the wound clean, to let the flavor of blood blossom on his skin. If he could not have the taste of his mate on his tongue, fresh blood would suffice. It would satisfy him for a time.

"I yield," Luis said.

Alek blinked, coming back to himself. He eased his grip on the dagger and stepped back.

"Was it wrong to...should I have run?" Luis rubbed his throat, smearing the thin amount of red until it disappeared.

"No. Never run. A beast will chase, and it will not have restraint. Instinct will demand a kill," Alek croaked. "It is better to find a hole to defend yourself than to run." He wiped sweat from his brow. "I think that's enough for today. You should bathe before the dance."

"Poor hygiene is generally frowned upon in society," Luis said with a grin.

"Sure, good society, but why would you want to impress a bunch of snobs?"

"It seems exciting. A pressure release." Luis headed to the door, but Alek stayed behind. "Don't you need to get ready?"

"No. I'm not fit company for any society, good, bad or otherwise." He ran his thumb along the edge of the silver dagger, the pure metal burning.

If he ever forgot why he needed to distance himself from Solenne, that was reason enough.

Chapter Nine

Solenne

Boxon

Vervain Hall

A dance before the summer solstice.

It seemed the height of arrogance as those affected by the curse would be increasingly vulnerable to the effects of the nexus. A dance filled with light and music and laughter and bodies crushed together might prove too tempting for a beast on the prowl.

Still, that didn't stop Solenne from donning her best frock, a lightweight, seashore green-striped dress. Luis wore a black tailcoat and matching trousers left over from his school days that did not look entirely academic. Despite the sleeves being a touch too short, she thought her brother looked rather dashing and did not comment on the small dagger he put in his boot.

Godwin came down the stairs dressed smartly in evening clothes, a black patch over his eye and wielding a silver-tipped cane. Solenne hadn't been sure if he would attend, but felt glad he went to the effort.

Alek stated he had no plans to attend and did not enjoy standing about in a hot room to be scrutinized like a show animal. As Solenne left the house, he watched her with covetous eyes. When she caught him looking, he turned his attention back to his book.

Vervain Hall was lit against the night like a beacon. Braziers lined the path to the front. Every door and window had been opened to the night air. Lively music and laughter drifted out.

Inside, they had pushed the furniture back and cleared space for dancing. People milled at the edges, nibbling on food and nursing drinks. If the chatter stopped when the Marechals entered, it was only a moment. This was the first time Godwin had been out in society —such as it was in Boxon—since the attack.

The dance had all the makings of a perfect summer evening, but something lurked at the edges, like a storm waiting to break, giving the atmosphere a manic feel. The revelers felt it, laughing too loud, drinking too much, and dancing with an almost desperate enthusiasm.

Solenne scanned the crowd, taking in the familiar faces and half hoping to spy Alek brooding in a corner. Of course he wasn't lurking about in corners with potted plants, waiting to dance the night away with her. That was wishful thinking. She promised Colonel Chambers a dance, and the sooner she completed that task, the better.

She spotted Charlotte in a vivid yellow dress with stiff white lace trim at the bodice and cap sleeves, standing next to her father by the terrace doors. She waved to her friend, who made her way across the room.

Luis stood awkwardly next to her, his hands twitching and flexing like he didn't know how to stand.

"Perhaps you should ask Miles to dance," she offered.

"He said he did not plan to attend. Said he wasn't the proper company to keep," Luis mumbled. "I had hoped he would change his mind, but no."

Ah. She understood that feeling exactly.

"Oh, don't you two look a lovely pair?" Charlotte said. Luis mumbled a reply, blushing.

"As do you," Solenne said truthfully. Charlotte's curls were on full display, tumbling and shining in the candlelight.

"How many dances have you promised? I haven't agreed to any," Charlotte said in a rush. "Papa says I'm being foolish, but Jase invited me. A personal invitation. Do you think that means something?" She fluttered a yellow silk fan, emphasizing her words.

"Just one dance," Solenne answered when Charlotte paused for breath.

"To Aleksandar, yes? Where is he? I bet he looks so dashing. Oh, as do you, Luis. The color suits you."

Colonel Chambers and his nephew approached. "Miss Marechal, Miss Wodehouse," he said with a nod. "No Aleksandar?"

"He sends his regrets," she said, which was a lie because Alek's exact words were much more colorful and contained zero regret.

"Not a worry. More pretty partners for us, eh, Jase?"

Charlotte laughed lightly, fluttering her fan. Luis tugged at the nearly too-short coat sleeves.

Jase looked bored at a dance held for his benefit. "If you say so. Country dances are a quaint amusement."

"But the company is so charming," Chambers said.

"If you can call this boorishly rustic aesthetic charming."

Solenne rocked back on her heels, stunned at Jase's rudeness. "I'm sure you're accustomed to grander affairs in Founding," she said, trying her best to keep her tone polite and not boorishly rustic.

"Not likely," Chambers said, giving a hearty slap to Jase's back. "This one was too sickly. Foul air in Founding, you know. Too much smoke in the air. Country life may be slower, but you get to enjoy it. Now, would you lovely ladies care to dance?"

He extended his hand to Solenne, who felt obliged to take it. Charlotte beamed at Jase, who gave her a cool look. "Pardon me, I'm feeling sickly, and nothing entices me to dance at the moment. My apologies, Miss Wodehouse."

He turned on his heel and left, leaving Charlotte quite red in the face.

Smoothly, Chambers offered his arm to Charlotte. "Forgive my nephew, Miss Wodehouse. He had a coughing fit earlier and is always in a foul mood after."

"Is he quite recovered? Should he be out?" Charlotte asked, because of course she was more concerned about Jase Parkell's wellbeing than her own insulted pride. Not to worry. Solenne was more than capable of being insulted for the pair of them.

"Confinement is seldom beneficial, in my opinion. He needs to exercise his lungs beyond expelling hot air. Now, please have pity on an old man. I don't know if I can keep up with a young lady such as yourself."

Solenne rolled her eyes, but Charlotte laughed, Jase's rude snub forgotten.

She felt content to watch the crowd and make pleasant conversation. Luis watched the dancers with raw greed on his face.

Suitable partners came over, traded pleasantries, but Luis never seemed to make the leap to asking them to dance, despite the clear yearning on his face.

"Would you like to dance?" she asked Luis.

"Would it be pathetic to dance with my sister?"

"Not as much as a spinster dancing with her younger brother. Oh, the burden he must bear, being seen with her in public society." She pressed a hand to her forehead, earning a small chuckle.

They joined the dancers, and almost immediately Solenne realized why Luis had been hesitant. He was terrible. All elbows and knees, he kept bumping into her.

"I know dance was on the syllabus at school," she said.

"For girls, maybe."

"We went to the same school, and there were plenty of boys in my dance class. Now, stop rushing me. Count if you must." She stepped back, letting Luis take the lead. She knew that he was not clumsy or physically awkward. Perhaps socially, but she had witnessed his archery skills. He possessed hand-eye coordination. He just had to ignore the people watching.

With each turn, he grew more confident. By the end of the song, he moved with the skill and grace of a hunter. Breathless, she allowed herself to be led to the side.

"The next dance is mine," a firm voice said. Alek wore his usual tailcoat, though sponged cleaned, and his cravat tied sloppily, but he was a most welcomed sight.

Without waiting for her response, he took her hand and swept her back onto the floor. He held her closer than proper, his eyes fixed on hers, and they moved together like familiar partners. Her body remembered his touch from when they sparred in their youth. She anticipated his motions, meeting him for every turn and twirl.

A thread seemed to connect them, drawing them closer than physical touch, though her skin tingled and fizzed where they touched.

Her eyes drank in the flush to his cheeks, the hungry look in his eyes.

He licked his lips, his fierce gaze never leaving her face. Her breath fluttered in her throat, suddenly overwhelmed.

The crowd vanished. Even the music vanished. Her beating heart provided the melody.

Eventually, she realized they stood still.

"The music stopped," Alek said.

"Did it?"

The moment felt too big to be contained. Her body hummed with excitement. She needed to catch her breath. She needed to sit for a moment.

She needed more.

Another voice interrupted. "Do you require a chair? A bit of air?" Colonel Chambers held out a glass of punch.

"I..." Alek tugged at this cravat, pulling the knot undone. His lips twisted, half sneer and half growl. He gave a clipped bow and left.

"Well," Chambers said, watching Alek's retreat, "I'd ask you to dance, but you look overtired. Perhaps I can show you the view of the garden from the terrace? There was a matter I wished to discuss with you."

"Thank you," she mumbled, accepting the punch and, by extension, the invitation to the terrace. Chambers wanted privacy, and she dreaded the reason.

A quick look around the room and she found Godwin watching them with interest.

She followed Chambers to the terrace, each step feeling like a march toward her execution.

The cool night air was a welcomed relief from the heat of the house's interior. Her eyes fluttered shut as she took a breath. She could do this.

Amiable and amenable. All the qualities one wanted in a wife.

Chambers placed his hand on the small of her back, guiding her to a secluded corner. She jumped, spilling the punch over her hand.

"Not to worry. These things happen. The cup was filled to the brim." Chambers produced a handkerchief and cleaned up the punch. He held her hand in his a bit too long, watching her reaction rather than the task.

Solenne tried to be gracious or beatific or however the heroines appeared in those novels she read when being doted on by a man they were expected to marry. Enthralled? Excited at being alone? Not the leaden weight she felt in her stomach.

His touch was unbearable. Wrong. Her skin crawled, not at all the way how it tingled and fizzed at Alek's touch.

Chambers leaned in. Solenne turned her face away, fearing a kiss and better for it to land on her cheek than her lips.

He sniffed her hair.

This was too much.

She snatched her hand away and the cloth. "I can manage, thank you."

"Ah, I see." He stepped back, frowning. "I do hope that you know I hold you in great esteem."

Yes, this was the proposal. She closed her eyes, wanting to be anyplace but there. Perhaps if she wasn't watching him, he would finish quicker.

"Your father is among my closest acquaintances. I want nothing more than your family's happiness. Particularly your happiness."

This was it.

"Colonel Chambers, I—" she started.

"You're charming and more than pretty enough."

Solenne cracked open an eye. Pretty enough?

"I wish you every happiness," he continued, "but I'm afraid that I cannot share that happiness with you. I know you're disappointed. Your father indicated, several times, might I add, that you would be receptive to my attention."

"You *cannot* share my happiness? I must confess, this is the strangest proposal," she blurted out.

Chambers took a deliberate step back. "My apologies if I've given you the wrong impression, but this is not a proposal. It's rather the opposite."

Oh.

Well, that made her unreasonably pleased.

"I fear I am a man ill-suited to marriage. I am rather set in my ways. I know Godwin had hopes of a connection, but I'm afraid I must disappoint. And, if I'm being honest, I believe your heart lies elsewhere."

Solenne felt herself blush, not realizing she had been that obvious with Alek. "Thank you for being forthright and clearing up any confusion."

"If I said or did anything to mislead you, I sincerely apologize." He gave her hand a perfunctory pat. "Enjoy the air. I believe I must return to my host duties."

When Chambers departed, Solenne pressed a hand to her chest with relief.

Aleksandar

Boxon Hill

Marechal House - the Courtyard

. . .

"Oww!" The wooden sword clattered to the pavement, and Luis rubbed his shoulder.

"Perhaps you would be faster if you had not drunk so much last night."

"Two glasses of wine! I'm hardly a drunk. Stop enjoying this."

"I am not enjoying this." Alek suppressed a smirk, noting that Luis did not deny being hung over.

He motioned for Luis to resume his stance, then sprang into an attack. Surprised, Luis quickly recovered. He placed too much importance on form and posture, as if a monster would wait for him to assume fighting stance number three. In the heat of the hunt, there was no time for formalities. Survival boiled down to action and reaction.

Truthfully, he had enjoyed little since his return to the Marechals. Well, he enjoyed the dance with Solenne. He did not enjoy the uncomfortable clothes he had to wear. He had not enjoyed leaving Solenne alone with that man last night. He did not enjoy watching them step out into the night for privacy. Loathing swelled inside of him, and the beast wanted to tear its rival to shreds.

It demanded that Alek march out and challenge his rival for Solenne.

He left, rather than make a fool of himself, because what did he offer her? Chambers had a grand house, money to splash about on frivolities like dances, and Alek turned up uninvited, wearing rags. Despite cleaning his coat and carefully mending the shirt, his clothes were worn and ill-fitting.

His only consolation was that Solenne appeared as miserable as he, which was a terrible thought. He should want her happiness, even if it meant his own misery. That morning, when the light crept across the bedroom floor, he could not find that spirit of generosity in himself. His beast was a selfish, greedy thing.

The practice sword smacked Luis across the shoulder. Again.

"You're too fast," Luis complained, rubbing his shoulder.

"So be faster or be dead." If his words were too harsh, he did not care. The reality of their profession was harsh. A single mistake ended lives. Hunter rarely got the luxury of growing old. "Perhaps this is a good place to pause for breakfast," he said.

Luis groaned. "I don't think I can eat."

"I have faith in you." Alek gave Luis a slap on the back, which sent him stumbling forward.

Cook had breakfast waiting in the kitchens. Luis turned an interesting shade of green at the plate of ham and eggs. "I think just toast this morning."

"Nonsense, Master Luis. Nothing cures a hangover better than butter and grease," Cook said.

"I would have thought hydration and a bit of willow bark tea," Alek said.

"Oh, no. Don't tell Solenne. She'll make me drink an entire pot of the stuff, and it is vile," Luis said.

"My ears are burning," Solenne said as she entered the room. Instinctively, his body shifted to face her, and he perked to attention.

Damn his heart for feeling like it would burst out of his chest.

"You look peaky," she said to her brother.

"I'm fine," Luis said, quickly shoveling an egg into his mouth. He chewed slowly, as if his stomach threatened to revolt.

She sat next to Alek at the table, the scent of her lavender and honey soap ticking his nose. At least she did not smell of that vile old man.

"Why is your nose doing that?" she asked.

"My nose is not doing anything."

"No, it's doing that." She wrinkled her nose, like there was a foul scent lodged inside.

"You are mistaken." Alek picked up his plate and moved to the end of the table.

"Oh, wow. I'm glad I'm here to see this," Luis said, planting his elbows on the table like he was in the front row of the greatest show imaginable.

Alek grumbled, stabbing at his plate.

"I don't know why you're so grumpy," Solenne said.

"I suppose congratulations are in order," he replied, every word hurting his soul.

The kitchen fell unnaturally silent.

"Quite the opposite, in fact." Solenne retrieved a plate from the cabinet. Her cheeks flushed, and she gibbered. "Colonel Chambers felt I had the wrong impression of his intentions, so he clarified his own affection for me. Meaning, none."

"No affection?"

Solenne slammed down the plate. "Must you drag this out? Do you enjoy my humiliation? No affection. No engagement. I am forever to be a spinster, it means."

"Don't worry, Solenne," Luis said, mouth stuffed with ham. "I'll always need you, even when you're old and all the village children think you're a witch."

Alek held his breath, expecting Solenne to send the dishes flying. Instead, she laughed, not her bright and mirth-filled laugh, but something darker and more tender. It unnerved him, and the beast whispered that he could fix this. He could have what he always wanted and make her laugh properly. Every morning could be this, ham for breakfast in a tidy kitchen, with her smile.

Alek shoved another slice of toast into his mouth to avoid making a fool of himself.

No engagement. It meant nothing to him, but it meant everything to the beast.

Solenne was his.

Chapter Ten

Solenne

Boxon Hill

Marechal House - The Summer Solstice

Heavy pounding sounded at the front door.

Solenne stilled, the cup of tea paused inches from her mouth, and listened. Cook placed a comforting arm around the maid, who whimpered. Travers reached for the wooden bat and looked at the ceiling, like he could divine who was at the door. Aleksandar, Luis, and Godwin had left for the stone circle, the epicenter of the nexus, as soon as the sun neared the horizon.

They were alone in the house.

Tension crackled through the air.

The pounding continued.

Travers looked to Solenne, waiting for instruction.

"This is unprecedented," she said. No one came to the house during an event. Solenne and the staff behind left alone had never been an issue. No one left their homes if given the choice.

"If they require aid, we must assist," Travers said.

"Yes, you are correct. Answer the door. I will be right behind you." She set down her teacup and reached for her silver knife. The blade wasn't much, but a good hit in a vulnerable spot would slow down anything, man or beast.

Up the stairs, Travers carefully approached the door. His hand paused on the bolt. "Declare yourself," he ordered.

"Open the door, man," a masculine voice said.

Travers looked to Solenne, who shook her head. She did not recognize the voice.

"I said declare yourself. Who are you? I am armed," Travers said, his voice losing the familiarly cool and polished tone Solenne knew.

"Jase Parkell," the man answered, muffled by the door. "I have a man. He's unwell."

"You are unknown to me, sir," Travers replied, looking to Solenne as if for guidance.

"Colonel Chambers' nephew," she whispered. After his disgraceful behavior at the dance, the man must be in dire need to seek assistance from the Marechals.

"Please. This is the closest house. My uncle's house is too far away," Jase said.

"Then I suggest your hurry on to your uncle's." Travers was having none of it. Gossip traveled fast in the village, and no doubt Travers heard about Jase's incivility.

"I found a man in the woods. He's delirious. He keeps saying he has something for Luis."

"Miles," Solenne gasped.

"It could be a trick," Travers murmured. "Mr. Bartram knows better than to wander the woods during an event."

Solenne nodded. Miles did know better, but if he were distracted or focused on a project, he might misjudge the hour. She adjusted her stance, wishing she wore something more substantial than a plain work dress and leather-soled slippers on her feet. If this was a trick, she and Travers would give a rousing good fight, but she'd move better in trousers and proper shoes.

Jase stood at the threshold, propping up Miles, who had an arm slung over his shoulder. Jase wore a ludicrously plum coat and a waistcoat in a matching print, expertly tailored and without a doubt expensive. His silk shoes were caked in mud, ruined. He had not dressed for a casual romp through the countryside.

"Miles!" she exclaimed, pushing her suspicions aside. "Is he injured? What happened?"

"I am unsure. I found him wandering in Uncle's property. He can't tell me a blasted thing. Apologies for my language."

No obvious blood or injuries, although Miles' eyes appeared glassy and his skin slick with sweat. She pressed her palm to his forehead. "He's feverish. Bring him through to the drawing room."

"I know I've been a terrible snob and I'm the last person you'd want to help," Jase said.

"Miles is a friend," she responded. None of this was for Jase Parkell. He could go rot for all she cared.

Travers helped Jase to carry Miles to the drawing room. Fortunately, the room was not far. They deposited the delirious man on a settee. "I say, life in the country is more exciting than I expected," Jase said.

Solenne ignored his attempt at humor or whatever *that* had been.

"Miss?" Cook asked from the stairwell that led to the kitchens below.

"Cool water, please, and a clean cloth. Miles?" Solenne knelt before Miles and held the man's face in both hands. He blinked slowly and his pupils were wildly dilated. "Did you eat something in the woods? A berry?"

Although it hadn't happened in years, flora near the nexus could shift. Benign fruit turned toxic overnight, just one of the many difficulties about life on the fringes of civilization. The sheep did well on because their stomach would digest most anything, nexus-twisted plants or not.

"N-no, no. I can't..." Miles slumped back onto the settee. The bag on his shoulder slipped to the floor. "Bite."

"A bite?" She frantically searched him for signs of blood and the cursed wolf's bite. Other than mud and sweat, his clothes were pristine. The dark fabric hid blood too well. Perhaps it was a smaller creature. She tore at buttons to push open the fabric.

"Miss Marechal!" Jase gasped in shock.

"Now is not the time for decorum. We have to treat the bite."

"Yes, of course. Allow me. I insist." He removed his own coat and unlaced Miles' boots. Constructed from sturdy leather, nothing should have been able to strike through the boot. Nonetheless, Jase removed the boots and stockings, and pushed up trouser legs to check his calves.

Nothing.

Solenne held Miles' wrist to push up his shirt sleeves. The man hissed and jerked away, nearly knocking a fist into her. The bite was angry and red, possibly already infected, and large enough to belong to a wolf.

"What bit you, Miles?"

"Doesn't matter," he mumbled. "Luis needs...the bag."

"Was it a wolf? A beast? This is important."

"So is the armor I made for Luis!"

Exasperated, she dumped out the contents of his bag. An undershirt slithered to the ground, almost soundless as the fabric flowed. Dull gray, it looked very much like the often-repaired armor Luis wore, only new and whole.

"Did you make this?" She retrieved the shirt, the fabric flowing as smoothly as water in her hands. Made of one piece of fabric, it had no discernible seams. "This is remarkable. Did you recreate the carbon nanofiber?"

"A close approximation." He sat up, wincing. "I spun the thread, and Mrs. Berry knitted the shirt. For Luis."

Solenne set the item to the side. There would be time to wonder if Miles had been intrigued by the challenge of making the armor or if he had been driven by the need to protect Luis. "We need to get that bite cleaned.

I'll need to fetch my kit. Stay here," she told Miles, then looked to Jase for support. He nodded.

"Miss, I will fetch what you require," Travers said.

She shook her head. She didn't know what she needed, exactly. Wolfsbane. Honey. "Yes. My kit. Wolfsbane. All of it."

A feminine shout came from the other end of the house. Travers paled. "See to that. We'll manage in here," she ordered.

"What can I do?"

Cook arrived with the water and clean cloth on a dull metal tray. Solenne took the woman's burden and set it on the side table. "Get his shirt off. Hold this to the wound until it stops bleeding," she said.

Her workroom was at the back of the house, in the original part of the building. The last expansion nearly a century prior added the front rooms laid out in a logical grid, with a corridor running down the center and a large foyer designed to impress guests. Narrow, twisting corridors filled the older section.

Poorly heated in the winter and poorly ventilated in the summer, the family seldom used this section of the house, other than to store weapons and artifacts. Her workroom was at the very end, a room with tall, narrow windows that faced the morning sun.

She ran, skidding precariously as she rounded a corner.

And nearly collided with a man.

"Colonel Chambers!"

He reached out a hand to steady her. "Are you well? The door was open."

"Jase…Mr. Parkell arrived with Miles. He's been injured," she said in a rush. "What are you doing back here? They're in the front drawing room."

"I thought I heard a noise, and the door was open." He ran a hand down her arm. The gesture was a touch more familiar than she appreciated, almost possessive.

She pulled away and stepped toward her workroom. "I require my kit."

"Was my nephew injured? He went out before dusk and did not return. I was worried."

"They were attacked in the forest, but he is well."

"Attacked? Here? Do you think something followed them into the house?"

She hadn't until that moment. Ice rushed over her. She told Travers to open the door, against every protocol, then had been too distracted to secure the door.

Her eyes darted to the iron door down the hall. Chambers followed her gaze, then touched the handle of the nearest door. Silver nails decorated the door in a grid, but time had tarnished the nails to a dull gray.

He drew his hand back when the handle did not budge.

"We must be prepared to defend ourselves, I fear," he said, shaking his hand slightly. "Can you open this door?"

"That goes to the basement. There is nothing of use down there," she said. Only the vault where the old and broken artifacts were kept, along with the few items too dangerous to leave unsecured.

"The weapons we use are here," she said, brushing past him in the narrow corridor. The skin at the back of her neck pricked at the proximity.

The door to the weapons room required a code to open the lock. The ancient keypad, numbers worn smooth on the keys, had not worked in more than a hundred years. Now a combination lock kept the room secure.

"Marvelous," Chambers said. He reached for a club studded with silver nails. It was a brutal piece of work. "This will do." He gave a test swing, lunging forward and stepping back.

Solenne elected to leave the room unlocked, in case they needed to make a mad dash for another weapon. Chambers went to join his nephew in the drawing room, and she finally made it to her workshop.

Dust and the scent of dried herbs hung in the air. Moonlight filtered in through the windows. She grabbed her kit and all the bottles of wolfsbane tonic. The supply was distressingly low. She felt certain she had more, but there was no time to count.

A loud crash made her jolt. She turned around, her elbow knocking over a bottle that should not have been there. It rolled across the table, heading for the edge. "No, no, no!" she cried, dashing to catch it.

The bottle smashed to the floor.

Everything was going wrong that night. She felt flustered and wanted to toss her entire stock to the floor. She made do with old equipment and limited supplies. Everyone said the family's work was important, valued, but those were only words. They did not offer tangible support. That smashed bottle cost money she did not have. She'd have to barter for a replacement.

Solenne touched the silver bracelet on her wrist. When things went wrong, her mother always said it was best to take a moment to decide why, rather than fly into a rage. As much as Solenne's natural inclination urged her to throw a tantrum out of fear and frustration, she needed to think.

Calm.

Someone had been in her workroom. They moved the bottles, carelessly leaving them in a location where it would be easy to knock them over. She had already caught Aleksandar helping himself to her wares. It was not inconceivable to imagine him doing so again and then being thoughtless enough to leave a mess.

They would have words once this horrible night finally finished.

She gathered up the supplies required for Miles' wound, then hurried through the corridors.

The air had shifted. First, Solenne noticed the scent of flowers that only bloomed at night. The air felt dry and crackled with static. Tension wound itself through every room in the house, tracing a path down the darkened halls, up the stairs, and into the secret, forgotten corners.

The front door was open. Again. Still.

"Travers. Chambers," she called.

No response.

Miles was alone in the drawing room, sprawled back on the settee. His skin appeared glossy. She pressed the back of her hand to his forehead. The fever had not broken in the slightest.

"What happened to Jase?" she asked gently, exchanging her kit for the bowl of water and cloth. She soaked the cloth, wrung it out, then placed it against Miles' forehead.

He jerked forward, his hand clamping around her bad wrist. His grip was tight, but not painful. "Oh. Apologies." He released her. "I'm not myself."

"You're having a bad reaction to more than the bite, I think. Were you stung by anything? Eat anything?"

"Nettles? I cannot be sure. Is that a difficulty?"

"Less than ideal," she said. Normal nettles were unpleasant but would not induce such a reaction. He could have been stung by an insect or pricked by a plant mutated by the nexus energies.

"Any difficulty breathing?"

He shook his head, then shivered. "No. I'm cold."

Finally, a bit of luck. If Miles were having an allergic reaction, his throat would be swollen and he'd be quite blue.

Solenne pulled the footstool to Miles and sat before him. Taking his arm, she ordered him to remain still. She swabbed the bite area with the disinfectant. It bubbled and fizzed. Miles watched, fascinated.

"It's funny," he said.

"Oh, this is a very humorous situation, getting yourself turned into a chew toy."

"No, the nexus. People say it's magic, but it's not. It has rules."

"How so?" She dabbed away the excess with the clean cloth. "Tell me," she prompted, content to let him lecture if it kept him still while she picked out the bits of leaves and grass from the wound.

"It's on a cycle. We've known that for years and years. And it only happens in certain places, which is weird. And things come through, we know that, but mostly what comes through is energy. We have our own form, of course. It's in the background, harmless to us. But what comes through the nexus, it waxes and wanes, but it doesn't go away. It changes. But that's what energy does, like heat. I use the heat from fire to transform metal."

"And the nexus energy does this? Can you harness it?"

"We tried, you know. Or others in the past tried. They built machines, but those didn't work. They failed. The energy is not compatible. Which is a shame, because it's *everywhere*. So we have this raw energy, like the heat from the sun or the wind, and it doesn't vanish. It forces mutations in plants." He paused. "In people."

Pausing her work, she gave him a serious look. "Miles, the bite carries a virus. It's not raw cosmic energy. This was the work of tooth and claw."

"Energy can't be destroyed. You can contain it or transform it, but never destroy," Miles said, as if he did not hear her. His head lolled back. "Transform is the wrong word. Disperse? Dissipate? Expend. Yes. Contain or expend."

Those words were familiar. She had heard them before. "Mother's journals," she breathed.

He nodded. "I have them."

"You stole them?"

Amalie had been an artificer, much like Miles. The older tech fascinated her. She spent countless hours trying to repair or recharge the artifacts in the vaults below the house. One such endeavor cost her her life.

"No, you misunderstand. She loaned them to me a fortnight before her death. I did not know how to return them. I feared—"

"I always thought Father burned them," she said.

Miles nodded. "Exactly. I fear Godwin would destroy them. Your mother had a marvelous mind. Are they still there? Below ground?"

"Probably. The only items we've bartered away have gone to you," she said.

"No. The batteries. The containment banks for—"

Glass shattered inward. Solenne raised an arm to shield herself from the flying shards.

The beast crouched, snarling.

Aleksandar

Boxon Hill

The Stone Circle

The moon aligned with the tallest stone, casting a long shadow. Energy poured through the nexus, the thin veil that separated the planes nothing more than a suggestion of division. The wayward energy hummed through the air, searching for a vessel.

With his eyes half-closed, Luis spread his fingers wide, like he could feel the current of energy in the air.

Alek could sense it, but only because of the combination of the summer solstice and the proximity to the nexus. The standing stone circle amplified the sensation.

At any other time, any other place, it was noise in the background. If he focused, he could feel it. Barely. Luis' gesticulation was a learning tool. As his skill grew, he'd lean less on the hand-waving and stumbling with his eye closed.

Godwin required no crutch to track the flow of the nexus energies and, by extension, any mutated beasts. The energies wanted to flow to the beasts, like a river rushing downwards. The full moon was a deluge.

Finding a trail in all the noise would be difficult, even for one as skilled as Godwin.

A useful mutation, Amalie had called it. Those who lived near nexus points had higher rates of mutation, mostly benign and unnoticeable. Tolerance for pollens that were not, strictly speaking, of this world. Natural pheromones that repelled insects. Very useful.

Violet blood.

This phenomenon had fascinated Amalie. In her crumbling, ancient texts, she found mention of a disease caused by a parasite born through an insect bite. Populations with this endemic disease developed a mutation in the blood cell that granted resistance to the parasite. This same trait could also affect the body's ability to deliver oxygen, often leaving the person fatigued, and the cells died early, leaving the person with a low blood count.

A useful mutation that had a price.

Luis pressed a palm to the largest of the stones, as if that grounding could amplify his senses. Perhaps it could.

Alek did not have to wonder what price Luis' useful mutation took. The cost was a lifetime in servitude to guard against the monster that prowled the night. A long-ago ancestor had shown an aptitude for the task, and it passed down through the generations.

As for what Alek sensed, it was a jumble of information. The nexus energy flitted about him, humming happily in his ears like bees in a summer field. He sensed nothing beyond his own nose.

Not true.

He felt a tug, the thinnest of connections between him to Solenne. It whispered *home* and *mate*. His beast agreed.

Alek tugged at his ear in a futile attempt to dispel the high-pitched noise. Every part of him itched. The silver on his neck, the bands on his arms, and the silver-inked tattoo over his heart burned. He wanted...

He couldn't form the instinct into words. To shift, to let the beast out in a burst of energy, but that would not only soothe his discomfort momentarily.

Home. Mate.

The connection back to Solenne anchored him, made the itching and the humming tolerable.

Godwin watched Alek with his one eye. "Anything?"

Alek scanned the ground, hoping to point to some trampled bit of grass or conveniently placed pawprint in the mud.

Luis and Godwin gasped at the same moment. The cord connecting him to Solenne vibrated, the tone of it black and red, ringing inside his head like a bell.

Wasting no time, he ran toward the house. The full moon cast a pale imitation of daylight over the ground. His boot heel skidded on the grass as he descended Boxon Hill.

"You'll break your neck!" Godwin shouted.

"The house," Luis said. "I can feel it."

Alek wasted no time. The house was under attack. The nexus energy parted around him like an eddy, surging toward something furious and hungry. Solenne needed him. Her fear...

He did not understand the connection, but he welcomed it. If Solenne was afraid, then she was alive.

His feet pounded the ground, and his legs pumped. He ran until it felt as if his lungs would burst. Not fast enough. Not strong enough. He needed to be unfettered.

With a growl, he grabbed the silver chain at his neck. Pain burned his fingers as he tore the chain away, but pain was momentary. Unfettered, he could breathe. The wild vitality of the nexus poured into him, filling him to the point of bursting. He could not contain it.

The shift started in his toes, elongating and the nails piercing through the leather like daggers. His fingers burned and flexed, claws out. A shudder rippled down this back, forcing him to bend forward. Fabric ripped at the seams of his coat.

Alek stumbled, falling to his knees. It was too much, like trying to fill a teacup from a gushing torrent. He wheezed, mouth opening and sucking in air, but nothing came. This curse had been smothering the life out of him for years, and it was, literally, smothering him now.

He pressed the heel of his hand to the tattoo on his chest. It burned, but that pain was a slight point of light in the overwhelming darkness. This cursed promised power, but it felt him trembling and weak. He fought to contain it, to control it, but the constant fight left him even more vulnerable.

Home. Mate.

The beast wanted out. It promised to strengthen him, faster. Fast enough to protect their mate. It tempted him. Teeth crowded his mouth, drawing blood. He couldn't do it on his own, he couldn't resist. He couldn't even breathe. He was drowning, and the connection with Solenne screamed and—

A hand thumped him hard on his back.

Alek gasped, breathing in.

"Come on. We need you." Luis held out a hand and hauled Alek up. The younger man gave him a curious look, then shoved him in the house's direction. "I can sense two. One is close."

Very close.

Chapter Eleven

Solenne

Boxon Hill

Marechal House - The Parlor

The glass fell to the floor. All she could hear was the pounding of her heart.

The beast stood on two legs, looking far more human than she felt comfortable with.

Miles stirred on the divan, struggling to rise to his feet, but his legs seemed unable to support his weight.

The beast's maw moved, and something like a croon came out. Was it trying to speak? She had never heard of such a thing. People under the curse were still, at least in theory, people, but they lost their minds from the pain of the transformation. She could not imagine how much it hurt to have bones snap and re-knit, for skin to stretch, tear and heal. Had this person come to her for help?

"It is an evening of unprecedented events," she murmured. Carefully, she inched closer to the sideboard.

The beast tracked her movement.

"I believe I can help. I'm going for my kit," she said. The beast snarled and snapped its jaws. She immediately paused. "All right. What do you want then? You obviously came here for a reason."

The man, obviously a male from the endowment nestled in a thick patch of hair between his legs, moved forward. She averted her eyes, looking toward the decanter and glasses on the sideboard.

He leaned in, muzzle against her hair. His hardened member pressed against her hip. She closed her eyes, willing herself to remain calm and not give in to fear, which clouded the mind.

Hot, foul breath wafted over her. He growled and snapped his jaws, making her jump with a strangled shout.

He huffed, as if amused.

Her fingers gripped the edge of the sideboard, more annoyed that the beast wanted to frighten her than actually feeling frightened.

A wet tongue licked the side of her face. Revulsion rolled through her body. The beast snarled and shook its head, one clawed hand scraping at its nose, as if trying to remove a foul taste.

How extraordinarily rude.

A shout came from outside the house. Luis and Alek.

"In here!"

The beast turned, grabbing her arm roughly. Solenne reached back to the sideboard, knocking over the decanter and fragile glasses. She struggled in the beast's grasp, his claws digging in, but she did not release the tray.

Alek filled the doorway, menace rolling off him in waves.

The beast yanked her forward to use her as a shield. Her grip on the tray held, glass shattering on the floor. Swinging with all her might, she brought the silver tray around and connected solidly with the side of the beast's head.

Its grip faltered enough for her to scramble away, still clutching the tray.

Alek and Luis surged forward, knives out. The beast swiped with huge hands, each claw a dagger in its own right. Each blow only seemed to enrage it, to feed its fury.

"Here," Miles said, pulling her back into a corner behind the divan.

Furniture creaked and groaned before smashing. So many things happened at once. Another man shouted; it was Travers, snagging Luis' attention.

The beast lunged, jaws dripping with spit.

Miles grabbed her hand in a crushing squeeze.

Alek jumped on the beast's back. His fingers dug into the furry backside and clung on, despite how the beast twisted and thrashed. One large arm sideswiped Luis, knocking him to his back.

Miles scrambled forward, weaving dangerously like he was intoxicated, which he was. He wedged himself between Luis and the beast, his arm raised to shield them. Dull gray material caught the light.

Massive jaws clamped around Miles' arm. He cried out, in shock or pain, she could not tell. From behind, Luis jabbed at the beast's face with a silver dagger. Alek clawed at the back.

The beast swatted at Alek, like a horse swishing a tail at annoying flies. Nothing seemed to make an impact.

Immunity to silver was impossible, yet it had a tolerance. Almost a resistance.

Solenne clutched the tray to her chest, suddenly realizing that the beast had to be ancient to have such strength. A decade, perhaps more, of living with the curse. She had only read of such beings in the family's journals. Each came with a high price.

As if it could sense her thoughts, it turned a luminous violet eye to her. Blood matted its fur, like wet hair plastered to the scalp, making the disfiguring shift even more apparent. Yet the eyes were familiar.

Its top lip curled back in a grin.

"Out," she said.

She had to get it out. It was not an unthinking creature. It came to the house for a reason, and she would not suffer to have it in her home one second more.

"Out!" She charged forward, swinging the tray and connecting solidly with that almost familiar face.

The beast squealed, stumbling back. Solenne labored under no illusions that she turned the tide, but three against one was not good odds. Four, including Miles. Luis and Alek would wear the beast down and corner him eventually. Until then, it was a battle of small gains and larger losses. Clearly the beast could withstand Luis and Aleksandar's blades. One good bite and it would be over for either of them.

The beast released Miles' arm, shoving the man back. One massive hand, disfigured with razor-like claws, swiped at Luis.

Her brother was not fast enough, catching the blow in the stomach. He stumbled back, dagger falling to the ground.

A roar—human and strangled with frustration—came from outside the window. Godwin leveled a crossbow at the beast and fired.

The shot went wide, catching Alek's shoulder. The second bolt also missed, flying close enough to Solenne that she could feel the air move as it soared past. The beast howled, as if someone had hit it. Perhaps it realized it was outnumbered now by one injured hunter, an untrained hunter, a one-eyed hunter, a woman with a silver tray, and a drugged blacksmith.

If she hadn't been so terrified, she'd laugh at their pathetic squad.

The beast reared back, throwing Alek to the ground, who snarled and snapped his jaws. Finally, the beast retreated through the window.

The tray clattered to the floor.

"What were you thinking?" Alek roared at her. He grabbed her roughly by the shoulders, nearly lifting her off her feet.

Aleksandar

His fingers curled around her upper arms, the claws not quite receded and digging into the light fabric of her sleeves. She felt altogether too fragile in his grip, nothing more than breakable bones in soft packaging, and he had already seen once how easily her bones broke. He wanted to shake her for being so reckless or to lock her away where her rashness and foolhardy nature could never endanger herself again.

She was his. His to protect and his to punish. *His* and she stank of another male. He needed…so many things. They wrestled for priority in his mind. Instinct said to cover her in his scent, to mark her so the other male would respect his claim. Reason said that he should unhand the hunter's daughter, lest he become prey. Ego took pride in that she thought fast during the attack, despite her fear pounding away in her heart.

He could hear it, feel her pulse thrum under his touch.

Thump. Thump. Thump.

His home. His mate.

His.

He was vaguely aware of others speaking, of movement in the room. It faded into background noise as Solenne stared up at him, her quicksilver eyes wide, as lost in the moment as him. He was so furious with her it was difficult to think with the beast howling inside, contained, but only because the beast allowed it.

"Alek, you're bleeding—"

He kissed her, hard, with too much teeth. The sane part of his mind hoped that they were only teeth and not dagger-like fangs. She melted against him, opening herself to him, deepening the kiss.

She tasted of copper, herbs, and fear. Delicious fear, sweet and forbidden, purloined right in front of her family. No one could stop him. No one dared. This pleased the beast, who wrapped an arm around her, shielding her, hiding her.

Her fingers tangled in his hair, pulling with force. He gave a playful nip at her lower lip.

They stood there, lips almost touching. The violet left his vision as the beast receded and normal sight returned. His hold relaxed, knowing he could release her and step back. Such an action would allow them to blame their impropriety on mutual relief or the heat of the moment.

She stretched up on the tips of her toes, brushing her lips to his, the barest of contact that meant everything.

Solenne pulled away, her face flush. A splatter of violet blood decorated her cheek; whether it was from the invading beast or himself, he could not say.

"My warrior, covered in the blood of her enemies," he said, using his thumb to rub it in.

Someone behind them loudly cleared their throat.

Chapter Twelve

Solenne

Boxon Hill

Marechal House - The Parlor

"You've got an arrow...just there, in your back," Luis said.

Alek reached over his shoulder and yanked out the arrow with a grunt. Violet blood gleamed on the silver tip. Using the sleeve of his shirt, he wiped it down and handed the arrow to Luis.

Miles wobbled on his feet, then sat heavily in a chair. The armor slid from his grasp into a puddle on the floor.

Godwin cleared his throat, crossbow slung over his shoulder. "Sorry about that. My aim leaves something to be desired."

"Where is Mr. Parkell?" Solenne asked, stepping back from Alek. "Colonel Chambers is also here. I ran into him in the hall."

Alek grumbled at the mention of the Colonel's name.

"What the devil were they doing here, tonight of all nights? And explain why the blacksmith is about to pass out in my parlor." Godwin used the stock end of the crossbow to knock out the broken glass from the window. The sound of broken glass hitting the stone outside was the sound of an expense they could not rightly afford.

"Mr. Bartram came to deliver a piece of equipment but was attacked in the woods. Mr. Parkell discovered him and brought him here."

"Not to Chambers?"

"No time," Miles wheezed.

"I expected better of you, Bartram. Gallivanting about on the solstice. Serves you right, but there's nothing to be done. You're here for the night," Godwin said, Miles already forgotten as his gaze settled on Alek. Her father's expression was inscrutable with the patch covering one eye. "Get patched up and go search for our wandering guests. Luis and I will track the beast.

It's moving slowly and will head to its den." With that, Godwin pivoted on his heel and left before anyone could question his orders.

Luis looked from her to Miles, bent over with his elbows resting on his knees, and back to her. "What's wrong with him?"

"Poison. A sedative, I think, but it is wearing off," she said, glossing over the bite. Luis did not need the added distraction of worrying about Miles.

"You'll stay with him?"

"Until you return. Go," she said, giving Luis a light push. He glanced at Miles once more, then departed.

Solenne smoothed back her hair, discovering that most, if not all, had fallen out of the bun. Her hand trembled, and she laughed. Now that the crisis had passed, her body succumbed to terror. Her heart pounded in her chest and her throat tightened, like she would never breathe again.

"Solenne, are you well?" Alek asked, taking her hand. The warm, solid feel of him grounded her.

"I've never seen one, a beast, before. Well, there's Tristan in the library, but alive, I mean. Never alive. I fear I'm babbling," she said, seemingly unable to stop herself. The beast had touched her and shared her air. "It licked me."

Alek's grip tightened on her hand, and a throaty rumble filled the room. A growl, she realized, the thought distant from herself, like an observation from afar.

"You did well," he said. His chest heaved, as if the words pained him. "If he had hurt you...but a serving tray? What were you thinking?"

"Silver," she said, irritated at his faint praise wrapped in concern. "For all good it did."

She twisted her arm, breaking his grip to switch holds. Lifting his hand to the light, she turned it palm up.

"No," he said, pulling back.

Solenne refused to let go, her fingernails digging in. He made no sound of distress, not that she expected her blunt nails to go against the rough skin of his hands. Thick dark hair poked out from the edge of his cuffs. Violet blood stained the fabric, but that was not what she wanted to examine.

The crescent scar laid pale and almost silver across the palm of his hand. Lightly, she traced the curving shape.

"I remember this," she said. Her own matching scar itched on the heel of her palm.

"We climbed to the top of the old mill to scavenge the solar panels," he replied.

Amalie sent up the two children, as they were lighter and, therefore, it was safer to be on the rotted roof. Except it wasn't, and the roof gave way. Solenne nearly fell, slicing her hand on a rusted nail as she gripped the edge of the hole. Alek pulled her back, also cutting his hand.

"I think Mama was more upset about the damaged solar panels than us nearly falling through the roof," Solenne said before she could think better of it. She glanced at the door and the smashed window, as if Godwin would hear her make a disparaging comment about her mother.

It's not that he never spoke about Mama. It was that grief had morphed Amalie into an irreproachable figure, incapable of flaws.

He broke her hold, picking up the heavy silver hammer and resting it on the injury-free shoulder. "I should find Chambers and this other fellow."

"Your wound—"

"It'll heal. It always does. He needs to rest. Stay with him. Lock the door," he said, already gone.

With a sigh, Solenne turned her attention back to Miles, who carefully examined the armor he crafted. "Were you bitten again?" she asked.

"No. The material performed admirably, but you can already see signs of wear and tear. Most distressing."

He held up a section to illustrate his point, but she could see no difference.

Travers boarded up the window to discourage other "unexpected arrivals," as he put it.

She examined Miles' arm. A vivid bruise was already blooming on the arm the beast had clamped its jaws around. Solenne applied a thick layer of salve to help reduce swelling and promote healing, then found a serviceable bed for Miles. She poured a cup of tea down his throat to help with pain, despite his protests.

"You'll hurt worse in the morning if you don't," she warned.

"I'll hurt in the morning, regardless. It tastes foul."

"That's how you know it's medicine," she said, even as she added a spoonful of honey to the cup.

She kept watched as Miles slept, in case he had a delayed reaction to the bite or whatever toxins flowed through him. With an old quilt wrapped about her shoulders, she settled into a chair to read. She absently flipped through the pages of an old primer, reading the signs of a beast's curse.

Faded ink listed the old-world names for the new monsters the original settlers discovered inhabiting the continent: werewolf, vampire, and witch. She could recite entire pages from memory, but the touch of paper and ink helped her to think.

The beast had been unfazed by the silver weapons. Pained, yes, but not grievously injured. According to the primer, with age, cursed creatures developed immunity to silver and other warding artifacts—the exact nature of a warding artifact, she did not know. The primer took it for granted as an obvious piece of information and failed to elaborate.

Immunity.

Beasts could resist the effects of silver. The devils who craved blood could tolerate sunlight.

She did not want to imagine such a world filled with ancient monsters who could shrug off attacks.

Her fingers ran down a list of the signs of infection and the means to test if a person had the curse: skin irritation to silver, violet-tinted blood, accelerated healing, though infected bites were slow to heal, fangs and other excessive teeth, and a violet light in the eyes. Behavioral changes comprised a long list increasing in severity from irritability to feral mania during the full moon.

None of it made sense. If Alek—

But she had seen the damage the silver-tipped arrow did to his back and the violet blood that stained his shirt. Unmistakable proof, yet his behavior did not align with what the book wrote. He should be unstable, unsocial, irritable with fits of fury and violence.

He should have shifted. How had he resisted the pull of the moon and remained human? Retained his mind?

The doorknob rattled, startling her awake from her rambling thoughts. The book fell to the floor.

"Solenne? Are you there?"

"Alek! Yes." She moved to the door, fingers hovering over the lock before she hesitated. Was this a trick? Had he slipped into a feral mania now? No, Alek sounded normal, but she wondered how many teeth he had in his mouth and how sharp.

"Do not open the door. Swear to me. Do not open this door."

Aleksandar

Boxon Hill

Marechal House - A Corridor

Alek leaned against the door, exhaustion finally catching up with him. Claws had receded, but his hands were still distorted and not entirely human.

Home. Mate.

Returning to the Marechals had been a mistake. He expected the proximity to the nexus point to exacerbate his condition, but he had not expected Solenne to affect him so.

"You're in my blood. Don't open the door. I won't be kind," he said, enunciating carefully around the teeth in his mouth. They were the sort of teeth made for snarling and biting, not eloquence.

Inside, the beast howled to tear down the door because she was in his blood and it promised to be anything but kind. It wanted to cover Solenne with its scent, to erase the lingering stench of the other who bared to touch his mate. Bad enough the house reeked of the musk, but an open window helped.

The door had to remain closed or he'd ruin her, in multiple, scandalous ways.

"What's happening? Talk to me," Solenne said from the other side of the door, her voice muffled by the door but safe. Safe as long as the barrier was in place.

"Don't open the door. No matter what I say. Promise me."

"I don't understand. What's—"

"Solenne!" His clenched fist hit the door. "Just promise me. Say it."

"I...I won't open the door."

"Good." He sagged against the door before sliding down to his knees. "You're in my blood. I don't know how, but I can feel you. That was how I knew to return to the house. It wasn't Luis or Godwin's tracking. I felt your fear. It was delicious, Solenne." He ran his tongue over his sharp teeth, drawing a thin laceration that healed almost immediately. "Does your blood taste as delightful? Or your—"

"Aleksandar!"

"Your skin. I want to lick every part of you, Solenne. Taste every part of you. Don't let me. I'll ruin you." He gave a mirthless laugh at how he had gone years without speaking to another soul, and now he couldn't stop the vile words from spilling out of him. "Half of me wants to fuck you until you can't walk and…the other half wants that too, but you wouldn't walk away. You'd run because you're my prey, and I would hunt you, capture you, and mark you so no one else would dare touch you."

Silence.

She anchored him. In the years since the bite that cursed him, every day had been a struggle to maintain control over the beast. It tore at him, wearing him down. Sometimes all he could do was let the leash slip a little to allow the beast to burn off energy. Each time left him shaky and half-starved, but ultimately more in control.

Being close to Solenne helped in a manner he had not expected. The beast's constant fight to run wild calmed. Now the beast only wanted its mate.

"But I won't. I swear to you, I'll keep you safe," he said.

"As long as I keep the door closed."

Replying seemed pointless. She knew the answer.

"Did you find Parkell and Chambers?" she eventually asked.

"I found no signs of them." He had found a discarded coat and a cravat caught on a branch near the back of the house, but no sign of either man. They were foolish to leave the safety of the house and dastardly to leave Solenne, Miles, and the household unprotected from the beast. "Cowards," Alek muttered.

"I am inclined to agree. How disappointing." Fabric rustled. "I had hoped they found themselves cornered by a beast or had barricaded themselves into a room."

Alek had thought the same. "No signs of a struggle and no blood. My best guess is they fled when the beast entered the house."

"I cannot believe that of Colonel Chambers. He's a military man."

Alek could believe it, but he kept his opinion to himself. Solenne had made it perfectly clear days ago that she could entertain no disparaging remarks about Chambers. Instead, he asked, "How is your patient?"

"Asleep. He was bitten, but only time will tell. Alek—"

"No, Solenne," he said, knowing what she would ask. Only a small percentage of those bitten by a nexus creature ever received the curse, perhaps one in ten. No one knew entirely why some were more susceptible than others, but where knowledge failed, superstition filled the gaps.

Some said that entire families had bad blood, that the line was tainted, and it was only a matter of time before the curse arrived. Or the person invited the curse because of carelessness or a moral failing. The curse was a divine punishment from a wrath-filled universe.

That one he could believe.

"Are you? I mean, I see the signs, but they make little sense."

"Tomorrow." He leaned his head against the door. "Ask your questions tomorrow."

"Will you be outside the door if I need you?"

His damnable heart stirred at the idea that she might need him. He could not risk being in the same room, so tenuous was his grasp, but he could guard her door. Sleep would be impossible regardless. "Yes. Anything you require. All night."

Chapter Thirteen

Aleksandar

Boxon Hill

Marechal House - A Corridor

A sharp, insistent prodding in the ribs woke him. "Get up already," Godwin grumbled.

"Is it dawn?" Bleary-eyed, Alek stretched and ignored the ache in his shoulder from a long night of sleeping upright. A pale gray light crept through the window at the end of the hall.

"Close enough." Godwin tossed down the silver necklace, which bounced off Alek's face with a sting.

Alek ignored the slight burning sensation in his fingers examined the broken links in the chain. It was too useful to toss aside and a skill smith could repair the damage. "Thank you," he mumbled, stuffing the chain into a pocket.

Godwin handed Alek a steaming mug.

Inhaling deeply, the warm, spicy scent helped to shake off the remnants of sleep. He wanted a long soak in a hot bath, preferably with a soap that would not strip off a layer of skin, and then he wanted an enormous breakfast. Warm bread, dripping with butter and honey. A half-dozen eggs, at least, and he'd take them any style the cook served them. And a slab of beef, still red and juicy in the center, the blood oozing out on the plate.

Alek licked his lips, fantasizing about a chunk of meat that a man could sink his teeth into. The bloodier, the better.

In the early years, concern about maiming an innocent person kept him confined under lock and key, but that captivity made the beast restless. It was better, he discovered, to ease his grip on his control, seclude himself in the middle of nowhere, and let the beast hunt a rabbit or deer.

His stomach rumbled, and he was not sure if that was because of the dream of a hearty breakfast or the taste of a wet, warm rabbit liver.

He glanced up to find Godwin watching him, a keen look in his silvery gray eye. He recognized that look. It was the look that shortly proceeded with a solid thumping during practice and a lecture on how to improve his technique. The older man leaned on a short staff like a walking stick, no doubt intending the staff to be the instrument of the thumping.

"I will not apologize for guarding her door," Alek said.

"Nor should you. The house was breached and unsecured."

Alek nodded, as if that were the reason he stayed outside Solenne's door. "Any luck last night?"

"I would thump you for suggesting I require luck to track a beast, but this one is a slippery devil. No. We found no trace of it, just a few prints in the mud."

"I found this." Alek dug in his coat's inner pocket and removed the cravat. Dirt and Alek's own bloody, smeared fingers stained the cloth. "No signs of Chambers or Parkell otherwise."

Godwin hummed, as if reevaluating his opinion of his neighbor. "The blacksmith?"

"Stable, she said, but that was some hours ago."

Alek raised his fist to knock on the door, but Godwin grabbed his wrist. "Leave them be. How is your shoulder?"

"I've had worse. Maybe next time, hit the beast."

The shrewd look returned. "I hit the target." He thumped the staff against the floor. "Come along. Let's see if they made it home safely or if we have to build them a pyre."

With a quick stop in the kitchen for a thick sandwich of yesterday's bread and cheese, they headed out into the already warm and humid air. Alek pointed them in the direction where he found the discarded garments. A few tracks in the mud led down the hill, into the trees.

"I forgot how early it gets hot here," Alek said, losing the collar at his throat. Warm, he nearly removed the coat. The shirt, stiff from dried blood, clung to his damp skin.

As if sensing his thoughts, Godwin said, "If you have not noticed, we're unconcerned about fashion here. Remove your coat if you wish. A bit of dirt and blood won't ruffle my delicate sensibilities."

"I'm fine," he lied.

"Whatever puts you at ease," Godwin said, waving his hand magnanimously. The man had been so stern, so serious when Alek arrived that he forgot Solenne learned her sarcastic delivery from him. "I will confess that I'm curious about how the wound is healing. You barely flinched when the arrow hit. Did it hurt?"

"Yes, it hurt." Alek took a larger than necessary bite of the sandwich, flashing his teeth and chewing aggressively.

"But is it still bleeding? You never know with your kind."

With his kind.

Alek finished the sandwich because whatever was about to happen would, doubtlessly, require him at full strength and both hands empty. He had been hungry enough in the past to never waste a perfectly good meal. "Same as you, I'd expect," he said, cautiously.

"I had hoped you'd draw out the beast. Like calls to like." Godwin continued on, using the staff to part brush and low-hanging branches.

"I'm sure I do not know—"

"Don't insult me, Hardwick. How long have you had the bite? It must be a few years now. You didn't even shift last night."

"Which hurt worse than your arrow in my shoulder," Alek said.

"Thank you for doing us both the courtesy and not denying it. Now, how long?"

"Seven, maybe eight years. How did you know?"

He had been careful to mask the symptoms of his curse. Obviously not careful enough. He thought back to when he first arrived at the Marechals' home and his encounter with Godwin at the front door. At the time, Godwin seemed cagey, but Alek had chalked that up to being protective over Solenne.

That tricky bastard.

"You knew when I arrived," he concluded.

"I've only one working eye. I'm not blind," Godwin said tersely. "You dared to come to my home, in your condition—"

"Then you should have shut your door to me!" His shout echoed through the trees. Enraged, his claws popped, and he needed to rend and tear.

With a snarl, he sank his claws into the nearest tree, scouring the surface. The bark and woody pulp underneath had a satisfying give, not as good as flesh or a still thrashing rabbit, but good enough.

Alek turned to the man, fangs on display and his mouth crowded with teeth. His top lip curled, displaying the sharpness and the potency of his bite.

There. No longer would he hide himself from Godwin. If it meant a silver knife in the back, well, it'd go nicely with the silver-tipped arrow he put there last night.

"Would you have honored a shut door?" Godwin asked, voice cool and unimpressed.

"You welcomed me into your home. You were so desperate that you'd accept anyone's help, even from me." Alek slurred around the extraneous teeth in his mouth, his voice more snarl and growl than civilized communication.

"End me now," he demanded. He threw his coat to the ground, revealing his shirt, stained a deep magenta from his dried blood, a color as unnatural as he himself was. Spreading his hands wide, he said, "Eight years I've been more beast than man. Finish me."

"Not while you are of use to me, Hardwick. Pull yourself together. If you cannot control yourself, then I will gladly put a knife in you." Godwin shook his head, then scratched at the edge of the eye patch, as if the healing skin itched. "I knew what you were when you were a child. I should have left you there, in your own piss and filth, but Maksim saved my life once. I owed him a boon."

Godwin's words shook Alek to his core. The beast receded in surprise. He swallowed roughly. Shifting teeth was a sensation he'd never grow accustomed to. "What? What do you mean?"

The older man brushed his fingers over the marks left on the tree. "How much do you remember about your parents?"

"Enough."

Truthfully, Alek's memories of his parents had faded, growing less distinct with each passing year. He was eight when a beast invaded their home and tore his parents apart. Alek had only survived because his mother locked him in a steamer trunk and covered that with a heavy quilt to muffle his frightened sobs. He could not be sure how long he spent locked in that hot trunk—hours, possibly days—until Godwin Marechal found him.

Sometimes he dreamed of them. The vivid memories came back with heartbreaking clarity, and he remembered all the details that time eroded. His mother smelled of herbs and washing powder. His father always had a bit of boot polish under his nails that he could never seem to scrub away. His mother's smile and how she would sing while her hands were busy with sewing or other work, but only if she thought she was alone. He and his father would sit outside the door and listen.

"She's my keystone, she ties me to this world and I'm nothing without her," his father said.

When Alek woke, the memories evaporated, only leaving behind the sense of loss.

"Hmm," Godwin said, the enigmatic bastard.

"Are you telling me I was bitten as a child and you, what? Took me to your home, trained me up, and waited for me to turn into a mindless monster?"

"You were not bitten as a child. Are you telling me your father never spoke about his father? Your grandfather?"

"No. Perhaps. I cannot recall," Alek said, growing frustrated. His grandfather had died before Alek's birth. That was all he knew.

"We'll discuss this another time. Now, tell me what you thought of the beast ignoring your silver blade? It acted as if you were attacking with a butter knife."

"No, we will discuss this now. What about my grandfather?"

The two men faced each other, both stubborn with their shoulders squared and feet planted in a fighting stance.

The breeze shifted, rustling the leaves overhead and bringing with it the scent of smoke from cooking fires. The house was starting the day. The sooner they located the missing men, the sooner Alek could have his feast and hot bath.

If Godwin refrained from planting a knife in him.

"Very well. Your grandfather was cursed. Maksim knew. We all knew. I studied with Karl for a year. He had such an iron will," he said, admiration creeping into his voice. "I'm not sure how he wrested control over the beast. He never shared those secrets with me, but I'm sure he passed them along to Maksim, as sure as he passed on the curse to his blood."

"My grandfather was like me?" Karl Hardwick had been a respected hunter and lived an honorable life. The village still sang his praises, decades after his passing. "And my father?"

Godwin scratched at the red skin around the eyepatch again. "I suspect not, but I don't know for certain. Perhaps it would have happened in time. Perhaps he had yet to encounter the right trigger."

"I went to the West Lands," Alek said, remembering the arid heat of the wild plains and the gruesome snapping of breaking bones as his body reformed into something alien. Monstrous.

Inevitable.

The idea settled in his mind and felt right. "The bite—it happened almost instantly. The books say it takes a month, possibly even a season, but I shifted that night."

Godwin nodded. "I know you have questions. I'm not sure I have answers."

"Fair enough." He suspected that no one could answer his questions about his family history. Did Grandfather Karl leave a diary? Journals? So much of the Hardwick home had been destroyed in the attack that killed his parents, and Alek had not been a good caretaker. He patched the roof but left most of the rooms untouched. Perhaps there was a trunk full of journals in some dusty corner, if the mice had not used the paper for nesting material.

"The beast was immune to silver. Not like you. You tolerated the arrow, but it hurt."

"Were you hoping I would lose control and shift?"

"Yes."

"With Solenne and Luis in the room," Alek whispered, disbelieving the man's callousness.

"Nothing went as planned," Godwin said, almost sounding rueful. "I thought for sure that the beast would be drawn to you, to defend its territory against a challenger. Instead, it went to the house. Perhaps the instinct to protect its territory is not as strong as I thought." Then, almost as an afterthought, he asked, "What happened to the beast who turned you?"

"I tore its throat out." *With my newly descended fangs.* He kept that detail to himself.

"You were in the West Lands? Yet Solenne wrote to you at Hardwick House. Did you not stay in the West Lands? You killed the beast. It was your territory."

The trees thinned, and Alek could see the road ahead.

The days and weeks immediately after his transformation were a haze. Survival instincts controlled him, prioritizing food and hunting. When he finally emerged from the shift, he found himself coated in sticky blood with feathers in his teeth. As far as he could determine, his victims had been mostly pheasants and other small animals. Every full moon that followed, Alek took pains to isolate himself so he only hunted game, not people.

He shivered, despite the humid heat, unable to say what he would do if he ever lost control and attacked a person.

"I stayed for a season, but home called to me," he finally said, even though that was not the entire truth.

Solenne called to him, but he knew he could not return to the Marechals, so the abandoned Hardwick House served as his prison.

"The immunity worries me," Godwin said, changing the direction of their conversation once again.

"As it should. The beast is old. I'd estimate he's suffered the curse for a decade."

"And he will not be alone."

Unsaid between them was the knowledge that older beasts often formed packs. Those newly cursed had little control over themselves or the urge to destroy. Young beasts often fought each other to the death.

That instinct to claim territory, to be a solitary creature, made a hunter's job easier. Those that rose above their base instincts and craved a pack were extraordinarily dangerous.

"On my way here, I encountered a pack. I eliminated a younger beast, but the other escaped," Alek said.

"It could be our trouble."

Or not, which was worse. A region infested in with beasts actively making packs was potentially more trouble than he, Godwin, and Luis could handle.

They crested a slight hill. The road curved to the left, but a large house constructed of warm cream-colored stones sprawled on the far side of an expansive lawn. Glass gleamed in the morning sunlight, and the pastel green shutters gave the house a picturesque quality. Crushed white gravel stretched in an elegantly adorned wrought-iron gate. Everything about the house's presentation announced the inhabitants' wealth and their impeccable taste.

Godwin turned off the main road for the gate.

"Vervain Hall," Alek said. When he attended the dance just two nights ago—it felt like so much longer—he had been too absorbed with finding Solenne. He barely noticed the grandeur of the house.

Wealthy enough, Solenne had said. Very wealthy, if he judged by the house's appearance.

"Let's see if Chambers and his nephew made it home last night," Godwin said, opening the gate to the gravel drive.

THE DOOR WAS OPEN, and the house buzzed with activity. Servants hurried through the hall, purpose in their steps, doors slammed, and voices shouted.

Godwin stamped his feet to knock away any mud clinging to his boots. The polished floors gleamed in the morning light, and the scent of lemon and wood oil hung in the air. A few pieces of simple furnishings sat at the side, speaking of quality and quiet dignity. The place made Alek feel grubby, not just because he was—and he was—but grubby in a soul-deep way that could not be scrubbed away, no matter how he tried.

"We need to speak with Chambers," Godwin said, grabbing a passing footman who carried a stack of folded linen.

"I'm sorry, sir. There's no time," the servant said, pulling away.

"Marechal! Don't stand there. Come in," a voice boomed from the top of the stairs.

"Chambers, explain why the devil you ran off in the middle of the night," Godwin replied.

A middle-aged man with salt and pepper hair descended, looking younger and far more fit than Alek recalled. He had dark circles under his eyes and looked haggard, like he hadn't gotten a wink of sleep. Beyond the exhaustion and rumpled clothes—which Alek shared—the man had an air of vitality about him. This was no retired military man come to play at being a gentleman farmer.

"It was Jase, my nephew—devil knows what got into him. He dashed out the door and practically straight into the maw of the beast." Chambers ran a hand through his hair and gave a weary sigh. "My apologies. I'm not a fit host at the moment. Jase is injured. A bad break in his leg. I've been with him all night."

"I'll send for Solenne," Godwin said.

Chambers shook his head. A servant approached, carrying a tray with three steaming mugs. "Please," Chambers said, accepting his own mug. "Solenne has remarkable talents, but the doctor is here. I've sent to Founding for Jase's doctor, seeing as I won't risk moving him, and I need to fetch my sister. I'm afraid I must leave immediately. There's no time to waste." Another sigh. "My sister will have my hide. She sent Jase here for the fresh air. His lungs are weak, you know."

Another servant appeared at Chambers' elbow—how many did the man have?—with a coat and hat. "Your horse is ready, sir."

"No rest for the wicked," Chambers said, hat in hand.

Godwin plucked the hat from Chambers' hands. "Don't be ridiculous, man. You're ready to fall over. I'll fetch the doctor and your sister."

Alek could scarcely believe his ears. Godwin's injury didn't make him incapable of riding a horse, but it left Luis and Solenne alone so soon after the beast had breached their home.

"I can't possibly ask that of you. Founding is too far to go on an errand and to leave your family unprotected," Chambers said, echoing Alek's own thoughts.

"This is an emergency, not an errand." Godwin leaned against the short staff as he considered the options. "Send Alek. He has the youth and energy to make the journey and back again."

Chambers turned to Alek, as if noticing him for the first time. Sun spilled through the opened front door and flashed on his eyes. "It's too great a task, and Christiana does not know him."

Alek looked from Chambers to Godwin. He did not want to leave Solenne—his mate— unprotected. Godwin would not take it well if Alek voiced how the beast refused to leave, whether at the implication that Godwin could not protect his family or at Alek's claim.

Last night his actions made his true feelings clear, and his condition. She was in his blood. He had never thought he could have a mate and yet his grandfather had suffered the same curse, had a family and an illustrious career.

He needed to think. Time on the road would be helpful.

"I insist," Alek said, ignoring the nudge Godwin gave him. "A letter of introduction from you would suffice and answer questions your sister may have."

Chambers held his gaze for a long moment, as if measuring Alek. "Very well. You may have use of my horse. I'll cover your travel expenses, of course. Send for a change of fresh clothes while I write to Christiana and the doctor. Blast that foolish boy."

The words sounded empty, like Chambers had not planned for his nephew to be injured on the full moon, but he wouldn't pass up an opportunity to send Alek away.

A quick scrub with a bowl of scalding water, a meal—finally—and Alek was on his way to Founding.

Solenne

Boxon Hill

Marechal House - The Greenhouse

. . .

The greenhouse had seen better days. In truth, all of the Marechal estate had seen better days, years, and decades. A patchwork of glass paneling, some old and some new, comprised the structure. Well, that was generous; wood boards replaced broken glass, and the greenhouse had slightly more patches than actual glass.

Still, it was warm enough and allowed enough sunlight to grow food stuff all year long. Solenne commandeered a few raised beds for herbs, because while she preferred to forage, demand for essential ingredients outstripped local resources.

Normally, work soothed her. The manual tasks allowed her mind to pick through problems, but today her thoughts spiraled.

Everything was odd, and nothing fit properly.

Solenne wished she had more eloquent words to explain the sense of restless unease in her gut. Miles stayed for a few days for observation, and Luis would not leave his bedside. Godwin announced he would devise a trap to capture the beast once and for all. She only saw her father at mealtimes and never for long, which frustrated her to no end. Mr. Parkell had broken his leg badly fleeing the house and now had a fever. Charlotte wouldn't leave his bedside, despite the appalling way he had treated her at the dance.

Three months had elapsed since the attack that took her father's eye, and she summoned Alek. They had three months to plan, and they had been woefully unprepared. They had another three months to devise a new plan, but she feared Godwin would try for more of the same.

They had been lucky to escape with as few injuries as they did. The beast had been in their home.

Had *licked* her.

Next time, they might not escape so lightly.

As for Alek, he scarpered off to Founding the next morning, answering none of the questions he promised to address. He left a week ago on Colonel Chambers' errand and had yet to send word. Solenne's worry increased with each passing day, and no one seemed remotely curious about his unusual hair growth during the solstice, his claws, fangs, or that he kissed her.

Her spade dug into the raised planting bed, turning over the soil with more force than strictly necessary.

In the days since the solstice, she kept herself occupied. Godwin ignored the serious repairs the house required in favor of tinkering with his trap. Luis was no better, obsessed with devising a stronger weapon to use against the beast.

More of the same.

So that left her to be the responsible adult and to take care of what needed seeing to. The glazier from the village repaired the window for two lambs.

Two.

Solenne didn't know whether to be humiliated at having to barter for basic repairs or insulted at the exorbitant fee. Beggars could not be choosers, but she didn't appreciate being reminded so coolly of that fact.

The spade plunged in the dirt, hacking away at a tenacious root. Besides the entire household acting out of character, no one would discuss the events of the solstice, like they all took a vow of silence. Travers walked away the last time she broached the subject. So Solenne was in the greenhouse, working her frustration out by prepping a bed for wolfsbane seedlings because her stocks were low, because the man she loved was a werewolf.

A werewolf.

Fury boiled in her gut, anger that such a thing happened to Alek, that it kept them apart, and angrier still that he just couldn't explain what happened to him.

Like he feared her rejection or hurting her. She honestly did not know, which added to her fury, because she would never reject Alek for a small...affliction and she knew would never hurt her despite being, you know, a werewolf.

No, she detested that superstitious term from the old world. She had used terms such as beast and creature her entire life and never thought twice. Now they felt dehumanizing. In the one and a half centuries since humans arrived on the planet, they should have developed a better vocabulary for the mutations that some population suffered.

She thought of Tristan—filled with sawdust, dressed in faded finery, and left in a corner in the library—and went cold imagining the same fate befalling Alek. Whatever happened to Tristan, he remained a person and deserved respect. *Beast* and *creature* were worse terms for his particular condition than werewolf.

Fine. Werewolf. The man she loved for as long as she could remember was a werewolf and no one would *talk* about it.

She gently tapped the spade's edge against the wood frame, knocking away dirt. Then she gritted her teeth and gave a choked scream, bashing the spade with all her might. She did not kneel like a lady, but squatted. The old frame groaned, wobbling because the rusty nails holding it together were nothing but powder, and that was one more blasted thing she could not fix. Then, as if out of spite, the wood handle on the spade separated from the blade. The blade sailed across the greenhouse. Stunned, she fell back onto her bottom.

Annoyed at her defeat by gravity and old tools, she gave a kick to the wood frame.

"I think you killed it," Luis said.

"Be quiet. You're ruining a perfectly good sulk." She tossed the useless wooden handle away.

"What are we sulking about?" Luis set down his satchel, fetched the pieces of the broken tool, and then joined her on the ground. He leaned back on his elbow and tilted his face toward the glass ceiling. A season's worth of dust clouded the surface, despite the steady rain. "This place really is falling apart, isn't it? Tell me about this bee in your bonnet."

Solenne eyed the satchel, heavy with books. She had never known Luis to be a great reader. "Money. Father. *You*."

"Alek," he said in a teasing tone.

"Be quiet." She wasn't in the mood for teasing.

"You're in a foul mood because your intended is a cursed beast."

"Don't say that."

"It's true."

"How would you feel if it was Miles?"

Luis paled. "Do not jest. It could be. We won't know until the autumn equinox."

Solenne turned her gaze to the garden bed, and the freshly turned earth. "It's a mean-spirited word. I know it's true. I'm not blind or oblivious." Once she had Alek snarling in her presence, at least. There had been signs, not even subtle ones at that.

Luis picked at the pile of discarded weeds, shredding the greenery and scattering dirt over his trousers. "I know you're not oblivious, and I don't know what other word to use except that one you always say is loaded with superstitious nonsense."

"Werewolf," she supplied.

He pointed a finger in her direction and tipped his head in acknowledgment. "I wanted to talk with you about our, uh, growly little problem."

"You saw the, um...blast! Why don't we have a better word for this? I dislike saying beast—"

"Because of Alek. Because he kissed you."

Solenne narrowed her eyes. How tiresome. "Yes, because Alek has been in our home for weeks and he's not a mindless beast, despite what we've been taught. If we're wrong about Alek—"

"What else are we wrong about?" Luis said, finishing her thought.

"Yes."

"An out-of-control creature attacked us. Whatever is going on with Alek, we cannot ignore the larger issue."

Solenne remembered how the creature sniffed her, the feel of its hot, disgusting tongue on her skin, and wondered how out-of-control it had truly been. It could have easily gutted her with one swipe of its claws but seemed to have enough sense to consider its options.

"The creature that attacked was old enough to develop immunity to silver," she said.

"Yes, exactly." Luis pulled a sheet of folded paper from the front pocket of the bag. "Father wants to devise a trap, but once the, um, target is contained, what are you going to do? Poke it with our little knives? Annoy it to death? I have a better idea." He unfolded the paper, and Solenne immediately recognized the handwriting.

"Where did you get this? How dare you destroy her notebook?" She snatched the page of her mother's faded scrawl.

Tidy lines filled the page, listing known facts. A small illustration sat in the center, distorted by fold lines. Finally, neatly numbered unanswered questions waited at the bottom of the page.

Blackthorn.

Mindful of the dirty fingerprints she left, she refrained from tracing the lines of the ancient sword. Knowing her mother, the illustration was meant to be based on eyewitness accounts but was most likely a product of

Amalie's imagination. As rigorously as her mother pursued her research, she had a nasty habit of using a handful of facts to paint an entire picture.

"I found it in Father's study, caught under a desk drawer," Luis said. "It's her handwriting, isn't it?"

"Yes," Solenne agreed.

"We need to find Blackthorn."

She folded the paper carefully and reluctantly handed it back to her brother. "That's a legend."

"The sword is real. Mother thought it was real."

"A magic sword that can turn vampires and werewolves into a pile of dust? No."

"Mother believed it was real." Luis pulled out a worn book from the satchel and flipped open the pages. Carefully, he tucked in the loose page.

Solenne recognized the book immediately, despite believing it destroyed. "Where did you find that? Not tucked behind a bookcase."

Carefully, she took her mother's journal from Luis' hands and flipped through the pages. The ink seemed fresh on the page, as if Amalie had written them recently. Inky fingerprints and smeared lead pencil smudged the pages. The scent of lavender and ink still clung to the binding.

"Miles had it. He didn't steal it," Luis added quickly. "Mama said he could read her old journals, and you know. When he thought to return them, Papa had burned her journals, so he kept them safe."

"I know, he told me last night. This is a treasure," she said, holding her mother's journal like the piece of wonder it was.

"A phrase Mama uses repeatedly is *not magic—*"

"But a mutation," Solenne finished. She could almost hear Amalie's voice.

"Yes. It got me thinking about mutations." Luis withdrew a stack of books from the satchel.

"When did you become a scholar?" she teased.

His back stiffened. "I read. We just don't share the same interests."

"My apologies. It was rude of me to interrupt. Please continue."

"Not if you intend to tease me," he said. She made a zipper motion over her mouth, which seemed to appease him. "Well, I thought about the nexus mutation. There are three varieties: werewolf, vampire, and witch." He paused. "Please don't yell at me for using those words."

"We really do need a better lexicon, but one problem at a time."

"Right. Three mutations." He held up a hand and ticked off fingers. "A shift in form. A shift in metabolism. A shift in matter. But we only concern ourselves with two of those."

"Because those suffering that mutation are—*can be* dangerous," she quickly corrected herself. "Alek aside, we know that the, um, newly transformed, often slaughter their own families, sadly." Many a hunt started in the remains of a home, torn asunder by blood and violence.

"But a witch with the ability to transform matter?" He opened a leather-bound book to a strip of ribbon marking a page.

Looking over his shoulder, Solenne recognized the passage. A written account of an early colonist who transformed water into ice. "That's a useful trick for the summer, but really. Lead into gold? Water into wine?"

"Liquid into a solid? You don't see how that could be useful?"

Solenne shook her head. The witch mutation was rare. So rare that she had never seen or even heard of a witch. None seemed to exist in recent memory. "If they were even real, which I doubt."

Luis shook his head. "The mutations are all about channeling energy from the nexus, yes? That's what Mama wrote. The crea—those like Alek have to shift to spend the energy. I've never encountered a blood drinker, but plenty of scholars agree that their metabolism consumes itself, giving them an unending hunger and a craving for, um, blood. Their bodies burn themselves up to spend the energy. And witches? They manipulate the energy to transform matter. Organic. Inorganic. That's useful, Solenne. Don't you see? Too useful to slaughter." He handed her book after book, each filled with ribbons to mark significant passages. The bindings positively bulged from his notes. "We're the witches," he said.

Solenne sat in disbelief. "Luis, no."

"Yes! Don't just dismiss this out of hand. People with the witch mutation were—are—useful. They were recruited to be hunters. Look." He opened another book, the title worn away on the cloth binding. The book fell open to a familiar page.

The Blackthorn Blade.

"Luis, again, that's a fairytale. A story."

"If the early hunters were witches, they could manipulate matter. Why not channel nexus energy into weapons? Blackthorn glowed under the moon," his voice changed as he read from the page. "Crafted by the most skilled smith and empowered by the hunter, the blade could turn the vilest creature into ash during a nexus event." He shut the book. "Empowered, Solenne, by witches. And if it was a focus for nexus energy, then it makes sense that it was at its most powerful during the solstice or equinox."

"Luis, you're talking about a magic sword."

"It's not magic—it's science!" His words echoed in the greenhouse. Clearing his throat, he adjusted his cravat. "This is science. The original settlers may not have had the best vocabulary to describe what they saw, but the other generations did, and they agree. Blackthorn was real. Our family made amazing weapons, the kind we just don't have anymore."

Even if the Blackthorn Blade were real, which she highly doubted, Solenne did not understand why it mattered. "Exactly. We don't have any functional weapons from the original settlers. We've got a heap of broken tech that doesn't work. We need to focus on what we have and what we can do."

"Mother believed it was real. I've read her notes—"

"And it got her killed," Solenne snapped.

Luis may have been too young to remember that day, but she remembered every moment with startling clarity. Amalie attempted to charge the battery of an old pistol with nexus energy. At least, that was what Alek reported. He had assisted her in her workshop that day.

The battery exploded with a force hard enough to shake the stone house. They found her in her basement workshop, shrapnel buried deep in her heart.

The scent of burnt hair lingered for *weeks*. The thought of the putrid odor was enough to make her stomach turn.

The color drained from Luis' face. "Yes, well. It's not magic. It is science, therefore it is reproducible. I'm certainly not a witch, and I don't suspect you are, either. Recessive genes, you know. Our best course of action is to find Blackthorn."

Solenne did her best to keep a neutral express but her foul mood won out. Blackthorn may have been a real sword, perhaps a fine one, but its extraordinary qualities seemed to have grown into the thing of legend. "No. Absolutely not. We do not have the time or the luxury to go on a quest for a magic—*scientific*—sword that's been lost for generations. We wouldn't know where to start."

"We do." Luis pulled out another book, green leather with gold gilding. Solenne recognized their book of fairy stories. He opened the book to a page featuring a wood carving of a very noble-looking man holding a sword aloft. Blackthorn glowed, if the black lines radiating from the sword were any indication. "Great-grandpapa Charles lost Blackthorn in a battle with Draven in the city in the mountains beyond the West Lands."

"A century ago."

Their great-grandfather had been a notorious gambler and drinker. His many vices heralded the start of the Marechal family's decline, but no one seemed to remember the way his debt emptied the coffers and brought the estate to the brink of ruin. Everyone fixated on the loss of one probably very fine quality but definitely not magical sword.

"No one ventures far into the West Lands anymore, and no one's reported defeating Draven. So, when you consider the long lifespan of a vampire, then Draven could still have the sword," he said in an excited rush. "Don't you see?"

Solenne snatched the book. She saw many things, none of which were flattering for her younger brother. His large frame and stature often tricked her into believing him to be older than eighteen until he spouted childish nonsense.

Magic swords, indeed.

"Great-grandpapa Charles was a drunk and a gambler. He lost Blackthorn. Indeed, he lost many of our family's treasures at the card table," she said in an even tone that masked her fury. "There is no vampire with a magic sword. To waste our time chasing this fable when we should think about our actual problems would be the height of foolishness."

"It's not a bedtime story. It's real," he said, voice firm and his chin lifted in stubbornness.

"You should research how to contain an older werewolf and help Papa devise a trap." And she needed to plant more wolfsbane because demand exceeded her current supply.

Luis rushed to his feet, grabbing the satchel roughly and causing loose papers and pencils to tumble out. "Pretend all you like that I'm being childish, but we have witch blood in us. You know we do."

Solenne opened her mouth to argue, but he continued, "No. No, I will say my piece. The air hums with nexus energy. I hear it every day. During an event, I can feel it moving like a river rushing around me. That's how Papa and I track the creatures. You might not understand because you don't have the same talent as we do, but it's a witch mutation. If I can feel the nexus, then great-great-so-on ancestor could have infused that energy into a weapon. And you know that our family is resistant to being cursed when we're bitten."

"Bite your tongue. I do not want to put that to the test," she muttered.

"We're not affected because we already have the witch mutation. It makes perfect sense when you think about it. When all this is over, I will find Blackthorn, and that's all I have to say about that." He took a deep breath, then nodded.

"Well, you sound determined to waste your time and energy on a fool's errand."

"Do not mock me. I'm serious." He gathered up his book and stuffed them back into the satchel. "Miles thinks it is a good idea."

"Then take Miles with you. No doubt he'd be ever so helpful fighting monsters." Despite her irritation, she had to admit that the blacksmith would be extraordinarily helpful.

"As opposed to what you do? Swing platters?" Luis mocked.

Brimming with frustration, she felt her entire body vibrate with the need to shout or say something spiteful, but she was a well-bred lady and such behavior was unbecoming.

Like it mattered. The only man she wanted suffered an irreversible condition that caused him to grow fur and fangs, and no one would discuss it. Her father would never allow such an unsuitable match, and Solenne was of the mind to tell her father to get stuffed because if someone in the family should marry for money, then he could blast well do the deed.

Unable to indulge her need to vent, she chucked a handful of dirt and weeds at him, like a well-bred lady.

Luis stood in shock, his mouth gaping open, so she threw a second handful at him. "Solenne!"

A clump hit him square in the face. He sputtered, swiping away dirt from his tongue. His ears went red, and Solenne hadn't seen her brother that angry since he was very young.

Dread washed over her. She went too far. Luis was an even-tempered fellow and hardly spiteful, but he was taller than her and he wanted her to eat a mouthful of dirt in retribution. There was nothing she could do to avoid it.

"I'm sorry," she said in a rush. "I'm so frustrated and nothing works and everything is hard—"

He hurled a clump of dirt at her. On impact, it scattered into tiny pieces, each finding its way down the front of her tunic. She spat out pieces of dirt.

"I accept your apology," Luis said in a magnanimous tone.

Solenne glanced at a bucket used for watering. It was probably empty, but if the bucket held even an ounce of water—

"Do not," Luis warned.

"Do what?"

"I know what you're thinking."

"Are your witchy senses tingling? Can you feel it in the ether?" She wiggled her fingers. While Luis was busy rolling his eyes, she dashed for the watering bucket.

Luis tackled her from behind. Her outstretched hand knocked over the bucket, spilling hardly a drop of water.

How disappointing.

On her stomach, Luis sat on her back, pinning her to the ground. He shoved a handful of mulch in her face.

It. Was. Disgusting.

Laughing despite herself and sputtering out the debris, she rolled to her back. Grinning like a fool, he grabbed both her wrists. Well, at least he could shove more mulch in her mouth. She raised one hand, reached across with the other, and kicked with all her strength.

"Oww!" Luis lurched away, holding his stomach. "Are you wearing lead-lined boots?"

"A lady never tells."

"You should have kicked the werewolf."

Both siblings looked at each other, spattered with dirt and bits of greenery in their hair, and burst into laughter.

"Swinging the platter was clever, but my heart nearly stopped. I thought he was going to eat you," Luis said, brushing away dirt from his shoulders.

"I thought the same," she confessed.

"Truce?" Luis held out a hand.

"Truce."

Chapter Fourteen

Aleksandar

Founding

Three days to Founding.

An eternity to return to Solenne.

Alek hated Founding. The crowded city perpetually stank of stagnant water and smoke. No matter how often he scrubbed his skin, the odor never seemed to disperse. At least he *wanted* to believe the malaise that hung in the air was stagnant water and not something fouler.

The original settlers planned the city in a grid pattern, and they had constructed the earliest buildings from the very ships that brought the settlers to the new land.

Over the next two centuries since humans spilled out of their ships, those buildings rusted in only a handful of years and were eventually covered over in brick.

The city outgrew the original grid, newer sections a free-for-all and the older quarters carved into smaller and smaller parcels. The result was a twisty maze of streets that never went where a person intended, and there were people everywhere. Too many people. Alek could not breathe for the foul air and the people in his territory.

With only the hastily drawn map Chambers gave him, Alek made his way through the city. The horse, more used to the crowded streets than Alek, seemed unperturbed by the noise and commotion. He, however, growled and snapped when the crowds drifted too close.

It took too long to find Dr. Sheldon, and then the sister, a Mrs. Parkell. He tried to wait patiently for the sister to cease weeping. Her capacity for this, he learned, was endless. Despite his urging to leave now and have someone send her a trunk, she insisted on packing herself. As a result, Alek spent an entire day in Founding.

By the time their party left in the early hours of the following morning, he wanted to claw off his skin, convinced he'd never be free of the filthy smog of the city.

The carriage made good time on the paved roads, but as they traveled farther from Founding, the roads transitioned into uneven stone, then crushed gravel, and finally dirt. Progress ground to a halt each time as the carriage got stuck on the muddy, treacherous roads. Mrs. Parkell's wailing that each delay kept her from her precious baby made everything worse. He did his best to ignore her while he helped the coachman free the carriage. He was thankful to have his own horse to ride and not have to share the carriage with the noisome woman.

"Do you intend to weep the entire journey?" Alek retrieved his coat from the nearby shrubbery, where he hung it to avoid sweat and mud.

"Oh, sir, how can you be so cruel? Why would my good brother send such a man?" Her hands fluttered, waving a heavily perfumed handkerchief.

"I believe he aimed to punish us both," Alek muttered.

"Back in the carriage. We can make Fallkirk by evening," the coachman said.

Fallkirk. Alek recognized the name. He had been attacked by two beasts near there, but he had only defeated one. The other still prowled the territory.

When they arrived at the tavern on Fallkirk, the sun had slipped behind the trees. Alek scrubbed off the dirt and the mud, and sent his clothes out to be laundered, despite knowing they would be just as filthy in a day.

He requested to eat in his room. Alone. Music and laughter drifted up from the tavern through the floor, but it was better than listening to Mrs. Parkell recite her numerous complaints to Dr. Sheldon.

A knock sounded at the door, and a young woman appeared with a tray. The aroma of roast, potatoes drowning in gravy, and warm bread instantly set his mouth watering. She set the tray down on the small side table by the window.

"You're that hunter who came through two months ago," she said.

"I am."

She lifted her chin, as if unimpressed. "You only did half the job. It's not safe outside after dark."

"It was unsafe during the day before I reduced the beast population." A thought occurred to him. Fallkirk was near Boxon but not part of the area the Marechals guarded. "Where are your hunters?"

"All dead, three years ago. Then that thing moved in."

"Why have you not requested Founding to fill the post?"

The woman gave him a look that suggested he was simple. "Oh, excellent idea. Why didn't *we* think of it? But we're only simple country folk—"

"I did not mean to imply—"

"You did," she said curtly. "The mayor and council wrote, and do you know what those stuffed shirts in Founding told us?" She continued without pause, not looking for an answer. "Offer a bounty. They wouldn't send troops to a backwater on the edge of nowhere, and the mayor can't find anyone to take the job. Don't suppose you're interested in finishing what you started? That thing helped itself to my ma's chickens. What are we supposed to do now? The ones that are left are too scared to lay eggs."

"Have chicken for supper, I imagine," he said, which earned him a frown and a slammed door.

As he ate, he pondered what the woman told him. The hunters were killed before the elder beast moved in, so what killed them? The beast itself? A pack that moved out of the territory?

When he had still hunted for bounties, Alek encountered many villages on the fringes of the civilized world with the same story. The local hunter families had died out, either through bad luck, poor health, or acts of monster. Drifters like himself filled in the gaps until local officials found replacements. But it sounded like no one wanted the job.

He couldn't blame them. Hunting was all danger, little to no pay, and every resident blaming you for chickens too scared to lay eggs.

The likelihood of two older beasts, a day apart from each other, worried him. He did not like such a threat so near his territory, his home and his mate.

Huh. He guessed Godwin had been right about the territorial nature of the beasts. He hadn't felt it before, but he had nothing he wanted to guard. Now he had everything.

And like called to like.

Alek mopped up the gravy with the last of the bread and decided.

"You can't leave us unprotected," Mrs. Parkell wailed far too loud for so early in the morning. She did not take too kindly to Alek's change of plans. "I can't imagine what my brother was thinking, sending you as his errand boy."

Alek wondered about that himself.

"I've encountered this beast before. It will follow me. You're safer without me. Dr. Sheldon was a military man. He'll keep you safe," he said.

Dr. Sheldon nodded. "I know my way around a pistol. Never fear, Mrs. Parkell. We'll be in Boxon by mid-afternoon."

Alek didn't linger while Mrs. Parkell's considerable luggage was packed into the coach. He saddled up the horse borrowed from Chambers and took off on a smaller, less traveled road that went through the heart of the forest.

He'd use himself as bait and lure the beast back to Boxon. With any luck, the two beasts would tear each other apart.

Solenne

Boxon

The Wodehouse Home

Charlotte barely left Jase's bedside, despite him being abominably rude to her at the dance.

Solenne felt for her friend, who was kind, clever, bookish, and forever being passed over for ladies who came with a fortune. Charlotte was too kind and forgiving. Jase did not deserve the care Charlotte gave when his leg became infected. She sat by his bedside with cool water and cloth.

"Father is making noise about sending me to Aunt Tessie in Founding for the winter. He thinks I'll have a better chance of catching a husband there," Charlotte said as she carefully poured the tea.

They sat in the garden behind the Wodehouse's home, tucked into a shaded corner nearly hidden by large, flowering bushes heavy with vivid blossoms. The arrival of Colonel Chambers' sister prompted Charlotte to give up her bedside vigil and limit herself to daily visits. Apparently, Mrs. Parkell had the bearing of a military commander and none of the charm.

"You'll have more variety and parties to attend," Solenne said.

Charlotte pulled a face. "I'll spend my day in the library, you know, and Aunt Tessie will despair that reading will give me lines around my eyes."

Solenne didn't bother to hide her smile or her titter of laughter. "Oh, the tragedy."

"Frankly, I'm too eccentric," she said, looking over Solenne's shoulder to some point in the distance. "I don't have a large enough fortune for those eccentricities to be overlooked, and I'm too plump and not pretty enough to compensate for the lack of a fortune."

"I disagree on all those points," Solenne said in defense of her friend. Charlotte was more plump than fashionable, but they lived in a village on the fringe of nowhere. Who cared about fashion? And she'd stab anyone who claimed Charlotte's russet curls and open smile were not attractive. Well, perhaps not stab; just a gentle poke, enough to draw a little blood and make a point about being rude.

"It will be a waste of time, but if Father insists, would you come with me?"

"To catch a husband?"

Charlotte raised a brow. "Unless you believe you have better prospects here."

Rather than answer, Solenne busied herself by refilling her cup and measuring out a spoonful of sugar. "No, there's no one."

"Really? Because I saw how protective Aleksandar was of you at the dance."

Right before he rushed off.

"No. You misunderstood." Solenne thought back to the night of the dance and the perpetual glare on Alek's face.

"Now you're going to spout some nonsense about duty and how you'll learn to find satisfaction in that, rather than the man you love, and I won't tolerate it. You deserve to have who your heart desires. And if it's money, well," Charlotte waved a hand as she spoke, "I imagine your situation won't improve, but it will not deteriorate."

The cup rattled on the saucer. "I would not say any such thing," Solenne weakly protested. "And I'd rather not discuss Alek."

A satisfied grin spread across Charlotte's face. "Very well, but only because you don't deny that you love him."

"What would be the point? My feelings for him have not changed since I was sixteen." As much as she wished they would.

"So you never felt an attachment to another?"

Solenne shook her head. "Only friendship."

"Not even Colonel Chambers?" Her eyes gleamed with curiosity.

"No. My father seemed more enthusiastic about a match than either of us." Solenne relayed the events from the night of the dance.

"I had wondered. He used to lavish attention on you and then, suddenly, he was distant."

"I wouldn't say *lavish*—"

"But he wasn't cruel about it? He does not seem the sort."

"No. The conversation was very businesslike and straightforward," Solenne said.

"Perhaps I can walk with you when you return home? Colonel Chambers wanted to borrow some of Father's books, and I thought of delivering them."

"Of course."

"You don't mind? If I deliver books to Colonel Chambers?"

Solenne paused before answering, wondering what her friend was trying to ask. "You didn't volunteer to nurse Jase because you feel affection for him, did you? He was a beast to you. To us both."

A pretty blush spread across Charlotte's face. Rather than answer straight away, she stuffed a cookie in her mouth. "The starberries are very sweet this year, don't you think?"

"Charlotte—"

"Colonel Chambers is interesting." Solenne opened her mouth to protest, but Charlotte continued. "He is. He's traveled and seen much of the world. He's interested in pre-colonial and early colonial history."

"He is." She knew of his collection, though she had not had the opportunity to admire it. Several pieces were removed for the dance.

"He's generous and rather handsome, I think. You should have seen how concerned he was for Jase! Hardly slept or ate. I had to convince him to rest. A man who'd wear himself ragged for his nephew has to have a good heart, don't you think?"

"Yes, I rather think so." Solenne had been so focused on the things she didn't like about Chambers—namely, not being Alek—that she did not see his better qualities. "He reads the most scandalous fiction, full of secrets and passionate embraces, and the best part?"

Charlotte leaned forward.

"When he's finished the book, he gives them to me."

The smile on her friend's face was radiant.

"I'm pleased for you. I only hope he has the good sense to return your regard," Solenne said with sincerity.

"As do I, when I won't need to go to Founding or stuffy Aunt Tessie." Charlotte made a pleased noise and then helped herself to another cookie.

"Speaking of your father's books, I was hoping to rummage through his collection. I can't find the information I need."

"Certainly. What are you searching for?"

"I'm not sure. Reasons a cursed beast would have control over their transformation? Be able to retain their mind and hide their affliction?"

"Oh, that's simple. They have a mate bond," Charlotte said.

Solenne's cup rattled in the saucer again. "What? No, there's no such thing."

"Yes, there is. Come along." Charlotte stood, carrying her tea into the house. Solenne had no choice but to follow. "It's odd. Colonel Chambers asked the same question. I have the books already pulled. There are some early colonist accounts and a local history."

"But people with that affliction don't take mates or have a mate bond. I'd have read that."

"Darling, you are my dearest friend. You're very well read on stabbing and poisoning, but little else," Charlotte said as they entered the study. Mr. Wodehouse's collection sat tidy and organized on floor-to-ceiling shelves that lined every wall. The collection did not compare in size to the library in the Marechal House, but it contained several obscure titles.

"Not true. I just read a brilliant novel with the most ingenious method of poisoning…oh. I see your point."

"If I want something dead, you are my first call," Charlotte said, amusement bubbling in her voice. She flipped through a book, searching for a passage. "Here we are. The mate bond acts as an anchor, keeping the afflicted partner grounded and negating the worst symptoms of mutation." She snapped the book shut. "There you are. To tame a beast, you must anchor it."

"But how?" And how was Alek tamed, for lack of a better word?

"The details are fuzzy." Charlotte pulled down a slender volume from the shelves. The book was little more than a cloth-bound pamphlet. "It seems to involve a romantic partnership, so one must assume there is an emotional component and perhaps a fluid exchange. Beauty soothes the beast."

"Like a kiss, blood or—" She thought back to the kiss she shared with Alek and how he said she was in his blood.

"I'm uncertain," Charlotte said, then plonked the pamphlet into Solenne's hands. "This is a firsthand account of an original colonist. Reprinted, obviously. You may take it home to read. Father won't mind."

"Oh, thank you. Is it rare? I wouldn't trust myself with something irreplaceable." The book felt unreasonably fragile in her hands. She'd make pains not to damage it.

"Not particularly. The account is rather scandalous and, um, *graphic*, so it's popular."

"A dirty book? I never." Mirth bubbled up at the sight of Charlotte's blush.

"It's history, blemishes and all," Charlotte said, struggling for a haughty tone in her voice. "One cannot censure the human experience."

Solenne flipped through the pages, searching for the naughty bits. "Oh. Oh my. Miss Wodehouse—"

They burst into laughter.

Chapter Fifteen

Solenne

Boxon Hill

Northern Pasture

The heat lingered well after sunset. Sweat collected in her lower back. No matter how many times Solenne plucked away the fabric, it clung to all her uncomfortable places with determination.

Near full, the moon cast enough light that she could see well enough to pick her way through the northern pasture. Luis did not want her to venture out, but Alek nearly consumed all her store of wolfsbane. The seedlings in the greenhouse would not be ready for weeks. She needed to replenish now, which meant a moonlight stroll.

Gathering the blossoms on the equinox or solstice was best for potency but impractical. A full moon was better, but gathering by moonlight would do. She didn't know how she knew those things; she just did. Luis would say it was a witchy instinct.

Nonsense.

The siblings made peace after their argument, but Solenne would never agree with Luis. His theory was, well, too much out of a storybook. Certain flowers blossomed at night. If certain flowers were more potent when gathered at night, then that was because of lack of insects gathering pollen or exposure to the nexus. Not magic, and not because she was a witch.

Solenne knelt at a cluster of the hooded purple blossoms, her basket at her side. Her silver dagger lopped off the flower heads with practiced efficiency.

Witches. She heard nothing so silly in her life.

The wind shifted, bringing cool relief.

A week had passed since Mrs. Parkell and Dr. Sheldon arrived, claiming that Alek went to draw away a beast to allow them to finish their journey without incident. He would be a day behind, perhaps two. Never fear.

A week. Too much time had passed. The distance between Fallkirk and Boxon did not warrant such a lengthy journey. Each day that passed, the likelihood of

Alek laying mangled and dead in a dark wood increased.

Distressed, she asked Godwin to set out to search for Alek. He did not seem surprised. "My dear, perhaps he has moved on. That's what his kind does, after all."

No. She knew in her heart that was wrong. Alek would not leave her.

She approached Luis, since he was keen on a quest. "Alek is skilled. He'll find his way back," her brother said.

He would not have been so blithe if it was Miles missing.

She couldn't sleep. How could she? Rather than chew her nails down to the quick, she read Charlotte's book. It proved to be as lascivious as promised. The author did not shy away from details, and Solenne was grateful that she kept this part of her research quiet.

After rushing through the first time, she reread with more attention to detail and took notes. The book was an autobiography of an original colonist. Two months after arrival, a crewmember was bitten and mutated.

Nothing seemed to quell the violence in the afflicted man. Not tranquilizers. Not restraints. The surviving crew believed that the only thing to be done would be a bullet to the head and end the afflicted man's misery.

Only the woman writing the account felt a connection with the man. She refused to think him a mindless beast. Desperate to avoid the man's execution, she locked herself in the holding cell with him. Such action was phenomenally brave and more than a little stupid.

Subsequent events were intimate in nature and described in such detail that Solenne felt her ears burn. The details didn't matter so much that on the other side, when the executioner unlocked the holding cell, they were bonded. The man was himself again, no longer a raging monster. The woman was his anchor, keeping him sane and human.

Solenne took notes. How could she not? Intimacy seemed to be key, though whether emotional or an exchange of fluids, the book never clarified.

She thought back to the kiss and how every part of her sparked with awareness, like she had emerged from a long sleep. Was that enough for a bond? Perhaps some scrap or injury in childhood led to contact with blood.

Better try all methods to be certain.

She pressed a hand to the center of her chest, willing herself to feel some tug or a thread between herself and Alek. She was in his blood, he said. They had a bond. She knew it. And Alek was not mortally injured on some empty roadside. She would know that too.

Footsteps rustled through the grass.

"Luis?"

Despite the moon's illumination, pockets of deep shadows lurked at the edges of the pasture along the stone fence and the tree line. The stone circle stood silently on top of the hill, dark against the night's sky.

The wind shifted, bringing the brittle scent of rain, parched grass, and something foul. Spoiled.

Death.

She gagged at the scent. It was too soon after the solstice.

A growl rolled through the night air.

Clutching her knife, Solenne moved to the direction of the house and resisted the urge to run. Running only encouraged a predator to chase.

Near the fence, she quickened her pace until she saw the figure blocking the path.

Hidden in shadows, it stood tall on two legs but was more beast than man. It lifted its head and sniffed the air, then crouched down. Two huge hands rested on the ground, as if ready to spring into action. Moonlight cast violet highlights on the shaggy coat as it crept forward.

"Alek?"

As soon as the question left her lips, she knew that was wrong. This was not Alek. If he could resist shifting during the solstice, why lose control of himself now? That delicate thread connecting them remained silent.

A growl, low and menacing, rumbled right through her. This had to be the beast that crashed into her home and licked her. The shadows hid much, and to be honest, she had not taken the time to look for unique features. The important point was they were not Aleksandar and they very much posed a threat.

Solenne stepped back. "Hello," she whispered. "You don't want to eat me. You're in pain. Confused. I can help." She moved to throw the entire contents of the basket but realized that she left the basket behind. All she had was her tiny silver knife, worthless for anything more than collecting herbs.

The beast crept forward, snarling.

She turned on her heel and ran toward the stone circle. The stones offered protection. She couldn't rationalize how she knew that, but imagined that she could hide in the shadows. The stone marked a nexus point, and she hoped the excess energy would confuse the beast.

But it wasn't a solstice or even a full moon. The beast should not have been there.

Her foot caught on an unseen rock, and she hit the ground hard. Her palms stung and her chest ached from the impact. Ignoring the pain and her ankle's protests, she lurched to her feet.

The stone circle loomed above, promising shelter.

The incline grew steeper. Solenne kept her eyes focused on the stones, not bothering to glance back to check on the beast.

Sharp claws swiped at her legs, catching on her trousers. With a cry, she fell to the ground. Kicking frantically, she freed herself long enough to make it another two steps.

The beast tackled her. One massive hand in the center of her back held her in place. Solenne kicked and screamed. Luis would hear. He said he would join her. Where was her brother?

The beast buried its maw into her back, its breath hot and putrid against her skin. For the second time in her life, she was being inspected by a beast, and it was as horrible as the first.

Her fingers dug into the ground, pulling up clumps of grass. Without hesitation, she hurled the wads backward, showering herself with dirt and leaves.

Claws sunk into her calves, the pain sharp and burning. Wiggling away exacerbated the pain to a blinding misery. Her mind went blank, and her body stopped fighting to save itself a little suffering.

As the beast pulled her back, presumably to some den or secret location, she screamed. Her tunic rode up as she bounced along the ground, rocks digging into her stomach and face, but she did not cease her screaming. She'd scream until her voice failed or the beast tore her throat out. Whichever came first.

Footsteps pounded on the ground. Finally, Luis.

The beast eased its grip, and she rolled away, despite the burning pain in her calves. Lifting her head, she saw the base of the giant stone slab and crawled forward.

The beast pounced, slamming her to the ground. It howled a terrible song of victory.

A second howl answered.

Icy dread washed over her. Two monsters, on a night that should have been safe. Nothing she thought she knew about the world made sense, but it did not matter because even if her brother arrived, he couldn't fight off two beasts.

Grass, dirt, and blood from a split lip filled her mouth. She stretched out a bloody hand to the nearest stone, the smooth surface vibrating at the touch, which had to be head trauma. The stones did not vibrate. The stones did not do much of anything, actually. They predated humans' arrival. No one knew who built them, but the why became obvious. Each stone circle marked a nexus point.

Solenne once read an old-world fairy story about how a fairy could be summoned in an ancient stone circle to grant wishes. A fanciful child, she left offerings of bread and milk. No fairies arrived to grant wishes.

Her fingers tingled as they brushed the unnaturally cold stone. The unknown makers polished the surface to a machine-smoothed finish. Exposure to the elements had not left a scratch.

All she offered was blood and terror. If she could have one wish, it would be for Luis to stay away. She didn't want to die alone, but she refused to die with her brother. He would live.

If the universe was so kind as to grant two wishes, she wanted to tell Alek she loved him.

Aleksandar

An unnatural silence followed Alek. At least it had until yesterday, when birdsong and the hum of insects and scurrying of small animals returned.

A week he spent on a fool's quest teasing the Fallkirk beast. It would chase him for half a day, then retreat to its territory. Alek persisted, determined to lure the beast, and believed he had succeeded. He felt it watching him, hidden in the forest and silent. The only clue to its presence was the absolute lack of noise from any other living animal. The creature had learned caution since their last encounter, when it had impulsively attacked the coach.

Yesterday it retreated, and he could not pick up the trail. Exhausted down to his bones, missing his mate, he returned home when the last of his provisions ran out.

Recognizing home, the horse picked up the pace. He couldn't blame it for being eager to return home. He was miserable company at the best of times, and a week of camping rough left him feeling sour and stinking.

"Looking forward to a bed of fresh hay?" He gave the horse a pat on the neck. It was an excellent animal with a calm, even temperament. Most horses, he discovered, were initially skittish around him, no doubt because of his curse.

After he tended to the horse, he planned to dump a bucket of cool water over his head to rinse away the worst of the grime before sinking into a bath.

A scream pierced the night. He knew it at once.

Solenne.

The connection between them pulsed with fear, much as it had the night of the solstice.

He urged the horse to go faster, growling in frustration. The horse flicked its ears back. The shift was upon him, brought on by his mate's distress.

Unable to navigate the forest quick enough for his liking, he leaped from the saddle and abandoned the horse.

When his feet hit the ground, he was fully shifted.

Solenne

Snarls and growls filled the air. She tensed, expecting a bite. Hopefully she'd bleed out quickly. Once, long ago, she saw the remains of a person torn apart by a cursed monster. There had been little left for identification as the face had been too badly beaten. Their boots had identified the unfortunate victim.

The image haunted her sleep for weeks. The savagery of it, teeth biting and tearing meat until only bloody pulp remained. That was not hunting for sustenance. That was cruelty for the pleasure of cruelty.

She hoped her monster was hungry and not in the mood to toy with his food.

A high-pitched squeal of pain pierced through her panic. She scrambled backward until her back hit the giant stone slab.

Two beasts wrestled, all tooth and claw. The challenger was massive, towering above her attacker. A distant, detached part of her mind wondered if age factored into the size of the beast. That same cool detachment catalogued the heavy scarring on the challenger. She had seen them before.

The beast lunged for Solenne, getting close enough for her to feel his hot breath. The challenger sank his claws into the beast's back and tore him away.

Hands distorted into claws swiped. Skin tore. Blood matted the fur. Teeth—so many teeth—sank into flesh. A pained cry ripped through the night, amplified by the stones, and the beast ran away.

The challenger reared back and gave a roar of triumph, the blood of his opponent on his face. He turned toward Solenne, eyes glowing violet. The shift distorted his face, making his brows heavy, excessive teeth pushing his lips back in a permanent snarl.

She kept returning to those eyes.

Solenne's entire existence narrowed down to that moment. Nothing human remained in those eyes. They were vacant, a luminous swirl of chaos.

It stalked closer.

"Stay back!" She held out a hand.

It crouched down, lowered his head, and gave a plaintive whimper. He shuffled forward. Her breath caught in her throat.

He paused, then moved back. The message was clear. He did not want to scare her, but she feared that it might be impossible. Her heart thudded in her chest and refused to quiet.

He tilted his head to one side, the moonlight catching on his violet eyes, and he made a hissing sound. Too slowly, she realized he was speaking.

"I don't understand. I'm sorry," she said.

He repeated the sound. "Sfff." He tapped his chest, then pointed at her. "Sfff wiff mee."

"Oh, I'm safe with you," she whispered.

The thread that connected them pulled taut. She knew this man. He was in her blood.

He shuffled forward, still low and, once again realizing too slow, submissive. She reached out, tangling her fingers in the mass of hair on his head. The hair had grown shaggy and felt coarse to the touch. At the base of his head, she felt a knotted ribbon that valiantly tried to keep his hair orderly. Every morning, her love's hair started in a tidy plait and worked its way free. It seemed impossible that this huge figure was known to her, but the poor ribbon confirmed it.

"Alek?"

Chapter Sixteen

Aleksandar

Boxon Hill

The Stone Circle

"Look at this mess. Why do you insist on a plait when you need a proper cut?" She gave the ribbon a tug. Placing her hands on either side of his face, she gently turned his head, as if inspecting him. "It's remarkable how little has changed in your face. Are you hurt?"

Dirt and an alarming amount of blood covered her face. He pushed back the fringe of hair at her brow. "You're bleeding. What were you doing out alone? If you ever do something so reckless again, I will lock you away in a tower until you're old and gray."

His tongue could not work properly with all the blasted teeth in his mouth. He felt like he was trying to talk around pebbles. Speech would only return if he calmed down, and how could he be calm when his mate stood before him, bleeding.

She blinked. "That sounded upsetting. I assume you're chiding me."

He pulled her into a crushing embrace, burying his nose in her hair. Her heart thudded, slow and steady, and it was everything.

"What am I going to do with you?"

He loved her so much, but he would strangle her for being so reckless. She was the only thing keeping him anchored to the world, to his sense of self, to his sanity.

Thump. Thump. Thump.

The easy, measured beats calmed him because they told him she was not afraid of him, even though he lost control. When he heard her scream, the beast took command over his body with startling efficiency. He had to protect their mate, protect Solenne. He would tear the throat out of anyone who hurt her. The beast roared approval. They were in agreement.

With each heartbeat, the beast calmed and receded. Alek felt himself slowly shift back, though the beast wasn't far below the surface. The curse had always felt like an entity taking possession of his body, an unwelcome invader to be fought and resisted. At the moment, it very much felt like a disapproving master ready to correct an incompetent apprentice.

Exhausted, he knew they should return to the house. Solenne needed her injuries cleaned and a doctor. She needed hot water, soap, clean clothes, food, and a soft bed. He wanted to provide those things, to carry her back to the house, but he could not seem to move.

She stirred in his arms. "I'm sorry. You're quite nude."

Alek looked down at his chest and his arms. The beast's thick coat had receded. "Side effect of the curse."

She snorted, then her entire body perked. "Oh, I understood that. Are you with me again, Alek?"

"I never left you." He adjusted her in his lap to make the most of the moonlight to assess the damage. His fingers brushed her temple. Blood matted the hair. A distressed noise sounded in the back of his throat.

She dabbed the injury, wincing at the contact. Her fingers came away bloody. "Head wounds bleed. They look worse than they are."

"How?"

"I think I hit my head. I tripped on a rock. Twisted my ankle."

He needed...

He needed to take inventory of every scrap and bruise. He needed to get her clean, warm, and safe, but first he needed to stop the bleeding.

Claws still out, he sliced off the tunic. Solenne protested, throwing an arm over her chest. "Stay still. Be quiet," he ordered, tearing the garment in half. One half mopped at the drying blood.

"Hold this," he said, pressing the fabric to her head. The other half he tore into strips. The fabric was soiled, but it would do for a bandage. He wished he had water, a clean shirt to offer, but all of that he abandoned with the horse when he heard her scream.

Carefully, he brushed his fingers over her exposed skin, searching for injuries. His touch remained clinical, and the beating of her heart kept him focused. *Thump*. A scuff on her chin. *Thump*. A split lip. *Thump*. An angry red burn on her abdomen. Her skin flinched at his touch, and she sucked in a breath.

"Hurt?"

"Tickles," she confessed.

He ignored his desire to touch her again and resumed his inspection, but her trousers got in the way. She wore too many garments. Grumbling, he undid the ties and tugged the fabric down.

A bruise had already bloomed on her lower abdomen.

Unacceptable.

She shifted. Sticky blood from an unseen wound smeared on his bare leg. Needing to know, he yanked on the trousers. Her hands knocked him away. "My boots," she said.

He tugged on the laces, growling in frustration as she kicked her feet. "I twisted my ankle. It will swell if you take off my boots, and I won't be able to get them back on."

"I'll carry you."

"No. Keep it in my boots until we can get ice on it."

Frustrated, his claw sliced down the trouser leg, exposing the scraped knees and puncture wounds on her calves. The wounds bled freely. As careful as he could with his disfigured hands, he tied the fabric strips around her calves.

"Is it bad?"

He grunted. She laughed, high-pitched and a touch frantic.

He gathered her back into his arms.

Thump.

Thump.

Thump.

Still alive. Still with him.

His thumb brushed her bruised lip. Leaning down, he gave into instinct and licked the edges clean. He had tasted hot, fresh blood from the hunt many times in his beast form. This was sweeter. Better than anything imaginable. He continued to clean her face, not understanding this need, until she batted her hands at him.

"Gross. Stop licking me. Do I look like a lady who enjoys being licked?"

Amusement rumbled through him. "You'll enjoy it when I lick you."

Her breath hitched. "Yes. All right," she said.

"Yes?"

"Yes." She moved to straddle him and pushed him until his back rested against the stones.

A bright, jolting charge surged through him at contact with the stone. Solenne moved off his lap, but he held in place. "It tingles. That's all."

She frowned, then gestured to a spot with a bloody handprint. "I thought so too, when I touched it. Alek? We're naked."

"You kept your boots on."

"And I am sitting on your lap." She moved just so, brushing her chest against his. His cock stirred to life.

"I noticed."

She leaned in, lips nearly touching his. Their breath mingled. She was in his blood.

"Ruin me," she breathed.

Stars above, yes. His brain sizzled at her words and the rare need in her voice. Careful of bruises, his hands skated up her back. He gripped the back of her neck, fingers wrapping around the delicate flesh, and drew her head back. Moonlight glinted in her eyes. Normally gray, they almost looked violet.

He wanted her more than anything, more than he wanted to see another sunrise, more than he wanted to hear his father's voice again, his mother's embrace. More than he wanted to be free of his affliction.

But not more than he wanted her safe and prospering. He could not give her the future she deserved.

"Solenne, no," he said, before repositioning them into a more modest arrangement.

She folded her arms over her chest. Not in modesty, he realized too late, but in irritation. "Do you think I'm stupid?"

"No." Far from it. Solenne was the brightest person he knew, in every respect: intellect, personality, and capacity for kindness.

"Then you do not think I know my mind?"

"How am I in the wrong for not letting you sully yourself with me when you're bleeding and traumatized? The adrenaline is making you say such things."

Her chin took that stubborn set he knew well. He imagined she'd march back to the house in the nude if her ankle could make the journey. Even if it couldn't, she might make it with the power of spite.

"I thought—I thought that thing was going to kill me. I made a wish on the stones. Do you know what I wished?" She barely paused, agitation mounting with each word. Clearly, she was not interested in his response. "Not that someone would rescue me. I wished Luis would stay away to survive, and I wished I had told you that I loved you!"

The words echoed off the stones and rang in his head, clearer than any bell.

"You love me?"

"Yes. Isn't it obvious?" Her shoulders sagged. "Do you remember when we went swimming in the river? I didn't want to go in the water and you pushed me? Then you immediately jumped in to save me. I was so angry with you, but I knew I could rely on you. Then. That's the moment I started loving you."

"You were—" He tried to remember how he had felt when he was that age. It seemed impossibly young. "Eleven. And then you asked me to marry you."

She lifted her hands in a helpless gesture. "I was overwhelmed with emotion and you did not say no."

"You were eleven." A child. He had been a child. From the moment he met Solenne, he knew she was his friend. His affection did not grow until much later. It astounded him she had been so sure of her heart even then.

"I never stopped. It's you, Alek. It's always been you."

Thump, thump, thump went her heart, even and true.

She moved upward, bringing her lips to his. Contact sent a jolt through him, fixing him in place in this moment. He barely moved, allowing her to take what she wanted. The injury to the bottom lip opened, and the taste of copper flooded his mouth.

She pulled away and smiled as she licked her lips. The split lip gave her a dangerous appearance. The beast inside him loved watching as she wiped the back of her hand across her mouth, unapologetic.

His heart quickened.

"Do not feel obligated to return the sentiment," she said, her tone nearly a purr. "I know how you feel. I'm your anchor. And if you're worried about sullying me, you're too late."

There were several threads in that statement that merited a follow-up, and he hated the idea of anyone—

anyone—touching her, but her heart skipped the tiniest amount.

She lied.

"Oh? You found someone in the village willing to brave your father's wrath."

She flushed. "At school. University. Papa sent Luis and me off to a boarding school in Founding after Mama, you know. Then I did two years at university before the money dried up. So if you're hesitant about ruining my honor, you need not bother. I ruined it long ago."

"Educated and worldly," he said, running an appreciating hand up her arm, "but a terrible liar."

She glanced away. "Alek, I could have died, and—"

"Hush. I hesitate not for a lack of desire but because you deserve better than a hasty fuck on the ground."

"Under the moonlight with the man who saved me." Her lips quirked up in a slight smile.

"Where did you hear about anchors?" Had Godwin divulged Alek's family history?

She breathed out, almost a pout. She would not get what she believed she wanted, though she tempted him. Mightily.

"In a book written by an original colonist whose husband had the same affliction as you." She yawned, covering her mouth at the last moment. "It's fascinating. I'm particularly interested in page 72."

"Page 72?"

Another yawn interrupted her nod.

"Sleep. When it is light, you'll explain this book." He pulled her to him and she snuggled against him, her head against his shoulder.

Thump.

Thump.

Thump.

Company arrived sooner than he liked.

"What did you do to her?" Luis stood over them, blocking the moonlight.

Alek cradled a sleeping Solenne to his chest. He curled around her to shield her nakedness with his body as best he could. That he was likewise nude and more than a little shaggy created an alarming tableau.

"Are you trying to eat her?"

"Honestly, Luis," Alek snapped. "Does it look like I'm feasting on her innards? She was attacked. I drove off the beast, but it's near."

Luis snapped to attention. "The beast that attacked the house?"

"No. I believe it is the one I encountered near Fallkirk. It followed me here."

"How serious are her injuries?" Luis crouched down, reaching out a hand. Alek snarled, and Luis jerked back in surprise. "She's bleeding. Let's go to the house."

"No." Alek's hold tightened on Solenne. "I can't leave just yet."

"Then carry her."

"You misunderstand. I cannot leave the circle. Not yet. It's not safe. The beast is still out there." He could not say why the stones were safer than heading toward the house, but he felt stronger there. Recharged. He wished he could better explain the compulsion, but they had to stay where they were until dawn broke.

"So you intend to keep my sister here, exposed to the elements while injured, passed out and wearing rags?"

"And whose fault is that?" Alek snapped, angered by Luis' condescending tone. "Letting her wander alone at night. Where were you? When she screamed for help? Cried out in pain?"

Color drained from the young man's face. "I told her I would join her if she waited, then we received word that the beast had been sighted down by the mill."

"In the opposite direction."

"Yes, blast it. Does it matter?" He ran a hand through his curls. "This is wrong. The timing. The moon. There are two more...beings with your affliction in my territory than I'm willing to tolerate, and I've spent hours chasing a rumor."

"Two? Does that mean you tolerate me?" A grin spread on Alek's face. Luis paled.

Ah, right, the teeth.

"Solenne has her heart set on you." His tone implied that he tolerated Alek for his sister's sake.

Alek sighed. "I know. I have tried to convince her otherwise."

Luis snorted. "Again with the jokes. Come to the house. Four walls are better than this." He gestured broadly to the stone circle.

"Because those four walls kept her safe last time?"

Alek held Luis' gaze. The younger man did not blush or look away.

"I couldn't track it," Luis eventually said. "You're standing right in front of me, and I can't sense you either. It's the stones." He strode over to the closest stone, the one Solenne marked with her bloody handprint. His fingers brushed the surface. If he saw the mark his sister left, he said nothing. "They hum, and it drowns out everything else. Why are your kind so drawn to them?"

"My kind?"

"You know what I mean. Do not be difficult."

Alek buried his nose in Solenne's hair before he answered, breathing in the scent of sunlight and summer heat. "I do not know. That is the truth. I've never been able to track as you do. The stones, the nexus point itself, are loud. They all are, but tonight it feels like a warning."

"Like a dog growling?"

"Now look who's making with the jokes."

Luis ran a hand through his hair again. "I have a long night ahead of me. If you insist on remaining here, I'll fetch a blanket."

"That is unnecessary." Possessiveness surged through him. He would provide Solenne with everything she needed.

"Is it? The nights get quite cool and Solenne does not have her own fur coat."

Good thing the smug look on Luis' face was hidden by shadows.

"I'll allow it. Go. Be quick about it," Alek ground out.

"I presume you will require clothes?"

Yes. Those. Details, details.

"In my saddlebag. I left my horse in the trees at the bottom of the pasture. The horse will also need to be seen to."

Luis gave a mocking salute before departing. "Be quick, he says, then gives me a dozen tasks."

Though he muttered, Alek heard every word. Such disrespect from anyone else would have thrown him into a rage, but from Luis it sounded like home.

Home.

He nuzzled her hair again. Sunshine and summer.

Thump. Thump. Thump.

He counted the beats.

ALEK COUNTED SOLENNE'S HEARTBEATS. The even measure of them as she slept kept him grounded in the present and not lost to chase down the fiend who hurt her. As the total reached four thousand, Luis returned with a hamper, a blanket bundled under one arm, and a saddlebag slung over his shoulder.

The young man approached the stone circle cautiously.

"I won't bite," Alek said.

Luis wrinkled his nose. "More jokes. You're clutching my naked, bleeding sister, your wolfy brain won't let her go, and you make *jokes*?"

"The bleeding stopped."

"Oh, then by all means, resume with the comedy." Luis tossed the saddlebag at Alek's feet. "That horse is the calmest creature I've ever met. You'd think it'd be scared out of its poor mind from the fighting, but no. Found a patch of rye grass and couldn't be bothered."

"She's Chambers' horse." Alek could not claim responsibility for the horse's temperament.

He set the hamper down. "I brought what I could pilfer from the kitchen, mostly bread, cheese, and cold ham. One thermos is water. The other is hot tea. I added in that powder she uses for fever and pain, but since that is bitter, I added sugar. Too much, probably. Make her drink it now because it's vile when it's cold. You've clean bandages in there because I'd really rather she not bleed out because you have to defend your territory."

And his mate, the beast added.

"She stopped bleeding before you arrived," Alek said.

"Oh, well, bully for you. I guess there's no need for hygiene. We'll catch a lovely infection, and it'll be grand."

"I don't remember you being a sarcastic little shit."

"I was eight when you left, but I assure you I have always been thus. There's a nightgown in there. Please dress her when you return to the house." He took a breath, as if mentally crossing off another item on his list. "That's it. Papa and I will find the beast. If you won't go to the house—"

"Stay here. I know."

He woke a reluctant Solenne, dressed her in the nightgown, and coaxed her to eat a bit of bread and drink the tea. When her eyes grew heavy with sleep, they resumed their position with her snuggled against him while he stayed on guard.

He counted heartbeats until dawn.

Solenne

Dawn crept over the horizon.

Solenne snuggled into the blanket, burying her nose against Alek's chest and allowing herself to soak up his heat. Birdsong warbled, and his hands brushed back her hair. Eventually, it registered that his chest was free of the excessive fur he wore the previous night, thus he was stark naked.

Because of the whole shifting into a werewolf thing. Trousers optional.

She had seen nude men before, specifically her brother, but that was her brother, and she had even seen Alek nude, albeit when they were children. Swimming in the pond and creek was practically a requirement on a hot summer day. She simply had not seen a nude man recently who was not related to her by blood.

The Young Lady's Guide to Etiquette failed to prepare her for the situation.

"You fake sleeping as poorly as you lie," he said.

Solenne pulled the blanket tighter around herself, dimly aware that she wore a thin nightgown. Outside the cocoon of warmth, the air held an unexpected chill. Autumn would arrive before long. She stretched, her shoulders making a terrible noise and her legs screaming in agony. Every part of her was sore. Exhaustion weighed on her, and she felt as if she could sleep the day away.

"Where did this come from?" She gestured to the now filthy nightgown, keeping her eyes averted from Alek's nudity.

"Luis delivered supplies. What are you looking at?" He twisted around, looking behind him.

"Protecting your dignity," she said, eyes fixed on the sky.

"I'm wearing trousers. Like I said, Luis delivered supplies." He leaned to one side to pick up a shirt, along with a needle and thread.

She looked down at his bare chest and disappointing lack of nudity. "You're mending your shirt? It's barely light."

"My eyes are better than the average human's, and there's a tear on the sleeve. Appearances matter," he said in a tone reminiscent of Godwin. "Have some water. You drank all the tea."

Her stomach rumbled at the sight of the hamper. "Did I dream about bread?"

One brow quirked with an unvoiced sarcastic comment as he handed her a chunk of yellow cheese and a thick slice of bread.

They were the greatest morsels she'd ever tasted. "More." She held out a hand.

"No more. How is the ankle? Can you stand?"

She flexed her injured foot, finding it swollen and stiff. "Better not."

Before she could suggest a solution, Alek scooped her up, blanket and all.

"Otherwise, how do you feel?" he asked.

"Exhausted. Grubby. Hungry. Sore. Chewed on."

His arms tightened around her as he picked his way down the hill. "You were not bitten."

"Oh." She felt a bit disappointed. "I told you about page 72, yes?"

"Repeatedly."

Disappointment morphed into embarrassment. She repeatedly mentioned page 72, and yet there was she, dressed in her nightclothes and frustratingly unspoiled.

Seduction was more difficult than novels had led her to believe, but she honestly didn't know what she could have done differently. She confessed her feelings. After Alek stripped her of her clothing, she felt sure that lovemaking was inevitable.

At least she kissed him. He seemed to enjoy that.

Well, he did not recoil.

Oh no. What if he hated it? What if he did not like for a woman to be so forward? What if he expected Solenne to be a shy, delicate flower? Amiable and amenable? If he expected that, then he barely knew her. She had changed. The years apart had changed them both, without doubt, but not that drastically.

"I will say it back," he said, interrupting her thoughts.

"But you will say it?" She couldn't even look at him. No need to ask to what he referred. Last night she had laid her heart bare at his feet. She loved him, only him and always him.

He adjusted her in his arms. "Yes. You cannot escape me."

She tucked her face against his shoulder to hide her smile. "How long ago did it happen? The bite?"

"Seven years, I think. I was in the West Lands, chasing bounties."

"That's dangerous to do on your own," she said. "Colonel Chambers' unit was deployed to the West Lands before his injury. If professional soldiers are not secure, what were you doing there alone? Of all the reckless things to do, Aleksandar Hardwick—" Anger seeped into her voice.

"I must beg forgiveness for being young and foolish," he said in a tone that implied his complete disinterest in forgiveness.

"Tell me how it happened," she demanded. Seven years ago, she was at university, attending classes when need be but spending every moment in the library. While she had been reading, safely tucked away in the library, Alek was mauled and forever changed.

He chuckled.

The brute *chuckled*.

"I apologize if my concern for your wellbeing is misplaced. There is no need to mock me. Set me down. I'll walk."

"You can't walk, and I'm not laughing at you, Solenne. Of all the topics I expected to discuss this morning, I did not expect to be chastised for that. You will not enjoy hearing the details."

Whatever he had to say, it could not be worse than the fight she witnessed last night. "Were you hopelessly outnumbered? Ambushed? Captured in a trap? Oh! You partnered with a treasure hunter who wanted to explore a ruined settlement and they betrayed you?"

"Did you read that in a book?"

"No," she lied.

He chuckled again because she was a terrible liar and he could always tell. "It's not exciting. A sudden snowstorm caught me unprepared, and I sought shelter in a beast's den. That was that."

"That was that," she repeated. "Luis spent all night hunting the beast that attacked me."

"Yes."

The house neared. She patted his chest to make him halt. "Wait. Before we go inside. I need you to know that I do not care about your condition."

"You'd be a damn fool not to care."

"I don't understand how you are the way you are. Every day I discover that I understood very little." So much had been kept from her either intentionally or from plain neglect. "But I'm your anchor, however it happened."

"I never intended—"

"Will you please stop interrupting me? I'm trying to tell you I love you and that I don't care how I get to have you. I'm not letting you go."

He fell silent. She held her breath, wanting to hide her face. She said it *again*.

He didn't have to say it back. Honestly. She just needed enough restraint to stop blabbering about her emotions.

"I did not intend to make another declaration, but I felt compelled to state my case as plainly as possible. You are exceedingly stubborn," she said, mustering what remained of her dignity.

"You won't let me go?"

"No. You're mine and I will marry you, then I'll bind you legally and with whatever this—" *don't say witchcraft, don't say witchcraft* "—mystical, definitely not magical, connection is." She grimaced, because that was worse than witchcraft.

"Your father won't like it."

"I fail to find myself caring."

"Are you at least going to ask me to marry you? Or shall I just accept your decree about our engagement?"

"I already asked you."

His brow furrowed as he remembered the details of their engagement. "You were eleven."

"You have yet to decline my proposal. I consider us quite engaged." She beamed her most charming smile up at him.

"I think you're spoiled and too used to getting your way." His grumble at echoes from an earlier, angrier conversation. Now his tone sounded light, almost teasing.

Good. She enjoyed him like this.

"And I won't keep it a secret this time," she said.

His brow furrowed. "I asked Godwin for permission, you know."

She could imagine how that conversation went. "I continue to find insufficient reason to seek Papa's permission."

He stood still, as if envisioning the moment Godwin learned of their engagement. "Let's get you cleaned and seen by a doctor. Then I'll give you an answer," he finally said.

"Alek! I waited all night. You promised we'd talk in the morning."

"We talked. This is us conversing. Mostly you prattled, and I listened."

"You honestly plan to make me wait?" She knew his answer. Had always known on some level. The thread between them hummed, warm and golden.

"You waited years. An hour or two is nothing in comparison."

Chapter Seventeen

Aleksandar

Boxon Hill

Marechal House - The Bathing Room

The household was on alert for their arrival.

"Send for the doctor," Alek said, carrying Solenne through to the bathing room. "She requires a bath, clean garments, a meal, and more of that tea. Get to it."

"Bring me my kit," Solenne added.

Travers followed Alek into the bathing room. Solenne lowered herself to a bench while he opened the taps. Travers lurked in the doorway with the maid peeking around him.

"Did you not understand my orders?" Alek asked.

"Sir, this is highly inappropriate. Surely a maid can assist Miss Marechal."

"Oh, it's quite all right, Travers. Congratulations are in order. We're engaged," Solenne said, speaking over Alek's grumbled response.

"Congratulations?" The man looked dubious.

"Congratulations, Miss," the maid said from behind Travers.

"Doctor, now," Alek growled.

Travers and the maid sprang into action.

An inspired ancestor had built a practical shelf into the tiles above the cast iron tub. Jars of various salts, bottles of perfumed oil, and canisters of little soap cakes lined the shelf. Alek sniffed the jars and, finding the scent pleasing, dumped in the contents.

"That's enough lavender," Solenne said.

Filled nearly to the brim, steam rolled off the water. He eased Solenne to the tub's edge. She ran a hand through the water and nodded, then accepted his help to remove the nightgown.

He crouched down to remove her boots. Carefully, he peeled away the sock from her swollen ankle. The injury looked serious.

She lowered herself into the water with a sigh. "Oh, it feels good to take those boots off."

"How bad is your foot?"

"Only hurts when I put weight on it. I can move my toes." She set her injured on the tub's rim and wiggled her toes. "Nothing broken."

She reached up for a cake of soap. Alek removed his shirt. The soap leaped from her grasp, landing on the far side of the room.

Alek grinned, flashing the tiniest bit of tooth and feeling particularly wolfy. "Can't have my shirt getting wet, can we? Imagine what Travers will say."

She reached up, hooking a finger around the silver chain around his neck. Momentarily, the sting of silver eased. He knew his skin was red where the chain rested. "I hate seeing the pain this chain causes. Don't wear this anymore."

"I barely noticed it," he said. The sting helped keep him focused.

"Then it's not working. Your tattoo." Her fingers brushed the sun emblem inked over his heart. "Why?"

"You're always with me," he answered. The pink flush pleased him greater than any material gain or temporary delight of the flesh.

He glanced down at the water.

And he had a lot to take delight in.

Before, when he removed her bloody clothes, he searched for injury. Keeping her safe and warm had been his top priority, driving all else from his mind. He hadn't really seen Solenne, admired her curves, her long legs, and the tumble of dark locks.

It seemed impossible that she wanted him still.

"The soap?" she asked, snagging his attention.

"Yes. Stay," he said, distracted. She laughed while he fetched the errant soap. "Lean forward and I'll wash your back."

"That's unnecessary."

"We're engaged," he replied.

Her face flushed pink. "I apologize if I was presumptuous. You're the only one I want to see me like this."

"Good. I'm the only one who gets to see you like this or any other way." Solenne probably meant seeing her in a moment of weakness or vulnerability. Alek was the only one privileged enough to view her bare skin, to appreciate the way the water glistened or her hair clumped in damp strands, clinging to the back of her neck.

With care, he lathered up her back, scrubbed with a cloth, and rinsed away the events of the previous night. Each touch was filled with adoration and promise.

This was his mate. She had seen him lost to the beast, with the blood of another on his tongue, and she proclaimed her love.

For him, of all people.

He washed and rinsed her hair, which turned the bathwater a distressing shade of pink. Letting the filthy water drain, he refilled the tub and continued to wash his beloved. He massaged her tender ankle with a small vial of oil that smelled of lavender. Mindful of each touch, he catalogued her sighs and moans, learning her responses. They were his too. Only his.

Finally, he washed her chest. With the same meticulous care, he lathered her shoulders and chest. He gently cupped her breasts, massaging the soap into a froth. Buff-colored nipples hardened as she arched into his touch.

Alek leaned forward, capturing her lips with his own.

"If you want me to stop, I will," he said, when he pulled away.

"Please, don't stop." Water sloshed over the sides as she leaned back.

Starting at her feet, he worked his way up her injured calf. The skin at the edge of the claw marks was red and swollen. Fortunately, they were not deep. She watched him with a slightly dazed look, her lips swollen and begging for another kiss.

Satisfied the claw marks were clean, he switched to her other leg. Soapy hands skimmed up her legs, creeping closure to the juncture of her thighs.

"May I?" he asked, hand nearly but not touching her there.

"Yes, please," she breathed.

Crouched at the edge of the tub, he positioned himself for a better angle.

Solenne jolted at his touch. "Sorry," she said, cheeks flush. "New sensation."

"You've never?" He wondered at the idea that Solenne had never touched herself.

"No, I have." She bit her bottom lip, then her eyes gleamed, like she arrived at a decision to be bold. "You were with me then too."

"Oh?" This he wanted to hear, about how she thought of him when she touched herself.

He pushed his fingers against her, encountering a tangle of hair and her silken folds.

"Alek," she moaned, sinking back.

"Let me be perfectly frank," he said, fingers stroking her folds, "I have loved you in some capacity since the moment we met."

Her gaze locked on his. Gently circling her tender bundle of nerves, he captured her mouth. Water drenched the floor.

"You're mine, Solenne. You always have been." He probed her entrance, finding it hot and tight. She tensed, then relaxed as he continued to stroke and tease. "You ground me. When we were apart, the memory of you kept me whole. You are my anchor. My friend. My love. My heart."

He worked his finger into her. She bit back a moan. Water drenched the floor as he worked another finger in. She was tight beyond belief and warm. Muscles clenched around him as he crooked his fingers, hitting that special spot. Her hips shot up and splashed back down, driving an enormous wave of water over the edge of the tub. The floor was in ruin, and there would be no doubt about what they had gotten up to. He didn't care.

Solenne was his.

He had tried to wait, to do the right thing and honorable thing, but that had only led to wasted years.

"I should have come for you," he said. "I never should have let anyone keep us apart. I'm sorry, love."

"You should be," she managed to say.

Alek was of the opinion that while she had managed to say something in that moment, he was doing a poor job of it. His fingers moved from her clit to plunge back inside, working a hard rhythm. She might have been inexperienced, but she met each thrust with enthusiasm.

"I can't wait to have you on my bed, spread out for me, a feast for me. I'm going to eat every morsel of you, love,"

"Yes, Alek." Her back arched again, and her feet braced against the side of the tub ten kicked, knocking over a basket of assorted washcloths. Her channel clutched him tight, pulsing with her climax.

He listened to her heart as her pulse and breath evened out.

Thump. Thump. Thump.

His heart. His love. His radiant daylight.

Solenne

Alek carried her to her bedroom, which was humiliating enough, but Travers' knowing look made her flush with embarrassment. Thank the heavens that her father and Luis had yet to return.

He pushed open the door with his shoulder. The room was not grand by any means, furnished with century-old furniture and cluttered with books and notebooks on every available surface. A decrepit green velvet chair sat under the south-facing windows, the bottom sagging and the velvet worn away on the arms. The windows let in enough natural light that she only required a lamp on the dreariest of days.

"It's not much," she said, aware that Alek had not been in her bedchamber since they were children.

Once safely settled on the bed, the book on the nightstand grabbed his attention. "Page 72?" He flipped through the pages before turning to the marked page and read the passage. His brows rose. "Well, that's certainly something to aspire to."

Dr. Webb's examination was thorough and efficient. The entire time, she worried that he would know what she and Alek had done in the bath. If the doctor had any suspicion, he kept that to himself. The maid who delivered a breakfast tray, however, gave Solenne a knowing wink.

The claw marks on her legs would scar, but it did no lasting damage to the muscles. Her ankle, however, was badly sprained. She was to have several days' bedrest, put no weight on it whatsoever, and he'd know if she defied his orders.

"Do not worry. I'll keep her in bed," Alek said. When the doctor turned to pack up his bag, Alek licked his lips and winked. Solenne nearly spilled her tea in a coughing fit.

"Sorry. I swallowed poorly," she said, grimacing at the lame excuse.

"Absolute bed rest," Dr. Webb warned one last time. Alek locked the door as he left.

She cleared the plates, barely tasting the meal as Alek occupied so much of her attention. Her mind kept spinning about what they did in the bath, what it meant, and his announcement of their engagement. Her proposal had been sincere, but she had not expected Alek to agree so quickly. She had been prepared to fight against whatever arguments he had to decline.

It was silly to feel disappointment at not having an argument. Simply silly. She loved Alek, always had and always would. His affliction changed nothing. He returned her sentiment, touched her, and had been inside her. So the matter was settled.

Well, they still had to break the news to her father, so she'd get her argument after all.

Eventually, she realized how intensely Alek watched her eat.

"Are you going to eat? There's more than enough for two," she said, the slice of buttered toast with honey hovering at her mouth.

He took the slice of toast from her hands, leaned in, and licked the honey from her lips. "I plan on eating," he growled, and she ached at his tone.

Carefully, he moved the tray to the floor, kneeling at the edge of the bed by her knees. Instinctively, she parted them, making room for him.

"Aleksandar, what are you doing?" she asked, though she knew.

"Is this not in your dirty little book?" He lifted her nightgown, exposing her bare thighs, and pushed open her legs further.

"Page 34." She read it several times and made notes.

He chuckled, because he saw the highlighted passages when he flipped through. His fingers brushed the gusset of her undergarment, then pushed the fabric to one side. "You will no longer wear these. I want nothing between us," he said.

Before she could protest, he gave the undergarment a tug, tearing the thin fabric.

"Oh," she breathed. He pulled her forward by the hips and she fell to her back. "Oh!"

He leaned to the juncture of her thighs and breathed. She felt a moment's self-consciousness about her hair and smell, but none of that seemed to bother Alek. He kissed the soft flesh of her inner thigh, working his way from her knee back to her sex.

She tensed.

"Relax," he murmured, switching to her other thigh. His kisses lulled and soothed her. She forgot about her awkwardness and inexperience and focused on the sensation of him touching her. His breath heating her skin. His lips caressing her flesh. Her fingers tangled in his hair.

"I imagined this," she said, eyes closed and voice breathy.

"You touched yourself thinking of me?" Hot breath gusted on her most sensitive area.

"Yes. So many nights." During her brief stay at university, frustrated and tired of waiting, she tried to form an attachment with another. Every man there paled to Alek. No one piqued her interest that way, and she developed a rather robust fantasy life to satisfy her needs.

"I've imagined this as well," he said, before leaning in.

His tongue, hot and wet, lapped at her inner folds. She jolted at the unfamiliar sensation. Not odd or unpleasant, but new and unexpected. Breathing out, she closed her eyes and let herself drift. Distantly, she was aware of the sound of his trousers being opened.

Alek growled against her sex, licking and sucking like a starved man. Her thighs trembled. Her fingers twisted in his perpetually messy hair. Before she could ask for mercy, her hips lifted as her climax broke. She was overheated and shivering at once, her flesh too sensitive.

"Gorgeous," Alek breathed, licking his lips. He rose to his feet, stroking his member. Thick and veiny, his cock stood proud in a thatch of dark hair.

Solenne slid to her knees, kneeling before him with her hands on his hips. She was fuzzy and tingling all over, flush with warmth, and she wanted Alek to feel the same.

His hand stroked from the base of his cock up to the head; his thumb smeared the leaking fluid across it. Her mouth watered, wanting to taste.

"Did you fantasize about sucking my cock?" he asked.

"Yes," she breathed. "So many times."

"Have a taste."

She opened her mouth obediently and her lips closed around his pre-cum coated thumb. The fluid was salty but not unpleasant, much like Alek himself. "More," she said.

He obliged, feeding her his length slowly. She licked the skin, relishing his salty taste, before swallowing the head. Her tongue swirled around, unsure what to do. She watched him for direction, but his eyes closed with a look of pure bliss.

With one hand, she held the base of his cock. Wet from her saliva, she worked the hand up and down, imitating how Alek stroked himself.

Using her other hand, she cupped his testicles. They were...odd. Warm, soft, and lumpy at the same time. The skin immediately contracted, growing dense and harder. She gave a light squeeze, and Alek groaned.

He tapped her head. "Solenne, I won't last."

Encouraged, she increased her pace. His member pulsed, and his fingers twisted into her hair. His body tensed, and her mouth flooded with his salty release. She pulled back, unsure what to do. The substance was more substantial than water, not so thick, hardly had a taste at all.

She swallowed.

Alek's eyes gleamed violet before he blinked, and they returned to his velvety brown. "My love," he breathed with utter reverence.

They stayed like that for some minutes, him stroking her hair and her nuzzling into the skin at his hip. The golden thread between them sang, filled with joy and contentment. She didn't want the moment to end. The sounds of the house drifted up through the floor. A soft breeze through the open window carried in the sounds of someone's arrival in the courtyard.

If she listened close enough, she could hear his heart.

"You need to rest," he said, breaking the silence.

"I'm resting."

"Doctor's orders."

"Only if you stay with me," she said, batting her lashes and giving her all at a sultry glance.

Alek looked as if he would deny her, then nodded. He helped her back into the bed, careful to avoid any weight on her injured foot, and elevated said foot on a pillow. He leaned over her, caging her in with his muscular arms, and gently kissed her. Sweet and soft. She wondered if she was still asleep in the stone circle and had dreamed the last few hours.

"Let me bathe. I'm filthy. I'll ruin the clean sheets," he said.

A fist pounded on the door. Alek tensed, as if he might fly out the window lest he be caught by a wrathful father and ruin her reputation.

She grabbed his hand, unwilling to let him leave. She loved him, but his dramatic noble streak made him act a fool. "Stay," she whispered.

"Solenne, have you seen Alek?" Luis asked through the door.

"Go away, Luis. I'm trying to sleep," Solenne answered.

"I must find him. Chambers has trapped the beast in his barn."

Chapter Eighteen

Solenne

Boxon Hill

Marechal House - Solenne's Bedroom

Sleep remained elusive, despite exhaustion. Solenne lay in bed, watching dust motes drift through the air. Her mind felt too full to concentrate on reading one of the numerous books stacked next to her bed. She kept replaying Alek's words and actions. Her fingers drifted to her lips, swollen and tender.

At some point, she must have drifted off to sleep because she woke in a sweat. Her entire body ached. Fumbling at her bedside, she knocked over the glass of water. The room was too bright.

Pain rippled through her stomach. Stumbling on one good foot to the half-bath attached to her room, she kneeled on the tiled floor. The cool porcelain tiles soothed her heated skin.

This wasn't right.

Aleksandar

Boxon

Vervain Hall

Flames already consumed the barn when Alek arrived. Rather than forming a bucket brigade to save the structure, people idly sat by, watching the blaze.

"They're just letting it burn?" Luis asked.

Godwin sat on the ground next to a full water bucket, soot covering his face. "They trapped the beast inside. Chambers made the call. Fire will kill it, even if silver won't."

"Are you sure it's the same one that attacked the house?" Alek asked.

Godwin leveled a stare at him with his one good eye. "What else could it be?"

"But did you see it?" Alex turned to Luis. "Did you see it? Can you identify it?"

"What else could it be?" Luis said, repeating his father's words. Meaning that no one caught a good look at the beast.

"Does no one think it unlikely that a beast old enough to ignore silver could be so easily trapped?" Alek asked, finding the situation unlikely.

"Easy?" Godwin lumbered to his feet, leaning heavily on his staff. Only then did Alek see the scorch marks on the back of his shirt. "Nothing about this night has been easy. Luis, Chambers, and I chased down the beast and finally cornered it while you were, what? Chasing a rumor in Fallkirk? We needed you here." The staff thumped against the ground, and his eye sparkled in the morning light.

Alek nearly bit his tongue. Godwin knew exactly how to rile him, always had, and seemed to derive joy from it. He remembered all that had transpired last night and that morning with Solenne, and he swallowed back the urge to lash out. He needed to be on Godwin's good side, at least for a few days, until he solidified plans with Solenne.

Discussing the trivial details of their spending their lives together had paled compared to the pure joy of celebrating that decision. He now faced several uncertainties.

Did Solenne wish to remain in Boxon with her family? Even with the beast eliminated, the Marechals needed another hunter. Or should they seek their fortune elsewhere? Fallkirk needed a hunter. He presumed plenty of other smaller towns and villages on the fringe of the West Lands needed hunters. Finding a post would be as simple as deciding where to settle, in theory. Did he even want to go back to hunting? Could he do anything else?

He always had his ancestral home. The house needed care, but it was solid and the land was viable. The tenant farmers did well enough. Raising any kind of animal or crop seemed preposterous to him, but he could easily imagine Solenne in a garden. The Marechals kept sheep and a greenhouse, so Solenne had more of an idea how to earn a living from the earth than he did.

Perhaps Solenne wanted more than to keep his household and teach him how to raise sheep? Did she wish to return to university? He had some money. Not enough for tuition, but he'd figure it out if need be.

Fuck. There were too many questions, and Godwin kept staring at him, like he could smell his daughter on Alek.

"Unless you were successful in luring the Fallkirk beast here?" Godwin asked.

Alek ran a hand through his hair. "I thought I had lost the trail when it doubled back but yes, it's possible it followed me from Fallkirk."

"Papa, the beast attacked Solenne. Alek saved her," Luis said.

"She what? And you didn't tell me?" Godwin spun to face his son, and Alek enjoyed the brief respite from Godwin's ire.

"We were busy." Luis waved a hand toward the conflagration.

"Well?" Godwin looked from Luis to Alek. "Report." Alek ran through what the doctor had instructed. "Good luck keeping her in bed," Godwin eventually said.

Alek grinned, unable to help himself. He had a few ideas on the matter.

He filled and hauled buckets of water when the fire threatened to spread when the wind shifted. They doused nearby buildings to keep the fire contained. By the time the sun reached the day's zenith, the barn was a smoldering ruin. If the beast still lived, it was badly injured.

"Dismember the corpse and salt the earth," Alek said, before dunking his head under a water pump. The scent of smoke filled his nostrils and clouded everything else. All he detected was char, burnt grass, and an acrid chemical stench of whatever Chambers stored in the barn. No longer used for livestock, it served as storage for any number of highly flammable items.

Convenient how Chambers' sacrifice cost him little. Such a loss would devastate any other farmer, even a gentleman farmer.

The wind shifted as a storm rolled in from the west, clearing the smoke. The dark clouds bisected the sky, one side summery blue and the other an ominous gray. Badly needing a bath and a meal, he wanted to return to the Marechal home before the downpour arrived. Beyond exhausted, he had pushed his body to its limits since last night. Even the beast required rest.

A fair-haired woman approached him.

"Aleksandar, may I speak with you?" She drew him to the side. "I'm sure you do not remember me."

"I remember you, Miss Wodehouse." When they were younger, Solenne and Charlotte burst into giggles whenever Alek entered the room. Since his return, he witnessed the same charming chatting and giggling like conspirators.

"Oh, excellent." A warm smile spread across Charlotte's face. "I need to beg for your help."

"If I can." Honestly, he did not understand how he could assist Charlotte. He was tired, covered in soot, and had burns on his hands and back. He wanted to return to Solenne as quickly as possible.

"I'm afraid this is rather delicate—" She glanced behind, as if to make sure their conversation would not be overheard.

"Miss Wodehouse, please," he snapped. Then gave what he hoped was a reassuring smile. "Do not be concerned about my delicate sensibilities. I assure you, I have none."

"Yes, I see. Well, I have a piece of news, and I know Solenne says she had no attachment to Lionel—Colonel Chambers, I mean. She seemed to encourage my affections for him but I'm uncertain. Hearts are tricky things. There's what we know and what we *know*." She gave him a look that implied he understood, which he did not.

Displeasure rumbled low in his throat. Solenne had no attachment to that man. None!

Charlotte paled, as if alarmed. "Yes, but what I want to know is would it upset her if Lionel and I were engaged?"

Such a tiresome way to ask a simple question. Alek rolled his shoulders. "Are you engaged?"

"Yes, as it happens, we are. Lionel proposed last night, and I accepted." A smile bloomed across her face. "Do you think it will crush Solenne?"

"No. She is already claimed."

"To you? Did you propose? Was it terribly romantic?" Charlotte clasped her hands and sighed. "Oh, this is wonderful. We'll have a double wedding, just like in the novels she reads." She frowned slightly. "Without all the stabbing, treachery, and doom, of course."

"I'll do my best," he replied, unsure what type of books his mate read.

"There's so much to plan and so many details to consider. A double wedding will cut down on expenses, I presume. I positively have a mountain of work to organize." Her eyes sparkled, as if she could think of nothing better. "This is wonderful!"

Charlotte launched herself at Alek, throwing her arms around him in complete disregard to propriety and cleanliness.

"What's this now?" a gruff voice said from behind them. Alek turned to find Godwin glaring at them. Correction: him. The glare was specifically for Alek's benefit.

Charlotte pulled away, beaming with excitement. "Mr. Marechal, it's the best news! Solenne and Aleksandar are engaged!"

Solenne

Boxon Hill

Marechal House - Solenne's Bedroom

. . .

"Solenne!" Heavy footsteps thundered up the stairs, waking Solenne from her fitful half-sleep. The air felt charged, as if a storm were about to break. "Explain yourself!"

She sat upright, head spinning. Food wouldn't be amiss, and perhaps a cool bath, though going downstairs to the bathing room seemed like an impossible journey. Hot and sticky from the fever, she had sought the cool tiles of the toilet floor. The small necessity was built into her room but only offered a wash basin, not a tub.

"Tell me it is not true!"

"Please, do not yell, Papa. I'm feeling rather poorly," she said, rubbing her forehead. Her entire body ached, like a werewolf had mauled her. Well, it stood to reason.

"Air this room out. It smells." She heard the rattle of the window being raised. Cool air flooded in on a strong breeze. "What are you doing in the toilet?" Godwin stood in the door, blocking the dim sunlight.

"Not vomiting, though my stomach is trying its hardest." Solenne set her hand on the closed toilet lid and pulled herself to her feet. She needed another dose of willow bark.

"Don't be vulgar." Godwin offered his arm as she hobbled her way to the bed. She sighed with relief as she sat down. He seemed to have finally noticed the bandage on her ankle and her leg. "How bad is it?"

"Nothing rest won't cure."

He pressed the back of his hand to her forehead and frowned. "You've a fever. Tell me what you need? That tea with the peppermint and ginger?"

She waved him off, her entire arm aching from the effort, as if she wore lead weights. "Where's Alek?" If anyone was going to play nursemaid, she wanted it to be Alek.

"So it is true. You've agreed to marry that...that..."

"That what, Papa?" She wanted him to speak those ugly, vile names. "The man I loved since I don't even know? The man who was my dearest childhood friend? The man who saved me from being mauled last night? The man who came to help us? That?"

"He's a monster, Solenne. You can't deny it. The evidence is obvious."

In retrospect, perhaps, but she had not been looking for symptoms. Alek captured her attention in so many other ways.

"I won't let you throw yourself away on this wastrel. You need to do your duty to this family."

"My duty?"

"Yes, your duty. I've indulged you, so some of this is my fault." Godwin paced the room. "I let you carry on this...this flirtation with Alek. I had hoped it was a passing fancy. You've always been so responsible. Luis is the fanciful one. I never expected my practical, sensible Solenne to entertain a man with such low prospects."

The words out of her father's mouth might as well have been in another language. He indulged her? Godwin had done nothing but make demand after demand on Solenne, always framing it as her duty to the family and letting her guilt make the difficult choices.

"I'll send him away. Immediately. He told that Wodehouse girl, but I can say she misheard in the confusion of the fire. Everyone knows that Charlotte is a silly thing, and Alek has not endeared himself with the neighbors. No one will believe it."

"Enough!" Her voice boomed in the air, and the wind stirred, whipping her hair in her face and rustling pages of the open book on the bed. "I gave up university for Luis' education. I run this household because you won't. I've been digging our finances out of this mess, and I even agreed to be the one to marry for money so that Luis could follow his heart," she said, nearly shouting. "What have you sacrificed?"

His face went red with anger. "No child should speak to their father with such disrespect."

"I'm not a child," she replied, her voice cold and even.

The sky outside the window darkened, and the wind picked up speed. Soon rain would pelt the glass.

"He's dangerous. His entire line is tainted. Your mother knew. She told me to send him away, but I owed a debt to Maksim. He's the reason she's gone. He cost me my Amalie," Godwin said.

Green curtains framing the open window snapped in the breeze.

"Mama was reckless."

"Do not speak ill of your mother."

"No. I'm tired of pretending that she was perfect in every way. I love Mama very much, but you know she was reckless. The accident was only remarkable in that she succeeded in killing herself." Amalie had minor accidents in her workshop regularly. No one thought anything of the flickering lights or the smell of smoke.

Godwin clenched his hand, then drove it into the wall. Solenne jumped.

"He was there! He was there, and he did nothing to help her. I should have slit that mongrel's throat when I found him and cleansed the earth of one more beast."

Lightning flickered across the sky, followed by the rumble of thunder. The hair on the back of her neck and arms stood on end. She had never heard her father speak with such hatred in his voice.

"He was dangerous then, and he's dangerous now. Don't you see? He broke your wrist."

Solenne unconsciously rubbed the fractured wrist. She and Alek had been sparring. He was taller and stronger than her and didn't mean to hurt her. "It was an accident," she said.

"No. I saw his eyes. The beast peered out that day. He slipped and lost control. That's why I sent him away."

"Then why did you allow him to come back if he's so dangerous?"

A shrewd looked passed over her father's face. "I'll admit, it is useful having access to someone with his abilities. Vile, but useful. His grandfather, who had the same affliction, was an unparalleled hunter."

"His grandfather had the same affliction?"

"He didn't tell you? My, my. What other secrets has dear Aleksandar been keeping from you?"

Thunder clapped, louder.

"Do not twist this around. You knew what he was when he entered the house. Did you know I was his anchor?" She did not pause for him to answer. "You suspected. What did you think would happen?"

"That you would behave with dignity and decorum," Godwin snapped. "I couldn't expect Alek to restrain him, but I expected my daughter to know her place. It's not too late. I can persuade Chambers to take you back, even in your soiled state."

Lightning flashed, and thunder boomed, deafeningly loud. Icy rain came in sideways through the window.

She hated her father at that moment. Godwin had been selfish in the years since Mama passed. She excused it as part of his grief. She had never thought him to be so calculating and mean-spirited, and all the more fool her.

"Marry me off and keep Alek on a leash like a dog. What a deplorable scheme," she said.

"Do as I say, for once in your wretched life. Chambers—"

"Will never take me back because he ended it. Him!" she shouted, voice nearly drowned out by the rain. "Close the damn window before the carpets are ruined. That's another thing we can't afford."

"I am your father. Do not speak to me in that manner," he retorted, but still closed the window.

She rubbed the bridge of her nose, exhausted. Her father's argument was nonsensical and boiled down to demanding her to obey out of filial loyalty. She found herself hard pressed for such feelings. "If you wanted to marry me off, why keep me here in Boxon? Why have I not been sent to Founding for the season?" Charlotte had gone often enough and always invited her.

"Dresses and parties? With what money? I needed you here."

The dissonance of his demands infuriated her. Marry well, but never leave his side.

He wanted obedience, pure and simple. He controlled every aspect of her life, and Solenne understood that she would never be free of him as long as she lived under his roof.

"The harder you try to control me and Luis, the more we'll fight. Eventually, you will lose us."

"Luis does as he is told."

"You hardly know him at all," she replied. Her brother had grown while he was away at school, and not just in stature. He had a questioning mind and a stubborn streak to rival her own.

Godwin crossed his arms over his chest. He likely intended it to be a stern gesture, but it read as defensive, protecting his belly. "I will not allow this union. You will not be allowed to stay."

"Alek is not without his own property."

"A ruin."

"Then we'll seek a charter in another town. There is always a need for hunters. If you force me to choose between my family or Alek, I will always choose Alek," she said, speaking with conviction.

He huffed. "Then we are at an impasse."

"So it seems." There was nothing else to say on the matter. She wished she really was a witch and could hex him, just a little. Instead, she fluffed the pillows on the bed with more force than necessary.

A throat cleared. Alek stood in the doorway, carrying a tray and teapot. His hair was wet and his face ruddy, as if he took a hasty bath. From his expression, he heard every word.

"Sir," he said coolly. "We won't stay where we're not welcomed. As soon as Solenne's ankle can bear it, we'll leave."

"That won't be necessary. You are...useful." Godwin frowned, as if the words were bitter in his mouth. "I can put you to use on collecting bounties, if nothing else." He left, slamming the door in his wake.

Rain against the window filled the silence. Alek set the tray down at the bedside table, the dishes clattering.

"Always pragmatic," Alek said, his voice almost sounding complimentary.

"I don't know how you can be kind to him. He said the vilest things about you."

"All true." He poured a cup of tea and stirred in a spoon of honey. She caught the bitter aroma of willow bark.

She accepted the cup, relishing the heat seeping into her aching fingers. "And your grandfather? Is that true? He was like you?"

"So Godwin claims." Alek poured himself a cup. "If he was alive when I was a child, I don't remember him."

"And your affliction? It's inherited?"

"I do not know. My father did not have this curse."

"Affliction," she said. "No one talks about my fiancé in such a manner."

With a brow quirked up in amusement, he blew across the cup before taking a sip. He grimaced at the bitter taste.

Curiosity spiked in Solenne. "Does it taste different to you? Foul?"

"It tastes like chewing on a tree," he answered.

"Ah, nothing unusual there. It's vile, but useful." Funny how Godwin had said those same words about Alek. "Add honey," she said.

"Does it bother you that any children we may have would be like me?" he asked.

She lifted a shoulder, tempted to share Luis' witch theory. Perhaps the witch and the wolf cancelled each other out. "It could be a recessive trait. Exposure via a bite activates it." She blew on her own cup of tea before sipping. "I hope they'll be smart enough to avoid the bitey end of a werewolf."

Alek sliced an apple, feeding her slice by slice. Mechanically, she ate. The bitterness of the tea masked the sweet crispness of the apple, or perhaps that was the effect of the fever. Rain continued to drum against the windows. Wind rattled against the house. Eventually, she yawned and her eyes grew heavy. Sleep had been so fitful and elusive, yet now she wanted nothing more than to curl up on the bed and listen to the rain.

"Sleep," he said, pulling her down. She rested her head on his chest, the golden thread between them humming with contentment.

Chapter Nineteen

Aleksandar

Boxon Hill

Marechal House

The fever broke the next day, leaving Solenne weak and listless. The headache lingered, making it impossible to read. Her foot kept her immobile, even though she hobbled about the room and thought she was being secretive, leaning heavily on furniture for support. Her pride prevented her from asking for help to the toilet, and he'd let her keep her pride.

Charlotte visited frequently with her notebook of wedding ideas that grew at an alarming rate. "You're not upset, are you? Alek said you wouldn't be. And why should you be? I have Lionel, and you have your Aleksandar."

"It is either the fever or the headache, but I don't remember agreeing to a double wedding with Charlotte and Chambers," Solenne said. He patted her hand and opined about the virtue of knowing when to go accept defeat.

So, that happened. A double wedding, just like in a novel.

Luis kept them updated on the werewolf that attacked her. The beast had been trapped in Chambers' barn and burned to death, so that situation reached its conclusion. Not enough of it remained for Luis to say if it was the one that attacked her and Miles on the full moon, but everyone agreed that it must be.

Alek made himself a constant fixture, of course. He only left her bedside to fetch a tray of food or more tea. She was beyond tired of tea. One morning he disappeared for a few hours, returning with the smell of woodsmoke and charred flesh. The beast that attacked her had not warranted a burial, instead it had been hacked into pieces and burned until only ashes remained.

Godwin only visited when Solenne slept, and then only briefly. It was as if Alek and Godwin could not abide being in the same territory together. They bristled and postured, but standing watch over Solenne was very much Alek's responsibility and he would not back down.

They did not speak. When one entered the room, the other left, which suited Alek just fine. He resisted the urge to ask Luis about Godwin's mood or how he took the news of their engagement. The worried look in Luis' eyes was enough.

When Solenne asked him what they would do if Godwin proved impossible to live with, he told her to rest and focus on getting better. He'd figure it out.

"Better? Bed rest is insufferably boring," she complained.

Alek knew what Solenne would never admit: with nothing to do and unable to read, her mind spun in circles, worrying about the problems she knew of and the problems she had no means to foresee. To give her the diversion she needed, Alek read aloud until she fell asleep, sometimes continuing on until his voice rasped. He chose the most worn, well-loved books, figuring they had to be among her favorites.

After five days, Dr. Webb declared her fit enough for short excursions. No long, rambling walks about the countryside. No running from monsters.

"I really don't plan for such things," she said. "Now take me out of this wretched room. I cannot abide it one second longer."

Alek took her to the stone circle on Boxon Hill for an outing. Invigorated by the cool fresh air and sunshine, her energy quickly lagged, requiring him to carry her to the top, where she found Luis and Miles waiting with a picnic lunch spread out on a blanket.

"This is marvelous. Thank you," she said, accepting a plate.

A bright, clear day, the prairie rolled out westward from the hill in waves of grass, turning gold after a long summer. Autumn and the harvest would be upon them soon, along with cold rains, snow and dreary gray days. From this vantage, Alek could not tell which were native grasses and which were planted by humans. At this distance, it all looked the same.

This was the edge of civilization. Humanity had settled further west, but the untamed wilderness pushed them back. It was hardly an inspirational story, but practical. Humans had not been on the planet long, in the grand scheme of things. Humans planted their seeds, bred their animals transported as frozen embryos—he had no idea what that meant or how it worked—shaped the landscape, and still, the land rejected humans. It was beautiful and wild.

"Is it true you went into the West Lands?" Luis asked. "How far did you make it? Did you reach the mountains? The city in the mountains?"

Luis continued to pepper Alek with questions until Miles interrupted to remind him it was time to return to the forge. "I'm making my own armor," Luis announced with pride. "Isn't that amazing?"

Solenne leaned her back against Alek. "Tell me I do not wear that ridiculous expression when I look at you."

"Do not ask me to lie," he replied. She elbowed him. When he regained his breath, he asked, "Are you well? Do you need to return?"

"Not yet. I missed the sun. The thought of returning to my bedroom feels confining," she said. Though she would not admit it, Alek could tell that the short excursion drained her energy. "Is it true about your grandfather? Tell me again."

"All I know of Maksim, I learned from your father. If there's more, we have to ask him."

Solenne frowned, clearly disliking the notion of speaking to her father. "I like that way you said we."

"You're my anchor." His arms tightened around her and the thread that bound them together sang with happiness. "You can't get rid of me."

"What are we going to do? Charlotte is planning this wedding, I have no idea how we can afford even half of it, and my father is...you know how he is." Stubborn. Inflexible. That went unsaid. "If we stay, he's always going to order you around like a servant."

Godwin did that now. "We can't live under his roof and avoid him forever."

"We can try. It's a big house. He's avoided me for the last few days."

"It's a bit easier when you're immobile."

"Alek, I'm serious. I don't think I can live with him after what he said, what he planned to do."

Yes. Marrying Solenne off to the highest bidder while keeping Alek chained to her side, unable to leave his anchor.

"Hardwick House is standing," he said.

"With four walls and a roof?"

"Yes." Barely.

"I noticed you failed to describe it as habitable."

"It was empty for a long time, but it is habitable. The groundskeeper kept it repaired. No broken windows and the roof is solid. Mrs. Suchet was the housekeeper when my parents...for my parents. I don't think she ever left or plans to leave. There are a few tenant farmers, but they're used to looking after themselves," Alek said.

The Hardwick's ancestral home was not as grand as the Marechal's house, but it produced some income. Since the curse forced him to flee back home to hide, he had not cared enough to make repairs or upgrades to the property. Now he regretted his lack of action.

"It has—had—a library. Nothing as extensive as yours, but the mice have not chewed up every book to pieces."

"How long would it take to travel there?"

"Three days direct but five by coach." It was not an easy journey with no direct road, requiring frequent coach changes.

"Oh. I don't suppose it matters. It's not like I'll be a frequent visitor," Solenne said.

He heard her grief at seeing her brother infrequently, if ever, and that hurt him. "Fallkirk needs a hunter. It is a few hours by coach."

"But your house—"

"Has done well without its landlord in residence and will continue to do so. The charter was granted to another after my parents' death." He imagined Mrs. Suchet would continue on splendidly without him.

Solenne made no reply, staring off into the distance. The sun neared the horizon, giving them perhaps an hour before it grew dark. The days were growing shorter, and the equinox would arrive soon. He wondered what that cycle would be like with his anchor firmly in place. Before, Solenne had been an idea, a hope, that gave him the thinnest possible tether back to his humanity. Maintaining control had always been a struggle. He felt stronger now but also stable, like shifting forms would be a choice, not an inescapable burden.

"I'm sorry my father is so difficult," she said, breaking the silence. "Call it guilt, depression, or grief, he's…I've been making excuses for his behavior for years and I'm tired of it. When I came back from university, the house and the finances were in chaos. Papa was stinking drunk most of the time. The tenants left, except for the shepherd. Thank heaven, because while the sheep mostly take care of themselves, we do need a shepherd. We're barely holding onto the charter. Charlotte told me that the village council is considering taking it away." She gave a weary sigh. "And I can't get Papa to care. At least he's not drunk all the time now."

He understood what she did not say explicitly. She felt obligated to remain to care for her father, Luis, and the household. "Your kind heart is one of the many things I love," he said, kissing the top of her head.

"But you don't know why I'm so devoted to Papa," Solenne replied.

"He's complicated."

"That's a polite way of saying he's an asshole."

"He did rescue me after my parents were killed."

"Because he thought you would be useful, which you are."

"See? Complicated. No one's action can be strictly black and white."

She twisted around to face him. "Please stop making excuses for Papa. I won't live in a house where you're merely tolerated. We'll go to Hardwick House. I want to see it."

"It's not much, truly."

"Your grandfather lived there. Perhaps there's a secret journal hidden in the floorboards. It could answer some questions."

Just like in one of her novels.

"I highly doubt it, but yes, after the wedding, we can visit. It won't be much of a honeymoon," he said, already mentally preparing the letter to have the house made ready for their arrival. The exterior needed a new coat of whitewash, as did all the interior rooms. Fresh paint would make the rooms seem brighter, but the furniture shabbier. New furniture then, at least for the master bedroom. Perhaps all the work would turn up a secret journal, however improbable.

Solenne

Boxon Hill

Marechal House - The Undercroft

THE UNLOCKED DOOR called to her. Dim light flickered at the bottom of the stairwell. For days, Godwin had avoided Solenne, and she hadn't sought his company.

"You're being childish," Luis said, before pushing her forward.

"He does not want to be disturbed."

"Talk to him."

"I cannot guarantee I will be civil." She grabbed onto the door frame, refusing to be bullied into a conversation with her father.

"Oh no, my delicate sensibilities," Luis said dryly. "Be an adult and talk to Papa. I'm worried. He hasn't been eating and you know how he gets."

She did indeed, and did not comment on the irony that Godwin's child had to be the adult in the relationship to take care of him.

"Please. You know him better than me."

"You know Papa."

Luis ran a hand through his dark curls. "I mean, you've seen him day in, day out for years. I only ever saw him on holidays from school and then he was on his best behavior."

"Holiday Papa," Solenne said, repeating the moniker she and Luis gave Godwin's jovial mood.

"Exactly. What I saw was upsetting. I'm worried about him." Luis somehow made his eyes larger and silently pleaded with those enormous eyes.

It was unbearable.

"Fine. Stop pushing me or I'll fall down the stairs." She switched on the solar-powered lantern to navigate her way down the stairs. Shadows hid the steps, so she made her way down cautiously, one hand on the shaky rail and the other holding the lantern aloft. The light was just enough to illuminate the cobwebs but not much else.

The basement held many relics from an age of wonder, all broken. The most dangerous—weapons her ancestors brought with them from the old world—had been locked away in a vault. Presumably, they held enough power or ammunition to be dangerous because Solenne couldn't see how the decrepit relics were dangerous now, unless she hurled them or used them as a bludgeon.

The bits of technology that worked were used until the very end, then patched together and pressed into service again. Hence, the flickering lights. The aging solar panels no longer captured enough energy to meet the needs of the house. Replacement panels were beyond the household budget. Solenne remembered scavenging panel parts with her mother. Too young to understand, she had thought it a grand adventure exploring empty buildings in abandoned villages.

The short corridor opened into a large workshop. To one side, the nexus batteries sat stacked on shelving units. Small readout screens glowed with violet light. Godwin perched on a stool by a workbench, bent over a device. Light pooled on the wooden surface around the lantern. The overhead lights flickered, casting strange shadows and illuminating little.

His hair was a tangled mess and his clothes dusty, but Godwin hardly looked emaciated and near death. Luis had drastically overstated the problem.

Solenne turned to leave, until Godwin spoke.

"Your mother had the patience for this." He pushed away the device.

"What is it?"

Godwin held up an ancient tablet, the screen a blank gray, and the back removed. "It's a reader, so my father claimed. It worked when he was a child. Contains hundreds of books in the memory banks, if we can get it to power on." He set it down, looking sheepish. "I thought you might like it for a wedding gift."

Solenne's anger softened. Her father spoke with actions rather than words, but she needed to hear the words. "An apology would also do."

He cleared his throat, voice gruff from disuse. "Yes, I suppose that's in order. I worry about losing you. Amalie was everything to me, and you and Luis are all I have left of her." He rubbed his chin, the bristles there more silver than Solenne remembered. "But you were correct. The tighter I hold on to you, the more you'll slip away. I'm sorry for not listening. I apologize for keeping Alek's true nature from you. I thought I was protecting you."

To keep from looking directly at her father, she inspected a shelf cluttered with bits and bobs, old cardboard boxes stained with dust and damp, and tools set down to never be put away in their proper place. Bits of shattered glass littered the shelf, and she realized with a jolt that she was looking at the detritus of the explosion that killed her mother. No one ever cleaned the workshop. Would she find bits of shrapnel in the walls? Blood on the stone floor?

"Solenne," Godwin said, grabbing her attention.

"Thank you," she said, not ready to forgive. Godwin's lack of an apology for his ugly words had not escaped her notice. If his actions changed, then yes. Her anger would dissolve.

She lined up boxes on the shelf. Labels, written in Amalie's neat hand, had faded with age. "I've been reading the handbooks. Older werewolves have absorbed more nexus energy, making them stronger and more resistant to silver."

"Yes, that's what the book says."

"The books never mention an anchor."

"No, I don't suppose they would," Godwin answered slowly.

"Why?"

He scrubbed a hand over his chin again. "Politics, I imagine. The first editions discussed anchors. What we have are later printings, after mention of anchors were purged."

"Politics."

"Yes, Solenne, politics. Not everyone is comfortable with the notion of a beast living among them, even a tame beast."

Her shoulders pulled back, ready for a fight. "Do not call Alek a beast."

Godwin held up his hands to placate her. "Maybe people and—what did you call him, a werewolf?—lived peacefully together in the beginning, but that changed. The mutations couldn't be contained. Entire settlements were lost in the West Lands. A few accounts of werewolves losing their anchors and destroying an entire village and people decided that they wouldn't tolerate any beast, anchored or not."

"So a purge."

"These notions are hard to unlearn. Wherever you go, if people find out about Alek's nature, they'll turn on him."

"His true nature, Papa, is a decent, caring man."

"Who turns furry and howls at the moon."

Father and daughter stared at each other.

"It'd be best if you stayed. People know him here. They'll be kind," Godwin said.

Still controlling, even when trying to make amends. The subtle digs at Alek, she didn't know if she could tolerate. No, correction. She refused to tolerate it, and she did not know if the protection Godwin reluctantly offered to Alek would be worth it.

"Thank you for the reader. I'm sure it'll be marvelous when you get it working," she said, retreating up the stairs.

Chapter Twenty

Aleksandar

Boxon Hill

Marechal House - The Library

"Alek, a word." Godwin did not wait for Alek to respond to his command, but headed into the library. He poured brandy into two glasses, handing Alek one. "My daughter has dug in her heels. Her heart is set on you."

Alek sipped the liquor, enjoying the burn as it slid down his throat. "I told you my intentions ten years ago. Nothing has changed."

"I'm not happy, Aleksandar. When you entered this house, you gave me your word."

"And I informed you that you misjudged your daughter."

The two men stared at each other until Godwin sighed heavily. He sat in a worn leather chair and rubbed where the patch rested against his check. "Never could tell that girl anything. Stubborn like Amalie." Another sigh. He drained his drink and contemplated the empty glass. "She won't forgive me until we make peace."

Alek's bit back his first instinct, which was to tell the old man that they did not need his permission or forgiveness, but he knew Solenne. She loved her family above all else. She could have gone anywhere in the last ten years, done anything, but she remained to help her father and brother. Her selflessness was more than familial duty. It was devotion.

She'd want to repair her relationship with Godwin. Perhaps not tomorrow or even the next year, but eventually.

"For Solenne," he said.

"Yes, I think we can agree on that," Godwin answered. "For reasons I don't understand, my daughter has her heart set on you. I shouldn't be surprised. You were always together as children, thick as thieves."

"Peapod," Alek said. Amalie had called them that, her peas in a pod.

"If I allow...no, I know you will tell me that there is nothing to allow. A poor choice of words."

"You need Solenne's forgiveness, not the other way around. I am not a child for you to scold or discipline."

"You don't think I know that?" Godwin snapped. "She was ill with that fever. I thought I could lose her and the last words we exchanged were hateful." He rubbed at the eyepatch again. "So, yes, I need Solenne's forgiveness and she won't do that until we are on speaking terms."

"We're speaking now." Yes, he was being obstinate and rather enjoying Godwin's face redden with frustration.

"Did you bite Solenne?"

"No, I did not," Alek answered.

"The family is largely resistant to the curse, but it is contagious. We're not a lucky lot, either. If you bite her —" Godwin stared at him with his one eye.

"I know the risk. I would never."

"And that other beast?"

"Laceration from the claws. Nothing else. Did you not discuss this with Dr. Webb?"

Godwin nodded. "I need two reassurances from you. One, you will never bite her and you will behave with decorum until the wedding."

"If I give you my word, you'll...tolerate my presence?"

"Insolent cur," Godwin muttered. He lurched to his feet. "If you behave like a gentleman and do not chew my daughter or sully her honor, then I will treat you like a gentleman."

Alek held Godwin's gaze, listening to the man's heart. It beat rapidly and his breaths were even. He sensed no dishonesty.

"Agreed, but I cannot make Solenne forgive you. Her mind is her own." He held out his hand, and they shook.

Solenne

Respectable ladies did not listen at doors. Fortunately, Solenne could never be bothered with appearances.

As heavy footsteps approached the door—she recognized her father's gait—she scurried away and ducked into a nearby door, which happened to be a linen closet. Lavender and soap made her nose itch, but she patiently waited until Godwin's footsteps vanished.

She entered the library, finding Alek holding a glass of dark liquor and staring at Tristan.

"Horrid, isn't he? Poor Tristan," she said.

He grunted assent then said, "We shouldn't be unchaperoned."

"Nonsense, I'm having a brandy. You're having a brandy. We just happen to be in the same place with the brandy. It's hardly scandalous." She poured herself a measure of what she assumed was brandy and took a drink. "Ugh, that's awful. You like this?"

"I never made that claim," he said with amusement in his voice.

"Waste not, want not," she said, downing the rest of the brandy before she could think better of it. The liquor seared a trail down her throat and warmed her gut. "We should ask Papa to give Tristan a proper funeral pyre and return his ashes to his family. It'd be, you know, a symbol of forgiveness and…" She groped for the correct word. "Wow, that is rather strong. I think brandy is growing on me."

"I think it's a good idea," Alek said, taking the bottle from her hand.

"Marvelous." She frowned. She had never been the type of person who proclaimed things to be marvelous. That was Charlotte. She was more the frown in vague disapproval and mutter under the breath sort of person. Perhaps brandy was not for her. "What did Papa want?"

"You know very well as you were listening at the door the entire time."

She grinned, unable to help herself. "Papa is trying to make amends."

"He's rather bad at it."

"But he's trying. You know, he tried to butter me up with a, what's it, a relic. A reader, he called it. No bigger than my hand, and it holds thousands of books. Can you imagine?" The device seemed too good to be true and she wouldn't expect it to work, but Godwin had picked the perfect token to win his daughter.

And then he reached out—albeit badly—to Alek.

Papa *listened* and, honestly, she could not recall that ever happening since she returned home from university.

"We should celebrate," she said, positively glowing with happiness and brandy. Mostly brandy.

She grabbed his hand and drew him to the overstuffed chair by the fire. Alek allowed himself to be pushed down, and she sat on his lap. Her arms wrapped around his neck and she leaned in for a kiss.

He responded with a quick press of lips, dry and chaste.

Disappointing.

"I promised your father to be respectful. A respectful man does not kiss his fiancée in her father's library."

She gave an anguished groan. "You can kiss and be respectful."

"Solenne—"

"This moral uprightness is rather bothersome. I can't say I approve."

"One kiss, then you'll go to bed."

"Just one," she agreed, already planning to wheedle more out of him.

Another dry peck on the lips.

"No, unacceptable," she said, slapping a hand to his chest. "A proper kiss or we keep practicing until you improve."

He leaned in, mouth on her. His tongue licked her lips, asking for entrance, and she opened for him. He tasted of brandy and the forest and wild things. Warm from the brandy or perhaps warm from proximity to him, her skin sparked at every touch. Fingers tangled in hair. Chests pressed together. Collars were hastily unbuttoned to allow for kisses. The chair groaned. She straddled him in an undignified manner and his fingers dug into her hips. She could feel him, the hard evidence of his want and desire.

She pulled back, chest heaving. Alek watched her, eyes dark with a touch of violet of a predator's eyes.

"Hmm. I believe this requires more practice," she said.

And they did.

Chapter Twenty-One

Solenne

Boxon

Vervain Hall

Charlotte had always displayed a high level of organization, but preparing for the double wedding catapulted her onto another level. Honestly, it frightened Solenne. When Charlotte appeared with her ever-expanding notebook and took out her rainbow-hued quill to make notes, Solenne trembled. Charlotte was not a woman to be crossed, which was how she and Alek ended up at Colonel Chambers' dinner party.

"I do not like this," Alek grumbled, tugging at the knot of his cravat. "This is strangling me."

"Stop fussing." She retied his cravat, then stepped back to admire her handiwork. Lacking evening wear, she dug an outfit out of the back of Godwin's wardrobe. Fashion moved slowly in the country, and Godwin was no longer as slim as he had once been.

The dark blue velvet coat, blue brocade waistcoat, and tan breeches suited Alek, even if he kept tugging at the cravat. "You look very handsome."

"This shirt itches."

"Can't be helped. Try not to ruin it. You only have the one shirt."

"I have many shirts."

"One presentable shirt," she clarified. She had witnessed Alek parade around in shirts with the collar open, sans cravat, the fabric so threadbare that he wore practically nothing. While she heartily supported his radical aesthetic, society placed many undue pressures on a person, including itchy shirts.

They approached Colonel Chambers' home, the gravel path to the front of the estate once more lit by braziers.

"It's one dinner. Eat what they serve. Don't growl. Laugh at jokes," Solenne said.

"I refuse. I am not an animal trained to laugh at a buffoon's japes," Alek complained.

"Well, that buffoon offered to pay for our wedding, so no growling." Chambers hadn't made any demands or intimated that his generosity came with strings attached other than indulging Charlotte. Still, better to be polite.

"I would be happy with a small ceremony at the magistrate's office."

"As would I, but this will be over soon."

"Four days."

"Yes." A tingle of excitement went up her spine. Four days until the wedding. It hardly seemed real, and there was much left to do, like the last fitting of her new dress and arranging travel plans. She wanted to leave the day after the wedding to Alek's house to arrive before the equinox, with plenty of time to spend lazing in bed in inns along the way. "I can hardly wait," she said, laying her hand on his arm as they approached the front steps.

The door burst open, and Charlotte spilled out, massive notebook and quill in hand. "Oh, thank the stars! It's a disaster. Come in. Hurry."

Charlotte ushered them to the drawing room, already occupied with Colonel Chambers and two other people she did not recognize. Charlotte made hasty introductions for Mrs. Parkell and the doctor from Founding, Dr. Sheldon. Nothing in the room made Solenne think they were amid disaster.

The room was decorated in a heavy-handed retired military man sort of style. Weapons adorned the walls, ranging from antique colonial energy blasters, more modern and gunpowder-based firearms, swords, the occasional spear and poleaxe, and a variety of daggers arranged artfully like a sunburst. Each piece was museum-quality, but more importantly, each weapon had the distinction of appearing well used, and maintained in a functional state.

As for the colonial weapons, Solenne wouldn't trust one of those to fire without taking off the shooter's hand.

"Admiring my collection? I picked up a few odds and ends in my travels. Let's have a drink while we wait for dinner," Chambers said. While he poured, Charlotte pulled Solenne to one divan.

"It's terrible," her friend lamented. "Poor Jase was examined today, and he absolutely cannot get out of bed for another three weeks."

"I thought he was improving," Solenne said. She had not spoken to Jase since the night of the solstice when he apologized for his rudeness, but Charlotte kept her abreast of his condition.

"Slowly, but this means we must delay the wedding because Lionel insists that Jase attend, which of course he must. Three weeks will put us at the autumn equinox."

Three weeks. Disappointing.

"Other than the delay, what is the disaster?" Solenne asked.

"It's not, you know, a problem?" Charlotte glanced across the room at Alek.

Solenne replayed the conversation they had when Charlotte gave her the infamous book. Had she inadvertently dropped a clue that implicated Alek? Or had Charlotte pieced it together on her own?

Probably. Clever friends proved such an inconvenience when one had a secret to keep.

She plastered a forced smile on her face. "No problem, other than the disappointment of waiting."

"Oh, I know, and I'm mightily apologetic. Though, I confess, I am glad to have you for a few weeks more before you run off to Alek's homestead. Waiting is so odious." Charlotte smiled at Chambers across the room. He returned the smile, which struck Solenne as odd. She had never seen Chambers wear any other expression than grim determination, even while he had been half-heartedly courting her. What a strange visage Chambers made while happy.

"Is there a problem, my sweet?" he asked.

"Just our mutual disappointment in delaying the wedding," Charlotte replied.

"Ah, yes, understandable but necessary. I've made arrangements for the day before the equinox, if that's agreeable to you and Aleksandar?" Chambers looked toward Alek, who joined the conversation.

"The day before? You're not worried about the beast?" Alek asked.

"The beast is dead. What better reason to celebrate?" Chambers gave Alek a hearty slap on the back. "Unless you think there's two beasts in one territory?"

Alek's lips pulled back into a smile that was a touch more menacing than charming. "No, that's unheard of. The day before the equinox is splendid."

Solenne swore the thread connecting them whispered that it wasn't too late to abscond to the magistrate.

Tempting.

"I told Lionel not to worry about the fuss of a big church wedding," Mrs. Parkell said, wandering over with an empty glass in hand. Her cheeks were flushed a rosy red from alcohol. "Weddings are all the same, and he's done it once before, but I suppose he wants to indulge you, Charlotte." She gestured with the empty glass until Chambers took it to be refilled.

"You were married before?" Charlotte asked.

"Oh, he hasn't told you? Years ago, when he was in the military. Margaret. Maggie. The drabbest creature I ever saw."

"Maggie died of a fever," Chambers said smoothly, his voice calm despite the irritation on his face. "As you said, it was a long time ago." The dinner gong sounded, and a look of relief flashed over him. "Come, I'm famished. Let's eat."

Aleksandar

Boxon

The Blacksmithy

The heat of the forge hit him like a wall. Not looking up from the workbench, Miles gestured for Alek to wait. He stayed in the doorway to avoid the sweltering heat, but still removed his coat. The blacksmith wore long sleeves, protective gear, and a helmet, and Alek did not understand how the man avoided melting into a puddle.

Miles turned off the propane torch, set down his tools, and stripped off his gloves and helmet. "Making a few improvements in the armor. The devil is in the details. Come on back," he said, waving to the storeroom in the back.

As Alek passed the workbench, he admired the skillfully wrought armor. "Another new set?" That would be the third set Miles made since the solstice.

"I'm not happy with the seams. They're the weak point. The material can resist a near infinite amount of damage, but it doesn't stay together after six or seven events."

"An event would be a bite?" Alek asked, not remembering to whom he spoke.

Miles paled. "Any sudden impact, but yes, a bite."

Heavy curtains kept the back room dim. The thick stone walls kept it several degrees cooler than the workshop. Miles pulled the curtains open, and light slanted through. He retrieved a small box from a shelf and held it to the light, and then revealed the contents.

Two silver rings gleamed in the afternoon light, iridescent and unnaturally bright, like forged moonlight.

Alek examined the smaller ring. A plain band, the design let the material shine. Literally. Colors shifted from blue to purple to pink and to gold, depending on how he turned it.

"Odreylium," Miles said. "Found only at nexus points. Difficult to find and tricky to work with, but I think I managed. It has some really interesting properties, such as its rigid to the touch. Give it a squeeze."

Alek gently squeezed the band, finding it firm and just like every other piece of jewelry.

"Right? But when hit with sudden force, it's pliable." Miles took the other ring and smashed it into the wall and then looked at Alek with something like triumph. When Alek failed to give appropriate noises of appreciation, he frowned. "Oh, um, well, it's hard to see. You must try it yourself. Flexible under stress. I thought it was a suitable metaphor for marriage."

"It is." Alek clenched his fist around the ring, attempting to crush it, and found it had give and bounce. Solenne would especially like the metaphor. "Impressive. Thank you. How much?" As he had never heard of odreylium, he expected a hefty price tag.

"It's a gift."

"Difficult to find and tricky to work with," Alek said, using Miles' own words against him.

"Yes, well, I consider Solenne a friend. I wanted to do this for her."

Alek accepted the ring box with thanks and tucked it into his coat pocket.

"Actually, there is something you can do for me," Miles said, nervousness creeping into his voice. He looked out the door to make sure the workshop remained empty. "Is it true that your kind, people with your affliction, can sense others?"

Alek's first response was to deny, but Miles saw his partial shift on the solstice. Even if the blacksmith had been too consumed with his own injuries to notice,

Luis would have told him. He asked, "How is your bite healing?"

"Dr. Webb tells me to be patient, but he is not concerned. Now is it true?"

"Usually. I can't really explain how, but like calls to like."

"And me? Can you sense it in me?"

Alek studied the man, taking in the mess of blonde hair, limp from sweat, and the high ruddy color to his cheeks. He had a deceptively lean build that was solid muscle. In a smartly tailored coat and a starched cravat, he could have easily masqueraded as a clerk or a banker or a barrister. Alek saw lots of things in Miles—his intellect, the power in his hands, and the worry in his eyes—but he did not sense the beast.

He shook his head. "Nothing."

Miles slumped, leaning against the door frame. "A month until the equinox. This uncertainty is torture. I suppose you had to wait and accepted it with grim stoicism."

Alek held his tongue. His first shift happened immediately, but Miles did not need to know that. Most people had to wait a full cycle. Instead, he asked, "And the need to make a lifetime's supply of armor?"

"For Luis, obviously. If the worst happens, I won't be able to make more." Miles dug a cloth out of a pocket and ran it over his brow. "Sorry. I know you're fine, and I won't presume to know how, but I can't expect the same in my situation. I have to prepare for the worst."

Miles looked to Alek, and he knew what boon the man would ask of him.

"Please don't," Alek mumbled.

"If the worst happens, will you—"

Alek gave a quick nod. He would not enjoy it, but he would if need be.

"Clean and quick? Luis is attempting to drown me in wolfsbane tea and he has this idea of a cage, but I won't. I can't do that again." He rubbed at his wrists. Alek remembered when a youthful Miles arrived at the village to be apprenticed to the blacksmith, a man known for his foul temper. He did not know of the man's history or what he suffered at his master's hands, and it seemed the wrong moment to ask.

"Luis has the right idea. The condition can be mitigated. Tonics are helpful. You see proof of that."

Miles worried at his bottom lip. "Yes, you're probably right, but if not? I care little for premonitions, but I have this recurring nightmare."

"Just dreams? Any other symptoms?"

Miles shook his head, and Alek breathed a sigh of relief. "Clean and quick," he promised. "Now, this need to armor Luis—" His tone teased, desperate to change the direction of the conversation.

"It's not like that."

"It's like that for him."

"I know." Miles sighed. "I enjoy his company and consider him a friend, but attraction has always come slowly for me. I can't give him what he wants now, and he's so young," he added, almost as an afterthought.

"You're a year younger than me. That makes it no more than ten years between you and Luis."

"Nine, but you know what I mean." Miles waved a hand.

Alek wasn't sure he did. Luis was very much grown. Alek had missed the day-to-day slow march from child to adult, though. Still, he had an air of youthful optimism about him, which Alek rather liked. "I imagine such a change would be difficult to accept."

The man's face brightened. "Yes. He is my friend, and I do care for him. That's why if the worst happens, I couldn't ask him to—"

"Yes, I see," Alek said. Miles cared too much to ask Luis to end his life if the curse befell him. The rings in his coat pocket felt heavier for the price Miles asked.

Still, if his only symptoms were bad dreams, then he would likely avoid the curse. Alek felt confident he'd never have to honor his promise.

Chapter Twenty-Two

Solenne

Boxon Hill

Marechal House - Solenne's Bedroom

It rained the morning of the wedding.

"Cheer up. It's not an omen," Luis said, delivering a tray packed with pastries.

Solenne turned away from the window. "I never said it was an omen, and are those almond croissants? Cook made almond croissants?" Cook usually saved those for a special treat, birthdays and the like. She stuffed one in her mouth, barely chewing. "Oh, these are so good."

Luis reached for one, and Solenne slapped his hand away. "No. Bad brother. Cook made them for me."

"Cook made them for everyone."

"On my wedding day. Get your own wedding day," she said, causing him to blush. "Fine. One. You can have the muffins." Starberries stained the muffins a deep magenta. On a normal morning, Solenne more than happily smothered them with butter before devouring, but there were almond croissants to be had.

Luis uncovered a plate with fluffy scrambled eggs, still steaming. "Cook also said to eat something besides sugar, or you won't last the day."

"Thank you. Pull the chair over. There's more than enough to share."

With the tray balanced on the bedside table, Luis dragged over the old green chair. "Nervous?" he asked, grabbing a muffin.

"No," she lied.

"Wow, you are a terrible liar. It's insulting how bad you are. Like, are you even trying?"

She kicked his feet. "I'm not nervous about the ceremony, just everything that comes after."

He nodded, which would have been sagely, but he stuffed another muffin in his mouth. "I wish you weren't leaving so soon. Papa calmed down."

She shook her head. Godwin's reluctant acceptance was only part of the issue. The atmosphere in the house felt electric, like before a storm. There would always be a reason to delay departure or stay.

She fell into that trap when she left university on a temporary break, to help Godwin set his finances in order and get the house under control. She fully intended to return, even though she had to pay her own way, but she kept putting it off until returning to her studies seemed impossible.

It was bad enough she and Alek had to wait out the effects of the equinox. Once that had passed, they were off because she feared that if she and Alek did not leave soon, they would never leave.

"He can barely speak a civil word to Alek. I won't let Papa treat Alek as inferior. I'm sorry, I can't abide by it," she said.

Luis nodded. "It'll be strange not having you here. You've always been…here. I'm envious, actually. You get to see the world, or at least bits of it."

"We're going to Alek's property. That's hardly traveling the globe."

"The only place I've ever been to is boarding school."

Solenne hid a yawn behind her hand.

"Did you get any sleep?" Luis asked.

"Nerves kept me up, so I did a bit of packing." Two trunks sat against the far wall.

"Wow. Alek will have to hire another cart just for your luggage."

"Oh, hush. I packed light. I don't know how long we'll be or what condition the house will be in."

"How much of that is books?"

"I only packed a dozen books." Two dozen, but why split hairs. Plus, she wanted to bring a decent stock of herbs and medicine with her. A few plant clippings would be helpful, too. There wasn't time. She had weeks to prepare, and there wasn't enough time.

She glanced at the rain outside the window.

"It's nearly time. Do you need help with your hair?" Luis brushed away crumbs as he stood.

"I thought I'd wear it down."

Already wearing the proper undergarments, Luis helped her button the back of the dress. It was a soft linen of deep indigo, embroidered with green leaves and hooded purple blossoms at the hem and neckline.

Wolfsbane, a common decoration for good luck. How fitting.

A knock sounded at the door. "The coach is waiting." Godwin entered, dressed in a finely tailored outfit of dove gray. Other than the waistcoat, it matched Luis' outfit.

"You look beautiful," he said, sounding a bit dazed. "Just like your mama. I don't think I've told you, but you and Luis are both made in her image. It's like Amalie never left me."

Solenne resisted the urge to fuss with her hair. "Thank you, Papa."

Silence stretched awkwardly between them.

"Luis, give us a moment," Godwin said, fussing with the cloak draped over his arm. When the door shut behind Luis, he said, "You really do look like your mother."

"The coach is waiting," she prompted, because the moment felt sticky, like it would trap her.

"Right, right. It's raining, and I thought you'd need something to wear." He presented the cloak with a flourish, rich blue velvet the color of twilight. Crystal beads decorated the edge of the hood and around the clasp.

The weight of the cloak settled over her, warm like an embrace. Godwin raised the hood and fastened the clasp. The length was ideal, stopping mid-calf. She ran a hand over the fabric, appreciating how it was made for her and wondering how her father afforded such a thing.

"Your mother wore this on our wedding day," Godwin said. Her eyes watered. Godwin cleared his throat, looking everywhere but at her. "I wish you wouldn't leave. I need you here, I'll always need you here, but I understand that you must go. I wanted you to know that you'll always have a place here, you and Alek."

Solenne threw her arms around her father, fully crying now and not caring if her dress wrinkled. "Oh, Papa, thank you."

Aleksandar

Boxon

The Chapel

Gravel crunched underfoot as Alek paced. He tugged at the cravat around his throat, somehow making it tighter. He hated how constrained he felt in his new suit, like the coat had been cut for a slimmer man. If he raised his arms, he felt the seams would rip.

He did not need a fancy ceremony with special clothes that seemed designed for discomfort. He only needed Solenne.

The clock in the village square struck noon.

Things happened, and he could not say how.

The coach arrived. He stood at the altar, awkward next to Chambers.

Solenne entered the chapel like the sun.

Thump. Thump. Thump.

The golden thread between them hummed and sang, and he was lost in the joy of it until only snapping out of his reverie when prompted to kiss the bride.

His bride.

Chapter Twenty-Three

Solenne

Boxon

Vervain Hall

Married.

Solenne couldn't stop smiling or holding Alek's hand. Not that she wanted to. She wanted to remain in this moment, blissful with the demands of the world at bay.

Well, not at this exact moment. She would very much like to skip ahead to the evening portion when she'd be alone with her husband.

Her husband. The thought made her heart sing, and the golden thread connecting her to Alek sang back.

"How long must we perform for the masses?" he asked, gripping her hand. Despite his grumble, she felt his genuine emotion of elation through their bond. It was a heady thing, being an anchor.

"It's a reception. At least until we finish the meal. I'm sure everyone will expect us to leave early," she said. "We'll muddle through, Mr. Hardwick."

"Don't leave my side, Mrs. Hardwick," he replied, looking entirely pleased with himself.

True to Charlotte's word, Colonel Chambers' home—her home now—had been decorated with restraint. Late summer blooms and greenery crowded nearly every surface, which seemed to be her one indulgence.

Solenne had feared, well, she wasn't sure beyond an embarrassing amount of money spent on temporary decorations like ice sculptures or edible gold flakes in the sparkling wine. She read that once in a book, and it seemed like the biggest waste of money imaginable, so it remained her gold standard—forgive the pun—for frivolousness.

Doors open to the terrace, allowing in the fresh air. The crowd milled about outside, and Solenne swore it was every person from the village and then some. She didn't know how the house could hold so many people.

"Is it too much? It's too much," Charlotte said, taking Solenne by the arm and steering them upstairs. Alek closely followed, despite Charlotte's withering gaze. "The gardener asked me what flowers I wanted and I couldn't decide, so I said all of them."

"No, it's lovely."

"Good. I know you're leaving soon, so thank you for indulging me. I wanted this last memory of *us* together before we're parted." She glanced back at Alek.

Subtlety did not work on werewolves.

"I'll be a few days away. It's hardly the other side of the world," Solenne said.

"But for how long?"

"I'm sure we'll be back in the spring."

Charlotte made a noise of disbelief. "You say that, but the roads will be poor or you'll be sickly or some other reason."

"The post does run to Snowmelt," Alek said dryly.

Another noise, this one more incredulous. "Even the name is horrible."

"Where are we going?" Solenne asked. Charlotte had led them into a part of the house she had never been before.

Voices sounded from down the hall. She paled, then pulled Solenne in through the nearest door. She closed the door carefully, as if to avoid any sound.

Voices approached, both male and sounding irritated as they debated some matter. Alek tensed, and she felt his alertness through the bond. The thickness of the door and the carpeting prevented her from making out the words beyond, "You will do as I say."

Chambers.

"Who is—"

Charlotte held up a finger to silence her.

Another voice responded. She recognized Jase's haughty tone. Their voices grew faint as the men walked past.

Charlotte sagged with relief. Somehow, her friend didn't appear as happy as she claimed to be.

Alek must have sensed her alarm, because he pressed Charlotte for an explanation. "You smell unhappy, and it is making my mate unhappy. Fix it."

Werewolves did not do subtlety either.

"Honestly, Alek."

"No, he is correct. I have doubts," Charlotte said.

"Doubts? Doubts! Then why did you go through with the wedding?" Solenne demanded.

"Because my imagination runs away with me and keep your voice down. Lionel does not like anyone in his study."

"Then why are we in here?"

"I need you to open this drawer," Charlotte said.

"I'm sorry, what?" The rapid change in topic could make a person dizzy.

Charlotte chewed on her lower lip, then leaned in. Her voice was hushed, nearly a whisper. "I have not been forthright with you. I fear Lionel is keeping something important from me. He did not tell me about his late wife. I only discovered that because his sister let it slip. What else is he keeping from me?"

Solenne's first impulse was to console her friend, to gently chide that she should have confided her doubts. Perhaps Solenne should have sensed the unease in Charlotte, but she had been ill and busy with the wedding.

No. Charlotte called on Solenne a dozen times to discuss wedding plans. Never once did she hint that anything was amiss, and she had never been shy about sharing her worries.

"You just want to be a nosy busybody, and I won't be part of it," Solenne said.

Light leaked into the room through the drapes. A large, heavy desk dominated the room. A bookcase lined one wall while a display cabinet ran the length of the other.

If Chambers had filled his home with weapons and souvenirs of military campaigns, this was an altar to the original colonists. Solenne recognized the heavy battery cubes, similar to the ones in her mother's workshop. There was a handheld device whose purpose she had no idea, the screen gray and blank. A helmet, pristine and without a scratch, sat next to a blue and green sphere.

Solenne peered closely at the sphere. It was unlike anything she had ever seen. A topographical map covered the surface, but it was not the familiar landmass she knew. These continents were unknown to her.

"Is that the old world? Earth?" Her fingers twitched, wanting to touch the globe but fearful of damaging the relic. Everything on display was priceless and belonged in a museum.

"Yes. This is Lionel's study and his private collection. I know there's something serious he's keeping from me and I know it's horrible to involve you, but please? Can you open the drawer? You're ever so clever with these things."

Solenne looked at the solid wood drawer and the rather sturdy lock. "I don't know how to pick locks."

"But you're so clever with tools—"

"Tools? What do you think I do?"

"Something with herbs." Charlotte waved her hand in a manner that suggested any number of things, like whipping up potions or being a master thief with an extensive set of lockpicks.

"I believe this is my area of expertise," Alek said. He grabbed a rather wicked-looking letter opener from the desk and shimmied it between the drawer and the desk. Clearly he had no compunction about invading a man's privacy, a flaw rooted in his dislike of Chambers. After a few moments of wiggling the blade, the lock clicked, and the drawer opened.

Alek gave her a triumphant grin, twirling the letter opener between his fingers.

"When did you become so dodgy?" she asked, a little breathless at the sight. Honestly, such a display was crass, but she found herself appreciative of her husband's less savory skills.

Her husband.

Solenne purred at the notion.

Alek quirked a brow, and that connection between them buzzed. Her toes curled, and she wanted nothing more than to skip the reception waiting downstairs and go directly to the wedding night.

"Oh, how odd," Charlotte murmured, disrupting Solenne's less-than-modest thoughts. Her friend unrolled a detailed architect's drawing of Marechal House.

"Why does Colonel Chambers have the blueprints for my house?" Several Xs and notations cluttered the map, written in a hurried hand.

The doorknob rattled, giving just enough warning for Charlotte to shove the papers back into the drawer.

"What's going on in here?" Chambers asked. He loomed in the door, somehow taking the light from the room. Solenne wanted to dip her neck and beg forgiveness.

"Oh, darling, I wanted to show Solenne your globe of the Earth. You know how she loves colonial history. I fully expect her and Alek to be too occupied to visit before they leave," Charlotte said, her voice bubbly and without a hint of mistruth. Even knowing the truth about the locked desk drawer, Solenne wanted to believe her.

When did Charlotte learn to lie so effectively? Could she teach Solenne?

"Hmm, it is interesting," Chambers intoned. His gaze swept over the room, as if searching for mischief.

"I can't believe how much of the old world was covered in water," Solenne said.

"And why are you huddled around my desk?"

Alek snatched a pencil and a blank sheet of paper off the desk. "I'm writing the address for our new home in Snowmelt. Despite popular opinion, the post does run."

"Well, hurry. Our guests are waiting," Chambers said.

Aleksandar

This house. Something about it made his skin crawl. Heavy drapes cut off the light and fresh air, giving the house a suffocating feel. Weapons of destruction had been strewn about like toys. Servants moved quietly, each footstep made with such care like they were afraid to make a noise. They might as well have been ghosts.

All because of Chambers.

He disliked the man, and not just over the rivalry for Solenne's affections. That had never been a contest. Her heart had always belonged to him, even when they both tried to deny it.

No, his dislike stemmed from something more nebulous and difficult to pinpoint. Something about how he moved, too graceful for a man who claimed an injury ended his military career. Or perhaps how he watched Solenne and Charlotte as they descended the staircase to greet the wedding guests. His eyes were too hungry. Alek recognized the look because it stared back at him from a mirror often enough.

Too many people crowded downstairs. There was too much noise and heat.

"Is that Vervain? *The* Vervain? Colonel Chambers, how did you find that?" Luis stood in front of a rather tired-looking long sword with a dull blade, rusted at the hilt.

"Drink. Enjoy. You're a lucky man," Chambers said, handing Alek a glass of wine before answering Luis. "One of my first pieces. The old man I bought it from claimed it to be so. I thought it was a fine example of early craftsmanship, if a bit worse for wear. I'm afraid I'm a bit sentimental for the old thing."

Luis made appreciative noises and pointed out features to Miles. The blacksmith held his own glass of wine and nodded, seemingly as interested in the antique longsword as Luis.

"I only wish Charlotte looked at me with half the devotion Solenne looks at you," Chambers said.

The women in question were standing at the foot of the stairs. Apparently, everyone in the village came and had to share words with the brides. Jase Parkell hobbled with the use of a crutch, his mother at his side. Mrs. Parkell had a pinched look on her face, but she always did.

Jase looked over his shoulder, as if he wanted to escape. Alek couldn't blame the man. The few days on the road he spent with the woman had been too many.

Charlotte smiled graciously. She was pretty with her curls and a laugh that drifted above the noise of the crowd, but she paled to Solenne. Everyone did.

"From the way you look at Solenne, I see the affection is mutual," Chambers said.

"It's more than affection," Alek said, speaking before he could guess himself. "She's always been my anchor. When I knew no one, she was my friend. When my family had been killed, she told me I was not alone. She's the bedrock of my existence. My purpose. My heart. Without her, I am nothing." Alek frowned at the glass in his hands. Wine rarely loosened his tongue.

"I must confess. I am jealous of the devotion between you. I had hoped—"

"Do not tell me you regret your marriage," Alek said in a sudden swell of protectiveness for the woman. He hardly knew Charlotte Wodehouse—Chambers—and could not account for it. "Charlotte may not shine as brightly as the sun, but she's a good person. A bit too kind-hearted, if you ask me, but that's not a flaw. Do not treat her poorly. I would not take kindly to that." He frowned, both at repeating the word kind and at his threat.

"What I do with my wife is no concern of yours," Chambers said. "You'll barely be able to keep your bride from freezing or starving this winter. I tried to convince her otherwise, but Solenne has this stubborn attachment to you." His tone made it sound like an infection.

"It's a bond between souls."

Damn this wine. He set down the glass on the nearest surface.

"I know very well it's a bond, and I'm not fool enough to break it." Chambers' voice was nearly a growl. He paused, smoothing the front of his waistcoat. A placid smile replaced his disgruntled expression. "Did you find anything interesting when you were rummaging through my study?"

He watched Alek keenly for a response.

"Couldn't get the drawer open," Alek said with a shrug. The lie came easily.

"Charlotte's idea, I imagine. She's too curious for her own good. Well, I guess I'll introduce my bride to her first taste of discipline a little sooner than planned."

Alek disliked everything about the man, from his superior tone, the waistcoat with embroidered bluebirds, and the way he licked his lips when he spoke of punishing his wife.

"Do not hurt Charlotte," Alek said, because an injury to Charlotte was an injury to Solenne. The warning sprang from more than a protective instinct. The thought this vile man desired Solenne, wanted to put his hands on her and would take pleasure from inflicting pain—

The beast wanted out. Now. This man was a threat.

Alek clenched his hands, claws digging into his palms. He hung onto his control. Barely. The bond between him and Solenne shivered with concern.

"Or what? Don't be greedy. One anchor is enough for man or beast, eh?" Chambers jabbed a finger at Alek, prompting a growl. A triumphant grin spread across Chambers' face. "How curious, Hardwick. Are you quite yourself?"

Alek brushed away the man's hand. He knew. Alek betrayed himself, and Chambers was the sort of man to press his advantage.

"You know, I never enjoyed hunting down your kind. It seemed cruel, chasing down beasts who were so simple-minded. There was no challenge to it, but you've been a challenge."

Alek wanted to deny it, to proclaim his status as an unadulterated human, but something in the man's gaze made that impossible. Alek was old in beast years. People with his affliction seldom lived more than a handful of months. The level of control, or power, radiating off Chambers was unimaginable. Alek felt the urge to bend his neck to the superior wolf.

The mask had come off. Alek knew before whom he stood. "Like calls to like," he said.

Chambers blinked, breaking the hold. "So it seems."

Alek stepped back. "I should make a polite excuse, but why bother. I'm finding my wife and leaving." She would be displeased with him, but she would be safe.

He found her in the dining room, sitting between Charlotte and Godwin. She laughed and picked at a plate with those little bites of food that never really satisfied a hungry person.

"There are too many people," he grumbled, unaware of the looks he drew.

"Alek? Are you well? You look...odd," Luis said.

He ignored Luis and rushed to Solenne, grabbing her arm. She lost her grip on her plate, sending it tumbling to the table. Those little bits of food scattered, ruining the clean linen. She gasped.

"We're leaving," he said.

Laughter from a nearby table. "Can't wait, Hardwick?" Jase asked, as if he were clever.

"What? Why?" Solenne's smile fell.

"I have no time for this." He scrubbed at his face. He was doing this wrong, and that frustrated him. His senses felt muddled. Alcohol did not have that effect on him. Chambers had dosed the wine with something, but he did not understand what. "Can you do as I say and not argue?"

Well, that was the wrong thing to say.

Solenne pulled back. "Excuse me?"

"Aleksandar, I think you need to take a moment to control yourself." Godwin laid a hand on his shoulder.

Alek jerked away, snarling. His hip bumped into the table, sending plates, glasses, cutlery, food and all the assorted detritus of dining to the floor.

"Do not presume to order me about," he growled. He turned to Solenne, forming his words carefully despite the sense that his mouth was too crowded. "Solenne, I would not ask you if it was not important." He glanced down at the overturned plate. "Perhaps Charlotte should come with us."

Godwin made more barking noises, blustering and without meaning. Luis appeared, pressing a glass of water into his hand. For some reason, Miles was there, retrieving the cutlery and plates from the floor. Alek rubbed his temples. Everything was too loud and too hot. He wanted to find a secluded corner and sit in the dark.

Solenne looked at him with concern. "Do you require something? For a headache?"

He nodded, his brain jiggling uncomfortably with the motion.

Miles gasped, dropping the fork. A vivid red burn branded his palm.

Chapter Twenty-Four

Aleksandar

Boxon

Vervain Hall

Alek turned to Luis, grabbing the young man by the arm. "Did Miles drink the wine?"

"What? Of course. We've all had some wine," Luis said.

Everyone spoke at once. Alek closed his eyes, trying to think. Chambers knew about Alek's condition, and he knew about Miles having been bitten. "Get him somewhere safe. He's not in control of himself," Alek said.

"Don't touch him!" Miles rushed toward Alek, snarling.

He sidestepped the man, moving more sluggish than he liked. Miles crashed into a table. Gasps echoed through the room.

"What are you doing?" Charlotte stood at the table, her wedding finery sparkling in the candlelight.

"I say!" Jase lurched up on his one good leg.

Alek snarled at the man. Distracted, he failed to notice Miles as he moved for Charlotte. Apparently, his irritation with Alek was forgotten.

In a quick motion, Miles had the bride by the throat and pulled her forward, across the table. Dishes crashed. Glasses spilled and rolled to the floor before breaking. She screamed, weak and thin as the blacksmith crushed the air from her throat. Her face turned red. People shouted, rushing for the door. Furniture overturned.

All the while, her husband watched with folded arms and a bored air.

Alek stumbled forward, his legs not responding correctly. He just couldn't move fast enough. It felt like lead weights held down his feet.

Damn Chambers. He'd tear the man's throat out with his bare teeth for this, and he didn't care who watched. His claws came out, and he felt his fangs descend.

Yes, ripping out throats seemed like a wonderful idea.

Godwin's cane appeared behind Miles, pressing against the man's throat. The man leveraged his weight, forcing Miles to release his grip on Charlotte or be choked.

Miles threw his head back, bashing it into Godwin's face. Blood poured from a likely broken nose.

Sweet blood. Godwin's injury pleased the beast inside him. The older man deserved to bleed for all the misery he inflicted.

Alek finally reached the grappling man. Miles twisted, slashing out with claws. He missed Alek, but Alek had not been his target.

He raked Godwin's stomach. Scarlet red blood bloomed across his evening clothes. He looked at Alek in surprise, as if trying to blame this on him, and then collapsed to the floor.

Miles was back to Charlotte. He swiped, she ducked, but he grazed her scalp.

Alek tackled the out-of-control man. "Calm. Do not make me hurt you," he said, growling behind his words.

For a moment, the man stilled, as if responding to Alek's command.

"Good. I will help you. You wanted me to help," Alek said.

Something in Miles' eyes snapped. He foamed at the mouth, all teeth and snarling. With surprising strength —it shouldn't have been a surprise, since the blacksmith was all wiry muscle—he flipped Alek onto his back. Claws dug into his gut. Alek twisted, trying to dislodge the man, but that made the claws dig in deeper.

"Not him! Her!" Chambers finally moved, grabbing his wife and shaking her by the arm like a rag doll. "What is wrong with you? Why don't I care if you die? Where is our bond?"

Solenne

Solenne knocked Chambers' hand away. It wasn't hard. The man wasn't expecting a woman to fight back. She placed herself in front of Charlotte, holding out her arms to create a barricade.

A self-satisfied smile crept across Chambers' face.

"This is your handiwork," she said.

His gaze slid over to her. In the confusion and the chaos, there was no mistaking the violet gleam in his eyes.

"You," she said.

"Me," he agreed. "I'm rather disappointed it took you this long to figure it out. You're cleverer than the average person but still failed to see what was in front of you. Twice." He nodded toward Alek, struggling to subdue Miles. "I suppose your uneven education is to blame. I wonder if Godwin knew."

"Leave my father out of this." She held his unsettling gaze, resisting the urge to look at her father on the floor. Bleeding. Unconscious.

Miles gutted him like a fish, like it was nothing. She pushed that horror away. She couldn't help her father if she fell to a beast. Survival was the most important thing at the moment.

Solenne nudged a butter knife with her foot, moving it away from the overturned table. She held out her arms, forming a barricade. Charlotte stood behind her.

Chambers gave a lazy shrug. "I suppose he might not have been so eager to give you to me, had he known."

"Solenne?" Charlotte's voice sounded so far away, despite being close enough that she stepped on Solenne's feet.

"What did you give Alek?" As soon as the question left her lips, she knew. Wormwood. A harmless anti-inflammatory, unless the person was a werewolf.

"Oh, not just Alek. Everyone. Wormwood. Wonderful little herb, isn't it? It lowers the inhibition and lets the beast out." That grin again, this time with too many teeth. His control was slipping.

"But why?" And then she knew. "Charlotte's your anchor. Or you tried to make her your anchor."

He growled. "She's *defective*. Useless girl. I intended you for that role, but your heart was already set on another."

"The anchor has to be willing," she said. If she kept him talking long enough, Alek and Luis could subdue Miles, then focus on Chambers.

"Receptive. She was certainly desperate enough. Practically fell to her knees thanking me." A vicious grin slithered its way across his face, and Solenne did not want to hear what other activities her friend performed on her knees. "But the connection just wasn't happening."

"So endangering her? That was the plan?"

"And it didn't work!" He growled, and the hairs stood up on the back of her head. "I bit Miles on a whim, but he proved useful. Now, enough chatter, give me my wife."

Charlotte pressed herself to Solenne, burying her face into Solenne's hair. Step by step, she eased them away from the table and away from Chambers. Her foot continued to nudge the knife along.

"Come, my sweet, I can smell your blood. You smell delicious. I could just eat you up." Chambers licked his chops, his face more beast than human now. He grabbed them both, tossing Solenne to the floor and lifting Charlotte. She kicked and squealed. His massive tongue licked her face.

"Stop!" Jase lurched forward, grimacing as if he stepped badly on his leg, and slammed a knife into his uncle's back. Chambers turned to snarl a warning, acting as if he barely noticed the blade. The color drained from Jase's face. He teetered on unstable legs, clutching the table for support.

Solenne took the moment's distraction and rolled to the side, aware of broken shards of glass cutting through the thin material of her dress, and reached for the butter knife. It was nothing compared to the beast that masqueraded as Chambers, but it was silver and the handle felt sturdy. She thought the past months of terror this cursed man brought to them and what he took: Godwin's eyes, mauled livestock, Jase's leg fracture, the beast that cornered her at the stone circle, and Miles. If he survived his first shift, if he found an anchor, his life would be forever changed.

Her anger grew with each slight. This pathetic excuse for a man wronged her. Took from her.

Finally, Charlotte, the best person she knew, who had so much love in her heart. He was going to kill her. Solenne knew it in her bones, and she couldn't let that happen. Charlotte was hers *first*.

The knife handle warmed to her touch. It nearly vibrated with her anger, demanding to be the instrument of retribution. Fine weapons decorated the walls, but none were in reach. This is what she had. A gust from an open window stirred through the room, whipping up her hair.

She'd make do. She'd make the humble butter knife make do.

Chambers opened his maw, lowering toward Charlotte.

Rushing forward, she jumped and grabbed what she could reach. Her finger dug into his eyes. She grabbed his earlobe and pulled with all her weight. He tried to shake her off, but she clung to him. Claws raked her skin, sharp. Charlotte fell to the floor.

Solenne sank the knife into his eye, causing a roar that rattled the windows. The silver stung her hand, but she did not let go. Twisting and pushing it in as far as possible, she clung onto him until he finally threw away.

Chambers stumbled blindly, heading for the door.

Luis rushed him from behind and ran a sword clean through. She must have hit her head when she was thrown because the blade glowed violet. "I knew it," her brother breathed.

Half-man, half-beast, and all monster, Chambers looked at the bloody point emerging from his abdomen. Such a blow would have ended any other werewolf. Hopefully, this weakened him enough to end this. He lumbered toward Luis, who darted back to the wall and grabbed the nearest weapon, a lovely silver-headed war hammer.

Chambers had decorated the room with the weapons of his own destruction.

"Mr. Parkell! Catch." Luis tossed the war hammer to Jase, who looked rather at a loss as to what to do with the weapon. A look of determination settled on his face.

Luis grabbed a set of handheld axes for himself, the silver blades gleaming in candlelight and mayhem. He nodded to Jase and the two men rushed the weakened beast.

Solenne looked away. Fortunately, the pounding of her heart in her ears drowned that out the sickening crunch of metal against bone.

Chambers fell. Luis hacked at the neck, severing the head. Blood splatter coated everything, his face, his finery, the floor and those unfortunate enough to stand nearby. Luis' jaw clenched with resolve to finish his gruesome task.

The beast did not get up again.

Chapter Twenty-Five

Aleksandar

Boxon

Vervain Hall

The silver circle was a testament to Luis' ingenuity. Silver forks, spoons, and knives had been hastily arranged around Miles. It was not a perfect circle, but it was unbroken and strong enough to hold a fledgling beast.

"Don't come any closer," Miles warned. Caught in a partial shift, cloth hung off him in tatters. Fur covered his arms and chest. Claws flashed. His face retained a human shape, if he had more teeth than usual.

He paced the circle, the claws on his feet tapping the ground.

"You promised, you promised!" Miles threw himself at the circle and bounced off an invisible barricade. He hissed, rubbing his shoulder. "Do it! What are you waiting for?" He slumped to the ground. "Please. You promised."

Alek clutched the blade. Silver hummed in his hand, insulated with the leather handle. He had stood here before, with a newly shifted beast pleading at his feet. Usually they begged for life or vowed revenge. None had ever begged for release.

The knife clattered to the floor.

"I can't. That was something I shouldn't have promised," Alek said, not sure if he spoke with mercy or cruelty.

Miles' face crumpled.

Cruelty then.

"Don't you give up," Luis said. He stood just outside the circle, the toes of his shoes pressed against the unseen barrier. "Don't you dare." He glared over his shoulder at Alek. "And don't you indulge his melodrama."

"This is no life—" Miles started.

"Idiot." Luis stepped over the barrier, into the circle, and pulled Miles forward into a kiss. It looked awkward and unpracticed, and Alek briefly wondered if he looked like he was trying to eat Solenne's face when he kissed her. "This is a life. Your life now. Ours."

"No, Luis."

"I killed one werewolf tonight. Don't ask me to end another."

"I'll hurt you. I hurt your father," Miles said, more snarl than words.

"Chambers poisoned you with wormwood. Both of you," Solenne announced. Kneeling next to her father, she tore at the fabric of her dress and pressed the wad against Godwin's gut. "He wanted you to lose control. He wanted chaos."

"This was his doing. Not yours," Luis said.

"No. I heard him in my head. I wanted to please him," Miles said, anguish plainly written on his face. "I'll do it again. How can you stand the sight of me?"

A firm expression flickered across Luis' eyes, not so different from when they sparred and the young man set himself against an impossible challenge. Solenne shared the same look.

"I'm your anchor. I know I am." Luis tapped his chest. "I'm not letting you go, so you might as well let me help you. Stay with me."

Miles slumped to the ground. Luis kneeled beside him, wrapping his arms around the blacksmith. "How can you tie yourself to someone like me? Pick someone better. Someone who's not cursed," Miles said.

"It doesn't work like that. I should know," Alek said. Both men lifted their heads in his direction. "I tried for years to forget Solenne, but I couldn't. She anchored me. She always had." Perhaps the connection would have frayed with time—another decade or so—but he doubted it.

Miles' lips pulled back in a snarl. "Don't speak to him! Don't look at mine!"

"Territorial. Possessive. The bond is already there, whether you like it or not," Alek said. He tossed the fallen dagger to Luis' feet. "Just in case he gets out of line."

"We're not going anywhere." He tucked the dagger into his boot. "How is Papa?"

"Breathing."

Dr. Webb and Sheldon worked on Godwin's unconscious form. The wound looked nasty and likely to fester. Unconscious was the best thing he could be.

Solenne arrived, blood splatter on her face and her hem soaked in her father's blood. Or Chambers'. Or Charlotte's. Probably a combination of all three. How preposterous to think she looked radiant, covered in gore and completely unflappable.

His mate.

The beast was so damn pleased with himself. Alek agreed.

He fished out a handkerchief from a pocket, pleased to discover it mostly clean. "How did he poison us?"

"Chambers dosed the wine," she said, accepting the cloth and proceeding to clean her face. "Wormwood is harmless to everyone except you and Miles. Lowers your inhibitions, I gather, and makes the wolf more dominant."

"Yes, that sounds right."

"It'll wear off. And you?"

"I want nothing more than to be alone with you, wife, but—" He looked about the room, at the overturned furniture, the destruction and the injured people. "What I want is irrelevant. Put me to work."

Solenne

She should not have been surprised by Charlotte's efficiency. After all, she had been helpless in the face of

Charlotte's organizing this disaster of a double wedding. As the lady of the house, Charlotte took control and coordinated the care of the injured and the cleanup.

She had a horrible feeling that people would refer to the day's events as the Double Werewolf Wedding. Technically, it was a triple event, but it hardly seemed the time to split hairs.

"How do we help him?" Charlotte asked, regarding Miles.

"Wolfsbane. It will calm him down." The herb acted as a sedative for a werewolf. So many people erroneously thought it was a repellent.

Charlotte looked as if she was going to question Solenne, but then shook her head. "I don't suppose you brought your box of tricks to the wedding. No. I believe Lionel has some medicinal powders in his bedroom. Let me check. Perhaps he can do something useful."

Chambers did, indeed, have a small medicine chest in his room, stocked with various herbs and pills. She found a packet of dried wolfsbane, labeled in her own handwriting.

Well, that solved the mystery of her diminishing supply cupboard.

"Give this to Miles. The entire thing," she said, handing the packet to Alek.

She watched her new husband and oldest friend dump the packet into a glass of water before pouring it down Miles' throat. Alek seemed distant. She didn't know how to explain other than he felt with her during the ceremony, as if they were one spirit. The connection between them was vibrant and alive. Now, it seemed muted, like he was pulling away. It worried her.

Did he think she held recent events against him? How could she? He saved Miles from making a terrible mistake. Alek was a champion in her eyes and the eyes of everyone in attendance.

Perhaps the number of witnesses was the issue. What was the saying? One person can keep a secret. Two can keep a secret if one is dead.

All those people saw his partial shift. He had to worry about repercussions.

Solenne cleaned the minor injury on Charlotte's head. It bled freely, giving her a ghastly appearance as a bloody bride in her wedding gown, but it was small and easily covered with a bandage.

When that was done, she switched her attention to Godwin. Dr. Webb carefully stitched together his lacerated abdomen. She assisted by fetching supplies, fresh cloth, and clean water. When Godwin moaned, she held his hand.

Chambers' body remained on the floor, covered with a wine-stained tablecloth. No one seemed to pay him any mind. Ignored and forgotten, it seemed a fitting fate. Soon his body would have to be burned, but that could wait a day. The living were more important, and no one seemed particularly aggrieved, other than Mrs. Parkell. She appeared with a basin of water and a cloth.

"It's my duty as his sister to clean his body. Even if he was a monster," she insisted. She dipped the cloth in the clean water and hesitated before she brought it to his impassive face.

"He's not contagious. Not anymore."

"I'm not worried about that," she said. "I failed Lionel. I hardly knew him. I thought I did. He never spoke about his time in the military. He never spoke about anything, really. When did this happen? How could he hide himself from me?"

Solenne left the woman to do her work. If she found any peace or forgiveness in her heart for Chambers, it was her own business.

Among the wedding guests, most injuries were cuts and bruises obtained in the panic to flee the room. The occasional person had a twisted ankle or knee, but nothing serious. Jase has not done significant injury to his leg. The only serious injury had been Godwin. When Drs. Webb and Sheldon declared him stable, they moved him upstairs into a bedroom. Solenne reluctantly allowed Dr. Webb to clean the claw marks where Chambers took a swipe at her. They seemed inconsequential to her father.

Eventually Alek took her by the hand. "You're exhausted."

"There's too much to do."

"You can't help anyone when you're ready to fall over. You need a bath and sleep," he said, his take-charge tone soothing her in a way she did not know she needed.

Bath and sleep sounded so good.

"I'm afraid I don't have an available room for you," Charlotte said, joining them. She looked equally exhausted, yet her eyes shone. This was her element. "I'm afraid we can't move your father. He has to stay for the time being. I imagine Miles will need to stay where he is?" She paused, waiting for Alek's response.

"Until he calms down," Alek said.

"Go home, get some rest and come back tomorrow," she said.

"I'll burn the villain tomorrow."

Solenne thought Charlotte might protest, that Chambers might be a villain, but he was still her husband and deserved a funeral service, but she only nodded.

"Tomorrow or the day after, I'll write to Snowmelt and tell them of the delay," Alek said. Everyone had to make compromises at the moment, such as they would not journey to Snowmelt in a few days. Solenne couldn't leave with her father injured. She felt gladdened that Alek instinctively understood this.

The return to Marechal House took no time at all. They stripped off their ruined finery and took turns scrubbing each other in the bath. Alek seemed...restless.

"You know, the original colonists had an endless supply of hot water on demand."

"Impossible," he replied, voice flat like he paid the conversation the minimal amount of attention.

"True. They bathed in stalls called *showers* where the water came in over their heads, but through an aerated sprinkler, not a bucket being dumped over their heads."

He huffed. "Sounds convenient."

"I agree." Waiting for the water to heat, filling the tub, and then splashing around took a considerable amount of time, especially when she just wanted to be clean enough to get to bed with her husband.

Her fingers brushed against the angry red bite on his shoulder. "That will never heal, will it?"

"It hasn't in eight years. It doesn't always look so—"

"Fresh?"

"A reflection of the cycle, nothing more. It doesn't hurt," he said.

She continued to scrub his shoulders and back, eventually moving to his front. Her hands strayed a bit far below his waist. Alek raised a brow. To say she eagerly anticipated the night was an understatement. Perhaps a more refined lady would be exhausted or too distraught to think of skin and kissing and every pleasure a man shared with a woman, but it was all she wanted. The events of the Double Werewolf Wedding —no, she would not call it that!—left her feeling tightly wound and in need of a release.

Alek, too, from the feel of him.

He leaned his head back and groaned at her touch. Before she could continue on, he placed a hand over hers, halting her. "Upstairs. You need sleep."

"That's not what I need, Aleksandar."

"Solenne, do not tempt me."

She pulled back, stung at his rejection. In the last few weeks, he had been insatiable, demanding touches and her attention. Now he acted cold and disinterested.

The thread between them? Silent.

Hastily, she reached for a robe. By this time, she had been nude before Alek several times, and he never made her feel anything less than desirable. Now she felt vulnerable and exposed. Naked in an entirely unwelcome manner.

"What's wrong?" she asked, tying the belt.

"Do not concern yourself."

"Blast it, Aleksandar." Frustrated, she threw a towel at him. He caught it with ease. "I know something is wrong, so tell me."

His eyes were cold. "It will upset you. Too many things happened today. Things you should not have seen. After today—"

"You're leaving without me," she said, ready to fall over at the words. All day she swung from nervousness, anticipation, then fear, then determination. Every moment fueled by adrenaline. There had to be a breaking point where her body couldn't keep up, no matter how her spirit drove her forward.

Her knees threatened to give out, and her stomach wanted to empty itself. She stumbled back against the wall. "You self-sacrificing bastard. You do not get to leave in some ridiculous notion to protect me! If you try, I'll stab you in the eye with a butter knife."

He surged out of the water, pressing his wet and very hard form against hers. "Solenne, be quiet a moment."

"So help me, I'll find the dullest and rustiest butter knife."

He kissed her, fierce and all-consuming. The connection flared back to life and she could feel his pulse thrumming. It whispered that he was here, here, here. She belonged to him and she couldn't make him leave with the rustiest butter knife in the world.

"Oh," she said.

His fingers dug into her wet hair, pulling to force her gaze to his. His eyes glowed with an intense violet light.

"I want nothing more in this life than to keep you safe," he said. "And you damn Marechals are so determined to throw yourself in front of every ravening beast you find. I thought I would lose you and it frightened me more than anything."

"Oh," she said. Anything else seemed unnecessary.

"So yes, I closed myself to the bond. I didn't want my fear frightening you. He had you, Solenne, in his paws, and I was too far away to do anything." He closed his eyes, as if reliving that moment. "I failed to protect you."

"You saved Miles and Papa. That's hardly a failure."

He opened his eyes and searched her face for what she did not know. Whatever he found, he nodded as if satisfied. "I will never leave you. Never. I will be your shadow because I can't trust you to not run headfirst into the maw of a beast."

"I hardly did that," she protested. Well, she did do that. Technically.

"And on Boxon Hill? And the night of the full moon? Every time, I arrived too late to prevent you from some foolhardy act of heroism. Since I can't trust you to have enough common sense to save yourself, I'll do it for you." Another crushing kiss, this one erasing her protests.

He growled, low in his throat, and her core clenched in response. "Now, wife, get in bed."

"I'm not sleepy."

"We will not sleep."

The beast would have his mate.

She was happy to oblige.

Chapter Twenty-Six

Aleksandar

Boxon Hill

Marechal House - Mr. and Mrs. Hardwick's Bedroom

The door slammed shut with a resounding thud.

"Nice room," he said, not taking his eyes off Solenne.

"Specially prepared for us."

A wedding night suit had been set up in a disused bedroom at the far end of the house, far away from the bedrooms in use. The room smelled of lemon furniture polish and dust.

Lips clashed. Hands grasped. Robes were discarded. Skin pressed against skin. Solenne backed across the room until she bumped into the bed. She pulled him down on top of her. The bed squeaked unforgivingly.

She buried her face against his neck and laughed. "Oh, for goodness' sake, listen to that." She shifted, the bed groaned in complaint. "I don't think anyone's actually slept in this bed in a decade."

"I didn't plan on sleeping tonight."

He hauled her to her feet, lips and tongues tangling to make his point. Her fingers twisted in his hair and pushed against him, driving him backward until he slammed against the wardrobe, rattling the wood against the plaster walls. "Careful," he said, earning him a growl from his wife.

His wife.

The thread connecting them vibrated, golden and joyous. He felt her want, her hunger. The stolen kisses behind closed doors, the brush of hands, had only stoked his appetite.

"I can't believe I've waited for you," he said in a low, thick tone.

"Not for my lack of trying to seduce you." Her eyes sparkled.

His fingers twisted in her hair, pulling the silken locks tight until her head tilted back. "Temptress."

"Please don't make me wait, Alek. I'm tired of waiting."

Every point their bodies touched sparked with an energy unlike any he had ever experienced. It sang in his blood. Strengthened him. Gave him sustenance. She gave him sustenance.

With a fluid motion, he lifted Solenne and carried her to the bed. She bounced on the mattress, her laughter easy and playful. Scrambling back, her dark hair tumbled around her shoulders. He pushed her down onto the mattress and loomed above her.

Hot, feverous kisses led to caresses and nibbles and licks. She gasped, pleading. He flipped her over, shoulders pressed down.

"You look so pretty on display for me," he said, brushing a finger over her damp curls. She whimpered and positioned her legs slightly wider. "And no one's ever appreciated this view."

His anchor. His mate. His love.

The steady thump of her heart grounded him even as the electricity of their bond coursed through him.

"Please, Alek."

"Such pretty pleading." He pushed a finger in her hot, slick channel. She groaned, then pushed back. Carefully, he worked her open and added a second finger. "Are you ready for me, wife?"

"Yes, please. I'm ready," she gasped. Her hips bucked, as if to make her point.

"Patience," he said, then licked his fingers clean. The taste of her, musky, sweet and luscious, burst on his tongue.

More. The beast would not wait.

Climbing onto the bed, he positioned himself behind her, his cock already dripping. Slowly, he pushed in. Wet and unbelievably hot, her channel wrapped around his cock like a sheath, like she was made for him.

She gasped at the intrusion. He paused, stroking her back. "Are you well?"

"Yes, it's just...an odd sensation."

"Good or bad?" He caressed the round globes of her ass, perfectly shaped for his hands.

"Good. Yes, good."

He gave a short thrust and felt her quiver around him. "Good. So good," he growled, his mouth crowded with teeth.

Slowly—painfully slow—he pulled back and pressed forward again, filling her. Stretching her.

His toes elongated into claws, shredding the bed linens and digging into the mattress. Vaguely he was aware of feathers and stuffing that kicked up as he gained momentum for his forward thrusts.

Every nerve sang with desire and delight.

Claws erupted from his fingers. Rather than mark her delicate flesh, he wrapped one arm around her torso and the other in her hair. He pulled back, holding her flush against him as he continued to pump into her.

"Page 72," he growled in her ear, nipping at the lobe.

She answered in a throaty moan.

Sweat rolled down his back. Close under the surface, the beast rumbled, still wanting more.

Alek flipped Solenne to her back. She squeaked in surprise but allowed herself to be positioned. With her knees pressed down until she was nearly folded in half, her feet hooked over his shoulders. He pumped into her, hard and relentless. The bed groaned in protest, but all he could hear was the synchronous rhythm of their hearts.

Solenne moaned his name and words of love, her feet kicking his back.

He gripped the headboard, letting it support his weight. The wood creaked and splintered as claws popped. He dug in harder, pushed harder, losing himself in her hot velvet embrace.

Pleasure coiled at the base of his spine, warning of his approaching climax. His fangs dropped, and he felt the razor-sharp teeth against his tongue.

The beast wanted to bite, to mark her smooth shoulders and leave evidence of his claim. The thought of her sweet blood made his mouth water. The beast did not care about the risk of contagion, it only hungered.

Alek rolled to his back, taking Solenne with him until she sat astride. Her eyes went wide, then her head fell back in a gloriously soulful moan. She rocked back and forth, finding the motion to please herself best. Watching her move, moonlight caressing her curves, was everything.

His hips bucked up, driving into her. She shuddered, then fell forward, her hands splayed on his chest. Her channel gripped him tight even as it spasmed around his cock.

Desperately close to his release, he grabbed a fist of her hair and wrapped it around his wrist. Her head jerked to the side, exposing the slender column of her throat. He snapped and snarled at the sight.

His mate.

"Alek!" Her limbs trembled and a look of bliss washed over her.

So lovely.

He lunged forward, jaws sinking into the thick length of hair held taut. His teeth chewed against the strands and the clean scent of her lemon and honey soap filled his nose. His hips pushed upwards, surging deep inside her, and he emptied his release.

Silence, except for the pounding of his heart and their ragged breaths.

Carefully, he untangled her hair from his claws. It fell in a curtain, the silken strands brushing against him. Her lips, swollen and red, twitched into a smile.

For the first time, his beast purred in contentment.

Solenne

"You bit my hair. Alek, what?"

He threw his arm over his face and groaned. "Better your hair than you." He lifted the arm to peek at the splintered wood of the ruined headboard. "Did I hurt you?"

"Not at all, but my *hair*?"

"Solenne," he said in a gruff voice that she knew was a teasing tone.

The bed collapsed, sending up a plume of feathers and fluff.

Alek's eyes went wide as feathers slowly drifted down like snow.

"That's Mrs. Hardwick to you," she said, without missing a beat. Pressing her lips together, she did her best to resist breaking into laughter.

She failed.

They burst into laughter.

"Do you think that was an antique?" she asked.

"I think the entire house heard," he replied. Reaching out, he plucked a feather from her hair. "I expect they'll be knocking down the door any moment."

"They knew what they were about when they put us in this room, far away from everything." Solenne extricated herself from the tangle mess of the collapsed bed and wrapped herself in a blanket. "I think my bed's big enough for two."

"Remember when your mama almost caught us in bed?" Moonlight pooled on the floor and the ruined bed, highlighting her husband's features. He licked his lips.

"I remember shoving you into the wardrobe and Mama acting as if she couldn't hear you." Solenne remembered the day well. They had done nothing more than exchange a few shy kisses, but Amalie and Godwin forbade them from being alone together in a bedroom. At the time, Solenne had been indignant. She had spent her entire childhood under blanket forts with Alek and in slumber parties, whispering stories to each other late into the night. The idea that they were *too old* for such behavior chafed, even if it were true.

"She said the ghosts were unusually active for that time of day," Alek said.

They grinned at the memory.

Wrapped in blankets, they snuck through the house. Floorboards creaked and they couldn't fight their shared mirth.

A fire crackling in the fireplace warmed Solenne's bedroom. A pitcher of cold water and a basket of sweet rolls waited on the bureau, along with a note from Luis reminding them to hydrate and keep the noise down. "Decent people have to work in the morning," she read, setting the note down on the bureau.

"He's not wrong. Eat. Drink. I'm not done with you." A wicked grin spread on his face and she shivered in anticipation.

She dropped the blanket. "Come to bed, love."

Epilogue

Charlotte

Boxon

Vervain Hall

Solenne and Alek stayed the winter in Snowmelt. She had been reluctant to leave Boxon Hill, but her father insisted. Luis was more than capable, and he had a fresh recruit in Jase—surprising everyone—to help.

After a few weeks to recuperate from the events of the wedding, they held a rather bizarre funeral for a stuffed werewolf. Adding to the bizarreness, Godwin presented Charlotte's father with the ashes. Apparently, the werewolf had been great-uncle Tristan.

From Solenne's letters, the description of the Hardwick House and Snowmelt, they were forced to stay the winter. Solenne never complained in their many letters, stating that the grounds held many useful and interesting medicinal plants. They returned to Boxon in the spring, just as Luis and Miles left for the West Lands on the other side of the mountains.

Charlotte remained the mistress of Chambers' farm, despite the best efforts of her sister-in-law to contest the legality of the union and, thus, inheritance in court. She might not have been married long enough for the ink to dry on the license, but she was legally married to Lionel Chambers, and he left no will. Why would he, when he lacked the humility to imagine his own mortality?

She felt there was a witty comment to be made about death caring not for hubris, but the simple matter was that Lionel felt himself unstoppable. Going through his private papers, Charlotte learned that when he was still newly enlisted in the military, he received the bite from his commanding officer. The presence of his master—she loathed that word—and military discipline kept the young wolf under control. Together they hunted creatures like themselves and looted the relics of old hunter families.

Alek had read the papers, too. Something like recognition flared in his eyes, but whatever connection he made, he kept it to himself.

Married and made a wealthy widow on the same day, Charlotte struggled with her new responsibilities and her new social position. Everyone in the village had an opinion, which they freely traded with each other. The vile accusations Mrs. Parkell flung against Charlotte in court—all of which the broadsheets published—did not help. She struggled to maintain a soft heart. Mrs. Parkell and Jase were just as betrayed by Lionel as she. In that spirit, she continued the allowance Lionel established for the pair and offered to cover Jase's university tuition and expenses.

He declined, having decided that he wanted to hunt monsters. He had known Lionel's secret for some time and had been forced to be his uncle's minion to protect his mother. Frankly, Charlotte could not imagine Lattice Parkell needing protection from anything. The woman was a force unto herself.

A year and a day later, Luis and Miles returned from the West Lands.

The man who climbed off his horse and strode across the courtyard was not the unsure young man who left. Time and the trial of the journey had changed Luis in more than physical appearance, but that had changed considerably, as well. His frame had filled out with thick, solid muscle, and exposure to the elements turned his complexion a golden tan.

Luis moved with confidence, and Charlotte hesitated to know exactly how many skirmishes had tested him along the way. Miles appeared equally worn, but he beamed at Luis like he hung the stars.

The entire household and then some had gathered in the courtyard to welcome the returning travelers. Godwin paced impatiently. Charlotte, who had spotted Luis and Miles on the road, had dashed through the woods with the news of their return. Sweat clung to the small of her back, and she did her best to mop up her brow.

Solenne gripped Alek's hand, and Charlotte averted her eyes, ignoring the pangs of jealousy.

Her friend pointed to the sun dipping near the horizon. "And what kind of time do you call this? You're late."

Luis crushed his sister into an embrace. Even from her distance, Charlotte smelled the distinct aroma of sweat, horse, and leather.

"Gah, you smell disgusting," Solenne muttered, her face pressed into his chest.

"I missed you, too," Luis said. "Are you shorter?" He pushed her away, hands on her shoulders. "You're shrinking. Must be all the magic. I do not approve."

"It's not magic," she said, knocking his hands away, "and you're a giant now. Everyone is shrinking from your vantage."

"Mystical werewolf bond magic." Luis wiggled his fingers.

Solenne laughed, sounding so pleased to have her brother back.

Luis and Miles made the rounds, embracing and slapping everyone they saw, including Travers who stood motionless, enduring the hug.

"Well?" Solenne asked. "Did you find Blackthorn?"

Luis gave a dramatic yawn. "We've been traveling for days—"

"Only because you were so excited to be near home that you refused to rest," Miles interrupted.

"Days without pausing to eat or sleep," Luis continued, as if he could not hear Miles. "I'd like a bath and a meal. Then we can talk."

Miles rolled his eyes. "Draven has the sword. Apparently, he's been waiting for someone to come and fetch it."

"So you have it?" Alek asked.

Luis shook his head. "He wants a trade that I was not qualified to make."

"What does the vampire demand?"

"A bride," Luis answered.

The crowd fell silent. The Marechals looked at each other, like they had lost the battle before they had fired a single shot.

"I suppose that's that," Godwin mumbled.

"Yes. I said I'd send word, but how could we ask—" Luis trailed off.

"An interesting fellow, but an unreasonable demand," Miles added.

That family. Charlotte loved them, but they lacked imagination and had a disturbing forgetfulness when it came to history. They squabbled among themselves, demanding to know the terms of the negotiation or if Luis just accepted the terms without protest. Luis refused to discuss until he had a bath. The more details Godwin and Solenne demanded to know, the longer Luis' list of demands grew.

Alek and Miles watched the exchange, amused and exhausted.

"I'll go," Charlotte said.

No one heard her.

"I will go," she repeated, raising her voice to an unladylike decibel.

The family turned as if one entity, as if they just noticed her presence.

"No," Solenne said. "Out of the question. You're not giving yourself to a blood drinker. They're dangerous—

"Don't be ridiculous. Send me. This is what I do, isn't it?" Charlotte retorted. "I marry monsters."

Afterword

Thank you for giving a Regency-style werewolf a chance. I know it's not my normal alien fare but I've had this idea knocking around my head for ages.

Please join my Facebook group to discuss Wolf's Bane and give me a piece of your mind.

https://www.facebook.com/groups/NanceyCummingsReadersGroup/

Not gonna lie. This year has been tough. We're all going through something. I've been fortunate that my husband could work from home. (I already do, but I do miss coffee shops.) I haven't lost any immediate family or friends to COVID, but I don't have to look far to find friends who have lost family members.

In an effort to turn off the constant worry in my head, I've been indulging in all the things I love. First it started with Jane Austen movies, then Lucy Worsley documentaries, then Agatha Christie shows and movies, jigsaw puzzles, knitting and playing with polymer clay. Anything to keep my hands busy and my brain engaged.

I also decided that it was time to write a book I wasn't sure about and I tossed in all the things I like. So that's how we ended up with this Jane Austen/Lost in Space + werewolves mash up.

Will there be more? Charlotte's story is in the works!

I have a whole slew of people to thank. My GargGirls have been there everyday for writing sprints, pep talks and general kicking my butt into gear. Thank you Stacy Jones, Stephanie West, Regine Able, Tamsin Ley and Abigail Myst. Marina Simcoe, Naomi Lucas, Tiffany Roberts are excellent cheerleaders. Bet McLynn is too damn funny for her own good. Honey Philips is a delight. Jeanette Lynn is the weirdest in the best way (and always poking me about the Jane Austen werewolf book). I think that's everyone. Apologies if I forgot a writer buddy.

Stay safe!

Nancey is a *USA Today* bestselling author. She writes fast-paced, low-angst books about kissing aliens, because that's how she rolls.

She once had an argument with her husband about being marriage in space. He claimed that marriage was a legal contract and ended when a person left orbit. Nancey said the vows were "till death do us part" not "until the spaceship departs."

She has written twenty books about being married in space just to prove him wrong.

Let's stay in touch! Join Nancey's newsletter and get a FREE copy of Claimed by the Alien Prince.

Get it at here:

https://dl.bookfunnel.com/jektemqay4

Let's hang out! Join Nancey's Facebook reader group for early teasers and whatnots.

https://www.facebook.com/groups/895051017325998/

Also by Nancey Cummings

Warlord Bride Index (with Starr Huntress)

Snowed in with the Alien Warlord

Alien Warlord's Passion

Warriors of Sangrin (with Starr Huntress)

Paax

Kalen

Mylomon

Vox

Warlord's Baby

Seeran

Rohn

Jaxar

Havik

Lorran

Ren

Caldar

A Winter Starr (with Starr Huntress)

Alien Warlord's Miracle

The Alien Reindeer's Bounty

Delivered to the Aliens

<u>Tail and Claw (Celestial Mates)</u>
Have Tail, Will Travel
Pulled by the Tail
Tail, Dark and Handsome
Tattle Tail

<u>Outlaw Planet Mates</u>
Alien's Challenge
Alien's Heart

<u>Valos of Sonhadra</u>
Blazing
Inferno

Splintered Shadow (Shattered Galaxies)

Taken for Granite (Khargals of Duras)

<u>Dragons of Wye (with Juno Wells)</u>
Korven's Fire
Ragnar

<u>Alpha Aliens of Fremm</u>
Claimed by the Alien Prince
Bride of the Alien Prince

Alien Warrior's Mate

Alien Rogue's Price

Made in the USA
Middletown, DE
09 April 2025